The crease split open and I took a step back. Towser had stayed back a couple of dozen steps, watching tensely. He's a good squirrel dog, but this monster had him spooked. Had me a mite edgy, too.

As the crease widened into a huge black and red pit and I took another quick step backward, Towser broke into barking and making stiff-legged hops back and forth. A slick, sticky-looking white tube shot out of the pit and wrapped him up. It was so quick, all I really saw was a glimpse of a struggling, yelping blob half visible inside the tip before it sucked back inside.

Doc immediately commenced to beating on the creature with both fists. "Dammit, Sprocket! Spit that goddam dog out! You know better'n to act like this!"

After a second, the eyeball reappeared and blinked at us twice. Doc picked up a crowbar laying in the grass and started whupping on Sprocket with *that*. He jumped aside when a hole appeared in the crease right in front of him and Towser jetted out, still yelping. He hit the grass running and kept going.

Doc beat on Sprocket a couple more times before he threw the crowbar aside. Then he turned to me, grinning. "Hell of a drilling rig, Henry Lee, but I can't say his humor is always in the best of taste. So to speak."

PETROGYPSIES

RORY HARPER

BAEN BOOKS

PETROGYPSIES

A Baen Books Original

Baen Publishing Enterprises
260 Fifth Avenue
New York, N.Y. 10001

ISBN: 0-671-69840-0

Cover art by Tom Kidd

First printing, September 1989

Distributed by
SIMON & SCHUSTER
1230 Avenue of the Americas
New York, N.Y. 10020

DEDICATION:

To the people who run my life, in order of seniority, with much love . . .

Maida Inez Harper
Cheryl Lynn Mayon
Judith Ann Miller
Rachael Victoria Harper

Also, I'd like to thank the guys at the Halliburton camp at Fresno for vast amounts of technical help, and for telling me four decades worth of preposterous oilpatch stories which I plan to file the serial numbers off of and turn into novels. Names will probably be changed to protect innocent and guilty alike.

Thanks,

Rory

Sprocket Goes
Down on the Farm

I glanced up from a shovel full of pig slop just as the Driller made the corner down by the dried up bed of Hanson's Creek.

The sun was about half set, so at first all I could make out was a long dark *something*, churning up a cloud of red-dirt dust. It was wide as the road and then some. And long—the front of the Driller must have been more than a hundred feet past the curve before the cloud at the end trailed off and blew away. I never saw nothing like it in my life before.

I yelled out. By the time it drew up down at the turnoff into our cattleguard, all eight of us, Papa and Grampaw and us four kids, plus two dogs, were clustered in front of the porch steps with three squirrel guns, a deer rifle, a hayfork, and a slop shovel pointed in its general direction. It stopped at the cattleguard and the dust started to settle. The lower flanks were streaked red and gray from travel, but the rest of it was black as a moonless night, only all slick and shiny like the intestines of a fresh-slaughtered bull. Hundreds of stumpy feet marched in place all the way down its length. I had a thought that shooting it probably wouldn't do much more than tee it off if it decided to come through the gate and eat us and the farmhouse.

It stood about forty feet away, with the people getting more quiet and the dogs getting more noisy every second, and then a head popped out of a hole that opened in its top near the front. The rest of a human body followed until a bearded man was free from its innards. He slid down the slope of its ten-foot high flank and walked toward us. He was wearing a gray jumpsuit with colored patches sewed all over it. On his head perched a battered silver-metal hat with a wide brim all the way around.

"Howdy, folks," he called out as he walked toward us. "I'm Doc Miller. This'd be the MacFarland place, I take it." He tugged leather gloves off and offered his hand for a shake as he drew near. He was a big, strong-looking man. He came nearly up to my chin height, and I suspected if we arm-rassled, it'd be a chore to put him down.

Papa nodded cautiously, handed me his gun, and stuck out his own calloused hand.

"Didn't mean to startle you folks. Pleasure to meet y'all." The man twitched his head back in the direction of the road. Holes had opened up in half-a-dozen places along the Driller's body and more men were climbing out of them. "We heard in Hemphill that y'all had been a little water-poor of late and came by to see if you'd be interested in a business proposition."

We hadn't seen rain for most of a month. We'd been managing to haul in barely enough water for man and beast, but the corn visible in the field behind the house had already started to turn from green and gold to brown and dead. Papa couldn't have said he wasn't interested even if he'd wanted to. Without water, and soon, this year's harvest would be ten acres of dry stalks. Last year hadn't been much to speak of, and this one just might be bad enough to run us off the land.

In the morning, Papa and the two youngest, Danny and Greg, took the buckboard to town after breakfast to see about getting a loan from the Grange Bank to pay the gypsies and buy lumber for the irrigation troughs. After I did my chores I wandered over with Towser at my heels to where the Driller squatted and watched while the gypsies got ready. They'd made camp at the far end of the pasture because the slope of the land was such that it was the best place to start running an irrigation system.

Doc Miller stood on top of the head of the Driller directing things. The pasture looked like the carnival had arrived. They'd pitched half-a-dozen tents of various bright colors, and they fussed with piles of strange equipment and odd-shaped boxes which littered the pasture's shady side. Towser stayed close beside me, every now and then growling halfheartedly. I squatted off to the side for about five minutes before I caught Doc's eye.

"Hey, boy. We been running a little shorthanded. You want to help out a bit? Drillin' is an exciting, romantic business, and you might learn something."

"My name's Henry Lee, sir, and I'd be pleased to help out."

"Hey, Razer!" he called out to one of the scurrying men. "You take over while I give Mr. Henry Lee MacFarland a tour of Sprocket." He slid down the

Driller's side and led me along its length, slapping it affectionately on the flanks as he went.

"This here is Sprocket. There ain't too many like him." He stopped where a bunch of large and small folds in its dark hide stretched for a dozen feet or so. "He's close to bein' the biggest Driller I've ever seen. And he still ain't got his full growth on him."

He rubbed an area about a foot above one of the creases. The crease unfolded lazily and an eyeball twice the size of my head poked out. It stared at us for a long second, then slipped back under its cover. Doc stopped and pulled at the blubbery edge of a crease that ran knee high for eight or nine feet. "He'll go down more'n twenty thousand feet—that's four *miles*, Henry Lee. There ain't a drilling rig in the world better than Sprocket at finding oil and making hole down to it."

The crease split open and I took a step back. Towser had stayed back a couple of dozen steps, watching tensely. He's a good squirrel dog, but this monster had him spooked. Had me a mite edgy, too.

As the crease widened into a huge black and red pit and I took another quick step backward, Towser broke into barking and making stiff-legged hops back and forth. A slick, sticky-looking white tube shot out of the pit and wrapped him up. It was so quick, all I really saw was a glimpse of a struggling, yelping blob half visible inside the tip before it sucked back inside.

Doc immediately commenced to beating on the creature with both fists. "Dammit, Sprocket! Spit that goddam dog out! You know better'n to act like this!"

After a second, the eyeball reappeared and blinked at us twice. Doc picked up a crowbar laying in the grass and started whupping on Sprocket with *that*.

He jumped aside when a hole appeared in the crease right in front of him and Towser jetted out, still yelping. He hit the grass running and kept going.

Doc beat on Sprocket a couple more times before he threw the crowbar aside. Then he turned to me, grinning. "Hell of a drilling rig, Henry Lee, but I can't say his humor is always in the best of taste. So to speak."

Sprocket's enormous mouth gaped open again and Doc stepped up on its lip. "C'mon. Let me show you his guts." He saw me hesitate and grinned again. "Hell, don't worry. This ain't his eating mouth. It's his drilling mouth." He pointed down at his feet. "See? No teeth." He stepped off the lip and marched inside the monster. If he could do it, so could I. The mouth closed behind us.

It wasn't dark for more'n a second, because Doc pulled open a curtain of flesh a couple of yards further on. We stepped into a hallway almost twice my height that must of stretched the entire length of Sprocket. It was lit by glowing warts spaced along the hall at head height, each about a half-a-foot in diameter. The walls were pink, shot through with darker red veins, and they moved in and out slowly. A musky breeze shifted direction every few seconds.

As Doc led me down the hallway, he pointed out holes and creases along the way. "Now this here, Henry Lee, is my bunk room." He pulled it open and I looked over his shoulder. Inside was a small round room holding a couple of chairs and a bed with a lamp over it. Colorful tapestries covered the walls and floor. A bulky wooden desk stood next to a set of rungs leading to a hole in the ceiling which let early morning sunlight in. "Since I'm the tool pusher on this rig, I get the room that's most forward." He closed it and walked on.

"Most of the rooms front on the tongue base are living areas. You know—bunkrooms, mess hall, head, that sort of thing. Now here—" We'd reached the tongue, a long, white snaky tube that lay in a groove in the center of the hall and gradually thickened as it led back to a hump about thirty feet further on. "Here is Sprocket's drilling tongue."

He peeled back white blubber from its tip and exposed a gleaming black bone, with three ratchet-edged pyramids angled off from its sharp point. "This is the drill-head and these here are Sprocket's drilling cones," he said, tapping one of the pyramids. "He twists 'em back and forth when he's making hole. They bite into earth and rock and chew it up." He let the blubber flop back over the cones. I'd gotten over worrying about being eaten alive and was starting to get interested in what he was saying.

We walked further down the hallway. The tongue got thicker, until it was higher than my head. At its very rear, it disappeared into the floor. Beyond it men hustled about, carrying things and calling to each other.

"The tongue actually goes back almost all of the rest of Sprocket's length under the floor. It compresses when it's not drilling, then stretches out as far as it's needed, the deeper we go. We're only going down to the aquifer on this one. Won't give it any kind of workout at all."

"Uh—no offense, sir, but how come you're finding water for us instead of being somewhere else drilling for oil?"

He leaned against the base of the tongue and pulled makings out of a pocket on his shoulder.

"Well, Henry Lee, we just finished doing a couple of wildcat wells up north." He grinned humorlessly as he shook tobacco out and rolled. "They all come up dry and the operator went broke before he paid us. It damn near busted us. We're heading down to a field opening up near Odessa. Looks like it's gonna be pretty rich. But a man's gotta eat along the way." He licked the endpapers and struck a phosphorus match off his hat. "Probably drill a dozen fast holes around here on farmsteads and then move on."

A man at the far end of the hall yelled at us. "Hey, Doc! We're ready to spud whenever you are."

"Be right there, Razer."

We walked down the hallway and out Sprocket's rear end. Doc made a final check of everything. A hose led from one crease to another and he yanked on it to make sure it wouldn't come loose. "Leads from his water bladder to his mud bladder," he explained. "Since we're going so shallow we'll just use fresh water for drilling fluid." Various machines and hoses were hooked into other creases and he checked all those.

Finally, we stood at Sprocket's head. A dozen men sat in folding chairs fiddling with various instruments in their hands. Doc stuck his arm in to the shoulder through a crease next to the mouth and felt around for a few seconds. "Pressure's good, Razer," he said to the man who'd called us and now stood next to him. "Let's get this show on the road."

Four men pried open Sprocket's mouth and walked inside. A minute later, they emerged carrying the tongue between them. Doc pried back the tip's cover for one last inspection of the cones, then laid it on the ground.

I'd been so interested watching him that I'd barely

noticed the movements and sounds of the men in the chairs.

Doc walked over to a crate in front of them and handed me two carved sticks that were on it. "Here you go, Henry Lee. Time to work." They didn't weigh much, and when I tapped them together made a pleasant hollow sound. I felt like an idiot standing there with them. What kind of work could I do with a couple of sticks?

Doc picked up the crowbar that he'd used earlier to get Sprocket to spit out Towser, and commenced to beating on him again, this time in a more rhythmical pattern. "Time to get to work, you lazy bastard!" he yelled. "We're ready and you're ready, and it ain't no use pretending you're asleep." This time I was far enough back that I could see it when both huge eyes opened and tried to stare cross-eyed at Doc. Satisfied, he backed off, reaching down to give the drilling tongue one last caress.

"Stokers ready?" he called out to a couple of men that stood next to a high pile of wood next to another opening in Sprocket's side.

"Bet your ass," was the reply.

He pulled a foot-and-a-half long wand from a narrow pocket I hadn't noticed before, that ran down his right leg. "Now, Henry Lee, I'm depending on you to help us out with this. You just watch my baton and hit those sticks together in time."

He raised the wand and took a deep breath. "Ah . . . one and ah . . . two and ah . . ."

The men in the chairs started blowing and rubbing and pumping their instruments all together, as his wand moved in graceful curves through the air. I missed the first few beats, but after that I did fine, the sticks' mellow clear sound following perfectly.

Oh, it was wild, blood-stirring music. That tongue jerked erect for a minute and then plunged into the earth, twisting and squirming. Sprocket's eyes squeezed shut, then popped open again. His sides heaved gently and his hundreds of feet tramped in rhythm with the gypsy music. The stokers off to the side began to chant in a language I didn't understand as they chucked logs into Sprocket's eating mouth.

We played for what seemed to be hours. I was in another world.

We didn't make music all the while he was drilling, of course, and I had work to do anyways. Papa got back from Hemphill after lunch. The Grange Bank had give us the loan, so we spent the rest of the day sawing and hammering, making irrigation troughs. Sprocket drilled close to five hundred feet, going below the aquifer to leave a reservoir of water in the bottom of the well. They finished late that evening. I did get to watch after supper when they snapped twenty-inch surface casing onto his tongue and set it in the hole, then mixed and poured a dozen sacks of cement around the wellhead to make sure it stayed in place. I talked with Razer and Doc some while I helped mix the concrete in a trough. They planned to move on down the road to drill another water well the next day at the Brewster place. Back to slopping pigs for me. I fell asleep listening to them partying in the pasture.

The next morning I'd already finished the morning chores before any of them stirred. The tents were still pitched where they'd been, but Sprocket had wandered over toward the back of the pasture. The dozen scraggly cows we owned gave him a wide berth. Doc was slouched over a campfire sipping from a battered tin cup when I walked up. "Hey there, Henry Lee," he called out. "You old enough to drink coffee?"

"I'm nineteen last month, Doc. I can do whatever I damn well please."

He squinted up at me. "Feeling kind of salty this morning, ain't you?"

I crouched and poured coffee into another tin cup. "Aw, I didn't mean nothing. I guess I'm sorry to see you going. Yesterday was fun."

"Like I said, it's a romantic, exciting way to live."

"Yeah. Looks like it beats dirt farming, anyway."

About that time the ground started to shake. A thunderous pounding came from Sprocket's direction. His hundreds of feet were stomping the back of the pasture into mud.

Doc jumped to his feet, looking disgusted. "Damned fool!"

"What's he doing?"

He threw the last third of his coffee into the fire. "Seismic testing." He shook his head. "Yesterday when we were drilling and he was marching in place he got one baseline. Now he's going for the other one."

"I don't understand." Sprocket's thumping speeded up.

"When he pounds the ground like that, it sends sound waves through the earth. Sprocket hears 'em when they slow down or speed up or reflect off different geological formations. Two baselines gives him a three-dimensional map of what's down there. The damned idiot's looking for hydrocarbons. Ain't no oil for two hundred miles in any direction."

Sprocket abruptly stopped and ambled back in our

direction. The men had all woken and stuck their heads out of their tents, cursing and groaning sleepily.

"Well, at least that foolishness is over," Doc grunted, as he picked up the pot to pour himself another cup. Sprocket reached us in a minute and towered over us silently. Doc stared at his protruding, rapidly rotating eyeballs.

Sprocket's tongue shot out of his mouth and began to drill furiously not three feet from me.

Doc threw his coffee into the fire again.

Papa didn't approve of the whole thing, but his eyes bugged out nearly as far as Sprocket's when the company man for Exoco pulled into the front yard in his brand-new, shiny red 1963 Ford pickup, hopped out, and showed him the numbers wrote down on the royalty contracts he offered. If the gypsies hit a good pocket of oil or natural gas, the first in an entirely undeveloped field, Papa and Exoco would make money beyond any human cravings. Exoco would finance the drilling costs and get the biggest share. The drilling gypsies would make out too, but not nearly as much.

Doc just shrugged when we talked about the deal. "Exoco's putting up some serious exploration money on this, Henry Lee. And we're drilling on property that your Daddy owns the mineral rights of."

"Yeah, but none of this wouldn't be happening without you and Sprocket! It isn't fair!"

He shrugged again. "You been around the oilpatch a little longer, you'd understand the economics of the situation. It don't matter a hell of a lot, anyway. We ain't in this for the money, much as I hate to admit it. It's the excitement and romance, son."

*　　*　　*

I thought the carnival had come to town when Sprocket first arrived. I was wrong. Within a week, the whole pasture was covered with strange beasts and strange equipment and even stranger people. The mud gypsies, the casing gypsies, the tool gypsies, the cement gypsies, and more—all converged on the MacFarland farmstead out of nowhere, all accompanied by one or more beasties that did something vital to the drilling of an exploratory well. In between chores, and building and placing the irrigation troughs that led from the water well to the cornfields, I usually only got loose after supper. I wandered among the tents and lean-tos they erected, breathing in the amazing sounds and smells and sights the gypsies brought with them.

The Exoco company man shouted and strutted about the camp like a little dictator. I started to understand why nobody knocked him upside the head for acting as obnoxious as he did when I realized that his company was footing the bill for everything and everybody in the pasture. Doc told him to go suck on sour gas, though, when he once made a suggestion about how to handle Sprocket.

Sprocket drilled twenty-four hours a day, his sides heaving with the effort. Illuminated at night by the light poles set up all along his length, the stokers fed him continuously the first week. Then the first of a series of bloated brown tankers showed up on the scene and hooked up to him. I was there when Doc himself stuck the hose firmly into Sprocket's eating mouth and we stood back as he began to suck on it like a calf at the teat.

"Ol' Sprocket'll eat just about anything, Henry Lee," he said with pride, "but what he loves second best is that refined, high-octane, lead-free, pure sweet gasoline."

"What's he like best?"

He grinned evil-like. "Fresh dogmeat." I hadn't seen Towser since the day Sprocket almost ate him.

"Just funnin'," Doc said before I could ask the awful question. "What he likes best of all, of course, is heavy crude. Oughta see the way he gets to shaking and shimmying and moaning when he hits a producible formation. You don't think he's workin' himself into a lather just because we play pretty music for him, do you? That's just how we sweet-talk him into doing favors for us, like drilling your little water well or trying out a wildcat some damn fool has a religious faith in, but he's in the business strictly to fill his belly with petroleum."

"And," he added, "for the romance and excitement of it all."

Eight nights after Sprocket started drilling, I snuck away from the house after bedtime. Papa hadn't come right out and told us young 'uns to stay away from them, but his mind was easy enough to see. I guess the rest of them was born to farm, but I'd lay in bed after breaking my back in the damned, boring-to-death fields, and hear pagan music, and the hum of many voices, and the whining, trembling noise Sprocket made in his search for the thing he loved best and I'd want to cry for some reason.

Doc was talking to a couple of casing gypsies when he spotted me coming. They stood in a half-circle in front of Sprocket, who was surrounded by half-a-dozen other oversized beasts. Doc didn't seem too surprised to see me. "Howdy, Henry Lee. Just couldn't stand it any longer, could you?"

"Sir?"

"I recognized the symptoms the first day, son. Not too hard to do. I got 'em myself about your age. Still got 'em."

There wasn't nothing I could say to him.

He turned to the casing gypsies. The reason I knew they were casing gypsies is they were all women. Casing gypsies always were. They wore dark green jumpsuits, but theirs fit a whole lot better than the men's. Over the next few weeks Doc told me stories about the wild ways of casing gypsies that I not only didn't believe, but due to my lack of experience, couldn't even understand half the time.

He spoke to the dark-haired woman that must have been their crew chief. "Ramonita, we're gonna be ready to start snapping on that twenty-six hundred feet of twenty-inch surface pipe in less than an hour. Big Red's hooked up and ready to cement. How come I don't see your pipe here?"

She swayed a few steps forward and tapped his chest with a black-tipped finger. "Because," she purred, "your half-smart *segundo*, Razer, moved Big Red and his bulk cement holder onto location ahead of time. They're blocking us out, as usual. They're asleep, as usual."

Her purr deepened into a snarl. "And it's your goddam job to straighten it out, not mine. We've been ready since this afternoon."

About that time, I wandered off, too embarrassed to listen to the rest of the conversation.

Ramonita was actually pretty nice once you got to know her. That night I helped her and her casing crew to snap on the surface casing. Sprocket pulled his tongue out of the hole for it. Each joint of casing was a twenty-foot tube of dark ceramic that their beast excreted. It unfolded in half lengthwise. They placed the first joint right behind his drill-head, so that his tongue rested on a double trough; then snapped it closed around the tongue and sealed the seams with a special glue. Then they hoisted the rear end off the casing vertical into the air with a sling hung from a tripod scaffolding they'd erected, and fed the first joint most of the way into the hole. The end of the length of pipe tapered in, then flared out again. The next joint's front end snapped right over that nipple, and so on.

After a few hours of lifting and snapping casing, I guess I should have been tired, but I wasn't. We worked to the rhythm of the music made by gypsies from half-a-dozen specialities, and it made that casing feel light as goose feathers.

When we were done I collapsed into a chair and watched while Big Red pumped cement down the inside of the casing and out the bottom and back up the outside into the annulus between the casing and the hole, bonding it in place. Doc strolled over with a cup and a plate heaped with sausage and thick pieces of bread.

"Here you go, Henry Lee. Oilpatch work may feed the soul, but every now and then you gotta feed the body, too."

I took a big bite of the sausage and it felt like my mouth had caught on fire, so I took a deep swig from the cup and the flames leaped higher.

"You've killed me," I finally managed to choke out. "What *is* this stuff?"

"Just boudain and a little heart-starter. Good stuff."

I took small bites of everything that was offered to

me afterwards. That heart-starter kind of growed on you after awhile, though.

A couple of hours later, I took another break and wandered over to the fire where a bunch of the hands was relaxing.

"I've been thinkin'," I said, to nobody in particular.

Doc and Razer both grabbed their hard hats and slapped them on. "Uh-oh!" Razer said. "Head for the hills!"

"Aww, come on!" I said. "I know thinking's dangerous, but I can handle the pressure."

They pretended to relax. "Well, if you're sure . . ." Doc said doubtfully.

"Seriously, what I been wondering about is—oilfield critters ain't like any other animals around. How come is that?"

"They're the last of the dinosaurs," Razer said.

"They're actually giant mutated catterpiggles created by atom bomb explosions," Big Mac, another one of Sprocket's hands, volunteered.

"They're from Australia," Pearl, the head cementer on Big Red, said. "Animals from Australia is all different from normal."

"Actually nobody knows where they come from," Doc said. "But I think they're aliens from outer space."

"You believe that old story?" Pearl asked. Half the guys around the fire hooted, but the other half just nodded.

"I read Marley Monmouth's diary in the library up at P&A," Doc said. Texas Petrological and Agricultural at Aggie Station is the main center of learning about the oilpatch. A couple of the guys on the crew had mentioned going there once or twice for vocational training on how to be better hands on their crews. One or two admitted to taking correspondence courses on occasion.

"I read that diary, too," Pearl said. "Ol' Marley had obviously slipped his transmission."

"If you'd been through what he claimed to have been through, you'd be a little funny, yourself."

"What was it he had been through?" I asked.

"He was out in the sun too long in the Anadarko Basin," Pearl snorted.

"Nobody has any record of oilpatch critters until about a hundred and twenty years ago," Doc said to me. "Until Marley Monmouth brought a herd of fifty-three of them down the main street of Duncan, Oklahoma. All the critters we know of now are descendants of that herd. He claimed that there had been almost two hundred of them, but the rest were dead. He said that he had been part of a wagon train pushing west a couple of years before. One night, strange alien monsters captured everybody in the wagon train. They took their prisoners into the wastelands where there was what we'd now call a very busy field being drilled. Marley and his people was used for slave labor to make the wells."

Doc paused for a moment as the bottle reached him.

"According to the diary, the aliens had captured several wagon trains and a bunch of Indians. They were not nice guys. They treated their hands like dogs, worked 'em till they dropped. Treated the critters awful poorly, too. There was only about two dozen of the aliens, but they had weapons that shot out rays that would burn up whoever they touched. Typhus started to sweep through the camp. The slaves got so desperate that they revolted. Most of 'em got killed. The critters helped 'em fight, and

most of them got killed, too. But some of them
escaped. Marley had half-a-dozen people with him,
including two Indians, inside one of the Cementers
when he got to Duncan, but all of them except
Marley had come down with typhus and died without talking. An exploring party went out to check his
story. Took a lot of guts back then, since it was
hostile Indian territory."

"Which is probably what really happened to his
wagon train," Pearl said. "Killed by Apaches."

"They didn't find anything but a lot of holes that
had been drilled in what is now the Anadarko basin.
No bodies. No other physical evidence. Marley said
the aliens must have disposed of everything else. He
died not long after. But by then he had explained
how the critters worked together to make a well."

"He come down with typhus, too?" I asked.

"Nope," Doc said. "Shot for bein' in the wrong
woman at the wrong time. Ol' Marley was pussy-crazy."

Razer took off his hard hat and held it over his
heart. "Our founder," he said piously. "We been
tryin' to uphold his example ever since."

"Personally, I think they're all just hallucinations,"
Pearl's *segundo*, name of Goose, said. "We're all
actually havin' the D.T.'s." He tossed me his bottle.
"Here. Drink enough of this, you wont' see 'em any
more."

I looked up at the sky and wondered.

I didn't get much sleep the next three weeks, what
with working all day in the fields and being with the
gypsies every night. I helped out on most all of the
critters at one time or another, learning how drilling
mud was mixed and why, or helping the tool gypsies
dress and move their tools when they were getting

ready to run in the hole for a squeeze job, or unpacking float shoes and collars to attach to the bottom of a string when they got ready to run it in. All of them was real friendly, answering all my dumb questions, and telling me stories about the far places they'd been and the things they'd seen and done.

But I kept coming back to Sprocket. The deeper he got, the more he had to exert himself twisting that long, talented tongue deep into the bowels of the earth, clamping his mouth over the wellhead to fight downhole hydrostatic until they could weight up the mud, whenever he hit a high-pressure zone. I got to know him inside and out, literally. Doc and the crew taught me how to care for him and keep him clean and feel inside his guts to monitor his vital signs so the stoking could speed up or slow down, or they could play music to calm him or spur him on.

They didn't need to spur him on much. He was drilling like his life depended on it.

The proudest moment for me came one night when we were down about ten thousand feet. We'd just started in the hold to hang some eight and five-eighths-inch liner pipe off the bottom of a ten and three-quarter-inch long string. I was standing at the wellhead when it slipped a little. Displaced mud gushed out of the hole, drenching me from head to foot. The second pair of coveralls I'd ruined. I only had one pair left.

When we finished up and I was kicked back sipping on some heart-starter, Doc strolled up with a cloth-wrapped package under one arm and a silver-metal hard hat under the other and dumped them at my feet.

"I don't mind you getting underfoot ever now and

then, Henry Lee," he said. "But I do mind you
doing it in them damned old messy coveralls."

I set down the cup with unsteady hands and un-
tied the string and shook open the package. Inside
were two gray, patched jumpsuits and a pair of steel-
toed work boots.

"If they don't fit, you're out of luck," he said.
"They're the biggest sizes we got."

"Thanks, Doc."

"Ain't a present," he said gruffly. "You earned
'em."

Then he strode off shouting at Big Red's crew for
not getting their cement downhole fast enough. I hid
the clothes under my bed during the daytime and
wore them at night when I went to the gypsies.

Sixteen thousand feet, seventeen thousand feet,
eighteen thousand feet, and still no strike. Sprocket's
hide began to lose its sheen and get wrinkled and
rough looking, but he drilled on, heaving and panting. He sucked gasoline in vast quantities, forcing his
tongue through rock that grew harder and hotter.
The mud circulated up practically boiling and we
began to coat his tongue with special unguents when
it came out of the hole, looking burned and chafed.

The camp grew quieter when he passed twenty
thousand feet, his maximum rated depth. More pressure, more heat, but no hydrocarbons.

I missed six nights while we got in the corn. The
weeks of no sleep finally caught up with me. I simply
couldn't anymore handle harvesting and working all
night, too. I worked like a zombie in the fields all
day, and couldn't bring myself to visit the camp
under Papa's watchful eyes when sunset neared. I

collapsed into bed right after supper each evening, sick as a dog, and slept without dreams until Papa shook me awake at dawn. Being sick don't matter when the crop's got to come in. When I saw Doc or one of the other gypsies I waved at a distance, but they only waved back and hurried about their business.

I came back the seventh night. They stood around Sprocket in silent little groups, no music, no laughing and joking.

Sprocket had somehow shrivelled. His hide hung in loose rolls all along his length and every few minutes a painful wheeze streamed from around the edges of his drilling mouth where he'd mashed it into the ground around his tongue. His head twitched spastically and his eyes were squeezed shut in agony.

Doc turned a dead face to me when I touched him on the shoulder. "Oh. Hello, Henry Lee."

He fumbled at his shoulder pocket and came out with a tobacco bag. When he saw it was empty, he let it drop.

"Sprocket's down somewhere around twenty-three thousand feet," he finally said. "We can't measure for sure, because he's refused to stop drilling for three days. We've got twenty-pound mud in the hole and he's still having to fight the bottom-hole hydrostatic. He's had his mouth dug in for a blowout preventer since noon."

I was frightened as much by the slurred, toneless way he spoke as by the meaning of his words. "Make him stop, Doc. The oil ain't worth it."

"He won't stop, Henry Lee. We've played to him, and talked to him, and shut off his gasoline, and he just won't stop."

He reached out and rubbed Sprocket's mottled skin. "Sometimes it happens this way. They just go crazy and won't stop drilling." His hand dropped to his side. "Until they die."

We stood together not saying anything for a long time. Finally I knew what I had to say, even if it wasn't true.

"You're wrong, Doc."

"What?"

"I don't believe Sprocket's gone crazy. You told me he's the best Driller in the world for finding and getting down to oil. Either you were wrong then or you're wrong now. Sprocket's going for the deepest, biggest reservoir that's ever been found."

His big hands clenched, but I guessed angry was better than the way he'd been before. "You don't know what you're saying, boy. You're just a typical worm. You run around here a couple weeks and you think you know it all. You—"

"I know one thing, Doc. Sprocket ain't in this business to kill himself. Like you said, he's in it for the petroleum!" I was shouting now, leaning right into his face, mad as hell for no reason I could say. "And for the romance and excitement, too, you son of a bitch!"

I turned around and started yelling at the other gypsies. "What's the matter with you people? Did you come here to find oil or not? How come you're standing around like a bunch of—" I tried to think of the worst thing I could call them and found it. "Like a bunch of dirt farmers!"

I rushed over to where the instruments lay in a pile and started throwing them at dumbfounded people. "Play, goddam you! Sprocket's doing his part of the deal. Least you can do is give him some music to work by if you're not gonna work yourselves."

I ran out of words and stood glaring at them.

Nobody moved. There was silence except for Sprocket's harsh panting and mine. I whirled, with a fist cocked to fly, at a scuffling noise behind me. Doc had his wand in one hand and the rhythm sticks in the other.

"I do believe you may be right, Henry Lee." His voice rose. "Come on, people. It ain't over till it's over!" In a lower voice—"I'm damned if I'll hold Sprocket's funeral while he's still alive."

I helped them hook him back into the gasoline tanker, and took turns massaging his heart muscle. We played and danced all night. I don't know if any of it did Sprocket any good. Along about daybreak I was sprawled against his side, right underneath an eye, beating my rhythm sticks together drunkenly in time with his weakening gasps while half-a-dozen gypsies kept up on their instruments. The rest had fallen asleep where they stood or sat. A long shadow fell across me and I looked up to see Papa's grim face above me.

"He's dying, Papa," I said. "He wants it so bad nothing or nobody can stop him."

"The family's in the fields finishing with the harvest, son."

"Not today, Papa. I'll be a farmer tomorrow, but please not today."

Sprocket's breathing stopped.

For a frozen second I sat there. Then I lurched up, almost knocking Papa aside. "Doc! Doc! He's not breathing."

Doc had fallen asleep in a chair, his baton slipping from his fingers to lie in the dirt. I frantically yanked him erect and dragged him to Sprocket. Shaking his head to clear it, he inserted his arm into a crease and felt around. "Pressure down to nothing," he muttered.

Finally, blessedly, I felt the tears streaming down my face. "It's over."

Then Sprocket's body started to shimmy; quick little waves travelling along his body. Doc jerked his arm out as the first real convulsion hit. Sprocket's eyes popped open, nothing but the whites showing. His body began to jerk and twist and hunch, carrying dozens of his feet off the ground at once.

Then a deep growling sound like a hurricane grew in the air and Sprocket's body began to tie itself in knots as we all backed away.

"Jesus, Son of God!" Doc yelled. "The well's coming in on us!"

I looked down at Sprocket's mouth and saw it grinding in the dirt, squeezed tightly around his tongue, and knew Doc was right. In addition to the normal bottom-hole pressure, Sprocket had drilled into a *real* high-pressure formation and the upward force was trying to blast everything out of the hole. Sprocket was fighting it with his last remaining strength.

The wrinkles in his hide disappeared as he swelled up. Doc began to backpedal. "He ain't handling the kick! His bladders are filling with mud coming up. Head for the tall grass! Blowout! Blowout!"

We all turned and ran like the devil was after us. The gasoline tanker, which was the only beast next to Sprocket, ripped loose, crashed through the fence into the woods bordering the pasture, and left a wake of shattered pine trees behind him. The rest of the beasts took off in whatever directions they were already pointed in. In the midst of the turmoil, I caught a glimpse of Papa high stepping his best. He was fresh from a night's sleep, so he was just about leading the pack. He didn't know what the hell was going on, but he was willing to find out from a safe distance.

I glanced back over my shoulder and saw Sprocket bloated like an enormous black balloon. Then he blew out. It looked and sounded like a tornado erupted full grown from the top of his head. A stormy dark gusher fountained a hundred feet in the air. I kept running. If it caught fire, I'd be fried to the bone in a second.

Finally, I fell face down between two furrows, exhausted. It started to rain on my back and I turned over. The rain was black. It was oil.

Fifteen minutes later, the gusher gradually grew smaller, and finally sank back into the ground. Cautiously, we slipped and scrambled among drenched wreckage until we came to Sprocket. Somehow, he'd held on and finally shut it in. He squirmed and wiggled happily in the middle of the mess, a deep dynamo hum vibrating his entire length.

Three mornings later the gypsies had washed off and repaired their belongings as best they could. The pasture and cornfields were covered with petroleum, black, clumpy globs of it drying in the summer sun. A welter of intersecting pipes and valves called a "Christmas Tree" guarded the hole that Sprocket had drilled. I stood on Sprocket's head and turned all the way around slowly. Papa and Grampa and my brothers clustered in front of the farmhouse.

A trail of dust led down the road back to Hemphill and places beyond, marking the departure of all of the gypsies except Doc's crew. Doc's head popped out of the hole beside me.

"About time for us to go, Henry Lee," he said.

I slid down Sprocket's side and walked slowly

toward my family. Behind me Sprocket's legs started to churn in place, limbering up for the march ahead of him.

When I hugged him, Papa tried his best to smile, because he loved me.

Sprocket's drilling mouth opened instantly when I tugged on it. We were halfway to the cattleguard before I made it through Doc's room and up his ladder.

As we looked back and waved good-bye, Doc said, "Damned if I understand you, Henry Lee. That well's gonna produce a whole lot of oil, and it's gonna be the only one around here, 'cause I don't think anyone else is crazy enough to try to get into a reservoir that deep. You could stay and be one of the richest men in this state."

I dropped my hand and turned to face the road. "Money's fine for them that value it, Doc, but I'll take the romance and excitement any day."

In-Between

We had settled down outside Waco that night. For the last week, we had mostly stayed on back roads, since Sprocket travelled slower than most any truck or car. His cruising speed was about thirty miles per hour. After dinner, Doc called me into Sprocket when I finished washing the dishes.

"How's it going so far, worm?" he asked. He stood beside a curtain that opened onto a room across the hallway from his.

"Just fine, Mr. Miller, sir. I lo-o-o-ve my job." As soon as I hired onto the crew, everybody forgot my name and started calling me "worm." Razer had explained that it was an old custom; everybody new to the oilpatch got called that until they demonstrated that they had learned the basics. Fortunately, the old custom didn't demand that I had to pretend to like it. Matter of fact, being disrespectful seemed to work better than any other response.

"Well, good," he said. "You seem to have mas-

27

tered the important stuff quick. So I got some more for you to do now."

I groaned. The important stuff he was talking about was washing or cleaning or painting or scouring anything that didn't move out of the way quick enough. I had put in fourteen-hour days since we left the farm, repairing steel hose, greasing bearings, cleaning Sprocket inside and outside, cooking dinner, cleaning up afterwards, and on and on.

It wasn't farming, and wasn't nearly as hard as farming, so I enjoyed every second of it. Of course, I didn't let anybody on the crew know that. I figured he had some more stuff for me to clean or fix.

"Hey, Sprocket, how about lightening up in there?" he called.

The warts inside the room began to glow softly, then brightened further.

"Today, we start the most important part of your schooling, boy." We stepped inside. I looked around the room. I only recognized about a third of the instruments. "You got a passable sense of rhythm," Doc continued, "but we need to get you up to speed on a real instrument."

The walls were covered with hanging tubas and oboes and trumpets and saxophones in three sizes. Black leather cases containing god-knows-what cluttered the floor. He pulled open the top drawer of a file cabinet bolted to the wall and displayed hundreds of music scores and books and further small instruments made of wood and brass.

"You got any preferences?"

I looked around the room, almost breathless. "Uh, not really. I always kinda wanted to play the fiddle."

"Huh. Afraid the violin is hard as hell to play well. Best to start on it while you're less than four feet tall.

I'd prefer we find something that you can sound decent on fairly quick. Besides, Razer already plays fiddle for us." He pulled a saxophone from the wall. "How about this? Tenor sax."

I took it gingerly and handled it for a second, looking it over. I blew into the mouthpiece. It made a sound like a horse throwing up.

"Well, maybe," I said.

I shuffled aside, fingering the keys on it. My foot bumped into a case leaning against the wall and knocked it over. The top sprang open when it hit.

It revealed my instrument.

Fifteen minutes later, we left the darkened room behind us. Doc carried the books and music folios he had pulled from the file case. I held my case by the handle. I had clipped to my belt the tiny battery-driven amplifier. The curving word "Pignose" was impressed in tin along its top, with a tiny metal snout poking out above the speaker grill.

In my room, we dumped all the goodies on the bed and I popped the case open again. Under the neck of the cherry-red instrument were extra sets of strings, a couple of cords for hooking up to the Pignose, and a flat box holding a couple of dozen picks.

I picked it up and, somehow, it felt immediately comfortable in my hands. I slipped the strap over my head and settled it across my chest. I smiled. I caressed the headstock, which was inlaid with the word "Epiphone."

Doc shook his head mournfully. "Just what the oilpatch needs. Another hillbilly guitar player."

I barely heard him. I was in love.

Sprocket Goes Courting

"It's a matter of pride to come into a new camp with your tanks topped off, Henry Lee," Doc said as we came off State 302 late in the afternoon. "Shows folks you been taking care of business."

The guy at the only filling station in town didn't act too surprised when the gleaming black hundred-and-twelve-foot length of Sprocket pulled up to the pumps and Doc and me popped out of a hole on top and slid down his flank to order eight hundred gallons of high-test. But he did want cash up front. Doc whipped out a roll big enough to choke a hog and started peeling off bills. After Exoco paid off on the well drilled on the farm, the Sprocket Limited Partnership was flush again.

I looked around and didn't see anything too interesting. Ain't many towns have a name that fits them. This one was called Notrees, and it fit like skin. Then again, we weren't out here because of what was above the ground.

I took off my goggles and wiped road dust from my

face with the bandanna I snatched out of Doc's back pocket.

Doc looked at me. "Hey, worm, get to pumping. Me and this fella's gonna be busy counting money for awhile."

"Yes, sir. Happy to, sir. Please don't beat me no more, sir."

Doc grinned through his beard and went back to business.

I pulled the pump hose loose and dragged it over to Sprocket and stuck it in his eating mouth. A quick, happy little ripple pulsed down the length of his body when he got his first taste of that sweet gasoline. I reached up and scratched hard at the crease a couple of feet above his mouth. He moaned in pleasure and the crease opened lazily, to reveal a deep green eye twice the size of my head. Sprocket and me stared at each other affectionately while he sucked his fill.

Presently, Doc and the filling station guy came around the side, talking.

"Farm and Market 181 crosses about five miles east of town," the filling station guy said, pointing. "Cut off to the left and the main camp's about a mile and a half further on. Must be about forty or fifty animals up there now. Say, which kind of animal is this one here? I still can't tell 'em apart."

"This here is the best goddam Driller in the oilpatch, Mister Oglesby. His name's Sprocket and he just finished making the deepest producing hole known to living man."

The guy shook his head admiringly. "You oil gypsies are the braggin'est people I ever seen. Every one I talk to says their animal's the finest there is."

"Most of 'em are liars," Doc admitted. "But I ain't."

Eleven of us made up Sprocket's drilling crew, and we'd all washed up and put on our best jumpsuits and tuned up the instruments that needed tuning. Sprocket's hundreds of feet fell into a loose dancing stroll as we rounded a bend in the road and sighted off to the left the dozens of tents and animals that made up the camp. Every man stood waist high, poked out of a hole on top of Sprocket. Being the pusher on the rig, Doc had the room most forward, so he poked out of a hole just back of Sprocket's bullet head. He faced backward toward us, raised his conductor's baton up high, then kicked the band into a jazzy tune called "Downhole Dreamer."

By the time we got to the center of the camp we were setting that song on fire. Razer poured out a flowing river of music from his fiddle, underlining and clarifying the complicated melody. I still had a long way to go before I'd be able to play guitar with the band, so I still kept time by banging the rhythm sticks together.

Before we were halfway through the song, gypsies from the camp had surrounded Sprocket, many of them adding their own instruments to the music-making. Sprocket danced in a rippling circle through the final, drawn-out chorus.

When the last note died away, Doc nodded and slid his baton back into the pocket running down his left leg. "If you boys worked as hard as you play, we'd all be rich." He surveyed the camp and called out. "Who's camp boss around here? We heard there was some hole bein' made in these parts and come for a piece of it."

An older man stepped forward from the crowd. "We can always use another Driller. Welcome to the field. I'm Zeke King, and I'd be honored if you gentlemen would allow me to buy you a round."

We adjourned to a large tent nearby, with folks following us in until it was pretty near filled. A couple of casing gypsies worked behind the bar.

After the first couple of doses of heart-starter and getting acquainted, Doc and Zeke got around to talking business. I only heard a few snatches of the conversation, due to the noise in the tent and the fact that the casing gypsy that served my drinks was cuter than a month-old foal. Kept stealing my attention, the way she gracefully sashayed back and forth, every now and then flashing electric-blue eyes in my direction.

"Hydroco's got the field purty well sewed up," Zeke said. "About a year ago, they came in and drilled a couple of test holes, then P-and-A'ed 'em all and left." I already knew what he was leading up to then, from bull sessions with Doc and the rest of the crew on the way here. You Plug and Abandon a well when you don't find any hydrocarbons worth producing. Sometimes companies do it to fake out the competition. "So, nine months later, when everybody had about forgotten 'em, their land men slipped in and quietly bought up lease options on damn near every piece of property in sight. A couple of small independents caught on toward the last and managed to get a few leases, but Hydroco's playing hardball." He shrugged. "Tough on the independents, especially while we're running past the full capacity of the camp here, but it makes for nice prices when it comes time to dicker for service."

Doc nodded. "Yeah, I see how they could pull off

something like that in this godforsaken wilderness. Must be costing 'em, though."

"They act like they don't care. It's a small field, but they figure there's enough petroleum down there to make it worthwhile to go for it all."

I lost track of the conversation for a minute or two again, because that little casing gypsy came by and refilled my glass. Her dark green jumpsuit was unzipped further than a preacher might like. In the process of pouring, she bent over a bit more than was strictly necessary and handed me a couple of glimpses of heaven. Paralyzed my mind for a while. The sweet smile she gave me didn't help, either.

By the time I regained consciousness, another fella had joined Doc and Zeke. He wasn't wearing a jumpsuit, just jeans, a white shirt, and work boots. They spoke in low tones, with the other fella's face changing from hopeful to frustrated.

Doc poured a dose from the bottle him and Zeke shared. "I'd surely be happy to do business with y'all if we can work out a deal, Mr. Mooney, but me and my boys just finished a week on the road. We'd like a day or two to rest and get the lay of the land."

The fella smiled unhappily. "Well, Mr. Miller, just keep in mind that I'm willing to pay premium prices for your rig time, with good bonuses."

Doc stuck out his hand and Mr. Mooney reluctantly shook it. "I'll keep you in mind, sir," Doc said. "We'll settle things one way or the other before too long."

The fella handed him a business card and started to drift away. "Remember, I got a room at the Driscoll Hotel in town."

Doc raised his glass and nodded. "Yes, sir. I'll remember that."

Shoulders slumped, Mr. Mooney left the tent.

I came up behind Doc and touched his elbow. He turned and grinned at me. "Oh, howdy, Henry Lee. Zeke, this here's Henry Lee MacFarland, new worm we picked up on the way over from that mess at Morgan City field I was telling you about. He'd appreciate it if you could tell him the name of that little honey behind the bar, the one with the black hair down to her sitter. And if she's hooked up with anybody right now."

I expect I turned red. Zeke laughed and stuck out his hand. "Pleasure meeting you, Henry Lee. Everybody calls her Star, and she ain't tied down that I know of. You got a fair shot at her, since I hear she likes 'em big and ugly."

I nodded and kept from crunching his hand to splinters. When I turned fifteen, Papa took me out behind the barn and convinced me to handle normal size people gently-like. They break too easy.

I turned to Doc. "I couldn't help noticing—"

"Yeah, I noticed that you couldn't help noticing."

"Uh . . . not that. I mean, it looked like you was turning down an offer by that Mooney fella to drill a well for him."

Doc nodded and took a sip from his shot glass. "Sure was. Don't believe in swimming upstream if it can be helped. He runs Mooney Producing. Him and anybody that works for him is going to have a hard time from Hydroco. Besides—" He looked at Zeke. "How many leases he got?"

"Three. And they run out in four months if he don't make hole on them."

Doc shrugged. "Hydroco may drill more'n a hundred wells hereabouts. You figure from there, Henry Lee."

It wasn't hard to figure.

"So," Doc continued, "long about tomorrow morning I'll make a call on the drilling superintendent for Hydroco and we'll do some business."

"Don't believe you'll need to wait till then," Zeke said. "He's coming in the tent now."

We swung casually around to look toward the entrance. Framed in the opening by the setting sun was a fella that looked to be the size of a grizzly bear. With not much less hair on him.

"Name's Jack Small. Everybody calls him—"

"Everybody calls him Tiny," Doc said in a voice so cold it must have hurt his teeth. "We've met." He leaned back and put his elbows up behind him on the bar, with the bottle hanging loosely from his right hand.

The fella at the entrance looked around the tent and spotted Zeke. He started through the crowd in our direction. About halfway, he saw Doc and stopped in his tracks. Their eyes locked up. After a second he moved forward again until he stood in front of Doc.

Doc stayed leaning back casually, eyes staring straight into Tiny's eyes. "Henry Lee, meet Mr. Tiny Small," he said, smiling. "I owe him a big favor. Four years ago he was the company man on a hole we was drilling down near Thompson's Bottom. I was *segundo* under Cutbait Benton. Nice old guy. I moved up to being Sprocket's pusher after Tiny murdered him. Thanks for the help, old buddy."

"You're a lyin' son of a bitch," Tiny growled. "It was a fair fight."

"Fair, my ass. Cutbait was half your size, and you didn't even give him time to back away before you broke his skull."

It happened quick. Tiny's right hand shot out.

Without even thinking, I grabbed his wrist before his hand wrapped around Doc's throat. It was like yanking on a crowbar set in cement, but his hand moved back a few inches. Meantime, Doc had smashed his bottle against the bar and pressed the jagged end against Tiny's stomach.

All three of us held in place for a couple of breaths, thinking about the next move. Finally, Tiny growled and stepped back, twisting his wrist loose from my grip and glaring at me. Then he turned on Doc. "Put down the bottle and we'll do some business, right here, right now."

Doc showed his teeth. This time it wasn't anything close to being a smile. "I ain't in the mood for dancing, old buddy. Druther carve you up seriously. Grab a bottle for your own self."

For just a second, Tiny looked around like he might take Doc up, then he turned and moved toward the entrance. "You ain't never working for Hydroco again," he threw back over his shoulder. "Not in this field nor anyplace else!"

Doc, me, and everybody else in the silent tent took a shaky breath when he was gone. Doc looked regretfully at the weapon in his hand. "Well, hell, it was almost empty anyway," he muttered.

The next morning, Doc and Razer vanished right after breakfast, taking Sprocket with them. I felt disappointed because Star's crew had been called out to location right after the little scene with Tiny. I hadn't even got to introduce myself. Now it looked like we might be heading on down the road before we even got properly settled in. But I wasn't as hungover as most of the crew, so I fiddled away the morning working on some junked-up hose connections that'd been left behind.

They came back around noon. We packed up and headed out to make location on one of the three Mooney Producing leases.

It was barren, flat, dusty country all the way. When we drew up on it, a mile from the nearest road, I saw that we weren't exactly alone. We all climbed out of Sprocket and Doc hurried over to the pickup truck in which Mr. Mooney had guided us to the lease. I tagged along. The way to graduate from being a worm is to poke your nose into everything that nobody stops you from.

"Goddam it, Mooney, you didn't say nothing about this!" Doc started off.

Mr. Mooney stepped off the pickup's running board and shut the door behind him. "Didn't seem important," he said mildly. "They're on adjoining leases. Ain't none of our business, really."

A half-a-mile away two other Drillers, accompanied by Mud Mixers and Gas Tankers, were making hole. Sprocket and them formed a roughly equal triangle. Doc pointed at the one on the left. "That one over there is a female!"

Mr. Mooney squinted and pretended to be surprised. "Well, so she is." He dug a tobacco tin out of his jeans pocket, opened it, and popped a chaw into his cheek. "Started drilling three days ago, both of them. Tend to make a man think there's oil somewheres hereabouts."

Suddenly Doc laughed. "You sneaky bastard! You acted like I was breakin' it off in you on the daily rig charge. With a female over there, Sprocket's gonna be drilling full tilt all the way to TD."

Mr. Mooney shrugged. "Still want to do some business?"

"Hell, yeah! You ever seen a mating drill before?"

"Nope. Kinda looking forward to it."

We drifted back to where the crew was clustered around Sprocket, joking and pointing at the other two Drillers.

Sprocket wandered around the lease for awhile, getting the feel of it. Eventually he stopped in one place and began seismic testing. His hundreds of feet drove hard in cadence against the ground, raising a powdery cloud along the length of his body for five minutes. Then he meandered some more and did it again in another place. Listening for oil-bearing sands.

The two Drillers on the adjoining leases made it almost a certainty that he'd hear something worth going after, but I noticed that all of us clustered together holding our breaths when he finally finished up and ambled in our direction. Sprocket wasn't hardly ever wrong. If he said no hydrocarbons, Doc would probably cancel the contract with Mr. Mooney. And I could tell he didn't want to do that.

Sprocket approached and towered over us. Suddenly his deep green eyes popped wide open, whirling madly. A groan of anticipation shuddered through his body. His drilling mouth gaped open and his tongue shot out, white and translucent, to wrap around Doc's legs. It yanked him to the ground, then flailed through the drilling crew, knocking men off their feet like tenpins. Shouting and laughing, everybody that was able to grabbed ahold of that wild, twisting, drilling tongue and wrestled with it. I got a grip behind the drill-head and held on for dear life.

We were going to make us some hole!

* * *

Mr. Mooney left location to make arrangements for Gas Tankers and surface casing, as well as lining up a Mud Mixer for later on. He seemed to feel that now that he had a Driller under contract he wouldn't have too hard a time with the rest. Doc wasn't so sure, but it wasn't his problem.

We spudded in around three that afternoon, with the usual gypsy ceremonies. Sprocket's gasoline reserves would let him drill for about three or four days before needing a refill.

Sprocket positioned himself facing the female Driller, his eyes fixed on her. Doc and the rest of the guys wouldn't tell me what was going on, just made the squiggly worm sign with their fingers and grinned when I asked, but it was pretty obvious. Him and the other male Driller was competing for her affections, as they say. I speculated the one that showed to be making hole the most sincerely would get her. But how would she know who was doing the best? It took me a while, but I come to the conclusion that she'd know who was drilling fastest by taking seismic readings while she drilled. I was awful proud of myself for figuring it out so good without any help.

We played music for about an hour after Sprocket started drilling. Afterwards, I was leaning against his side, watching him get it on and feeling the screaming hum that vibrated through him, when Razer walked up and squatted beside me. Me and Razer got along fine. He was about ten years older than me, and rough as a rooster in a brand-new henhouse. Talked a lot about the baby-dolls he'd known and the fights he'd lost. He was a good old boy. He was holding a shovel in his left hand.

"Time for you to get some more technical education about making a well, worm." I looked at the shovel. He patted it. "We plant to make about twenty-six hundred-foot of twenty-inch hole before we set surface casing."

I nodded. "Just like you did on the well you drilled on my farm."

"Yeah, Doc usually likes to start off that way. That's about as deep as the Railroad Commission will generally let you drill before getting on your butt to lay pipe." He pulled a little book with a red cover out of his back pocket and started thumbing through its dog-eared pages. "Yo, here's your lesson for today. Capacity of Hole." The page was covered by a table of numbers. No words, hardly. Just numbers, I followed his pointing finger. "Twenty-inch hole has a capacity of 2.1817 cubic feet per linear foot. Sprocket makes about four hundred-foot of hole on a good day. And he's gonna have a lot of good days, this being a mating drill. Let's us figure three days before Mooney gets us a mud crew out here. Twelve hundred-foot of hole. That calculates to a tad more than twenty-six hundred cubic foot of cuttings coming up out of that hole. Them cuttings have to go somewheres."

"I gotta dig a reserve pit," I said.

He clapped me on the shoulder. "It's a pleasure schooling a young worm as smart as you, Henry Lee." He handed me the shovel. "Me and Doc figure a pit ten deep by fifteen wide by twenty long will do just fine until the mud crew can get here and make their own big one."

I couldn't believe what I was hearing. "Razer, digging a hole that size will kill me dead!"

"Do the best you can, worm. Me and Doc have confidence in you."

I moaned. "What if the mud crew don't show up in a couple of days?"

He stroked the end of his moustache. "These shovels is built solid-like. Don't wear out for a *long* time."

When I drag-assed around to the other side of Sprocket I saw all of the fellas on the crew standing in a circle about thirty feet away. All of them had shovels in their hands. Behind me Razor snickered and pushed me forward. "They been waiting for you to make the first shovelful, Henry Lee. We gonna let the worm spud in on this particular hole."

We worked late into the night on that damn pit. Of course, the mud crew arrived the next day before dinner time. Burned me up.

I shouldn't admit it, but there's usually a fair amount of time for screwing off when you're on location. Oh, sure, Sprocket needs caring for, and so does the hole, but a lot of it is just standing back for a day or a week and letting him do his business, then stepping forward and working like an animal as long as necessary. Trouble is, you got to pay attention, because it can change from off-duty to assholes-and-elbows in a matter of minutes.

This one started lazy in its own way. We got a good mud crew, and that can make or break you right there. Seems Tiny had hacked off their mud engineer, too. I never heard it spoken, but it seemed to me that him and Doc figured to make as many holes for the independents in the field as they could, just to mess with Tiny; then move on to where matters weren't so tense. Good thing about being a gypsy is you don't have to kiss nobody's butt unless you got a taste for it. Just pull up stakes and find somebody more reasonable to do business with.

Until we got to setting our first string of casing, there really wasn't a whole lot to do, besides maintenance chores. I practiced guitar steady. Doc said his main instrument was the piano, but he was a composer and arranger, so he knew how to play everything a little. He spent as much time as he could teaching me the basics. I had trouble with the instructional materials sometimes, since I never was much for book-learning. At first, I couldn't make a musical sound at all, but after I learned a few chords and the movable Major/Relative Minor scale, it started being fun. My hands and fingertips ached all the time.

Sprocket drilled and sucked from a Tanker full of gas, every now and then wanting some music played to keep him happy. We started with fresh water in the hole for mud. We'd move on to the more exotic and complex mixtures as we got deeper and encountered formations requiring them. Mr. Mooney moved his trailer onto location and wandered around sticking his nose into things. He was polite about it all. Mostly because he was a naturally polite fella, I think, but also because he sure as hell didn't want no personal problems with the crew of the only Driller he had any chance of getting to make a well for him.

I ran chores for everybody. The worm on the rig does everything from bringing coffee to looking for the left-handed pipe wrenches. In between chores and guitar practice, Razer broke me into the mysteries of the red book. I never would have believed all the figuring you have to do to make a well. You got to be able to figure volumes and heights, displacement and capacity, buoyancy factors, hydrostatic pressure and fluid weight conversion, chemical and physical properties of various gases and liquids as they affect the well, and on and on till you want to puke. Razer told me we'd just get a running head start with it on this well. I wasn't all that hot with numbers either, and the red book about broke my mind on occasion. I'd be schooling for years before I could balance all that on the fly. Made me realize that digging that reserve pit was one of the easy jobs.

The crews on the other two rigs were friendly enough. Even though they were drilling for Hydroco, that didn't mean we was enemies. We visited back and forth and partied together a couple of nights. The female was named Munchkin, and her crew was tickled pink that she had two males courting her at once. Spanky Blankenship, the male Driller's pusher, didn't seem to mind the competition from Sprocket. Uncle Foots was a strong, young, deep rig almost as big as Sprocket, and he had a three-day head start on his hole, though I didn't know till later what kind of difference that could make in the contest.

On the sixth day after we spudded, Sprocket reached twenty-six hundred feet. We'd moved to a light, gel-based mud containing some particulates because we'd been losing returns on the fresh water. Nothing serious, just meant we had gone through a water zone and it was taking circulating fluid into it. The gel and particulates caked up and helped seal off the zone from the hole until we could cement it. Sprocket started coming out of the hole, getting ready for running surface pipe, so Doc figured it was a good time to clean his mud bladder. Sometimes you have to wash him out by hand because running water through the bladder won't do the job well enough, what with the particulates settling out and sticking to the walls.

It was messy work. I climbed around inside the bladder, scrubbing with a soft brush while Sprocket trickled water in. Whenever it got about knee-deep I'd bail out the solution with a bucket, dumping it into a tub set in a framework a couple feet off the ground right below the sphincter that opened on the outside world. The tub had a nipple on the bottom, and I'd knocked together a couple of lengths of suction hose, leading them off to the reserve pit, so at least I didn't have to worry about emptying the tub when it got full.

I finished up after a couple of hours. I guess I must've looked like the Abominable Sludgeman. I climbed out of the bladder rear end first through the sphincter, feeling behind me with my feet. Just as I straightened up, standing in the middle of the tub, something touched my ankle. Startled the hell out of me. I yelped and twisted halfway around, slipping in the gunk that was still on the bottom of the tub. Before I knew what was happening, the tub flipped out from under me and I fell backwards onto whoever had touched my leg.

I ended up on top. I might have guessed who it would be. The zipper on her jumpsuit mashed against my mouth. It was located down about where it had been the last time I watched it. I moved my head back a few inches and saw I'd smeared mud all over her. Confused, I untangled my hand from her hair and tried to rub some of the mud off her chest, then froze, realizing what I was doing and exactly where I was doing it.

She giggled. Her hand moved to cover mine, but

didn't seem to be in a hurry to move it. I knew I should say something to apologize, but I couldn't figure out what. Some girls have that effect. Make you turn stupid.

Finally, she squirmed out from under me and sat up and finished brushing herself off as best she could. "Looks like we could both use a bath, Henry Lee. You are Henry Lee, aren't you?"

I nodded.

"Well, Henry Lee, you know any place around here two people can take a bath?"

I felt sorrowful. I shook my head.

She ran fingers through her hair, untangling the snarls as much as possible, taking a deep breath or two. I tried to keep from fainting. "Aw, too bad," she said. "Maybe some other time, huh?"

I nodded.

"You do talk, don't you, Henry Lee?"

I nodded. She looked at me like she was waiting for something.

"Oh . . . oh, yeah," I said. "Uh, pleased to meet you, Star."

"How'd you know my name?" She stood up and started brushing off her jumpsuit.

I had an answer for that one. "Same as you know mine. I asked somebody."

She extended a hand to help me up. "I didn't ask anybody your name. Doc just requested me to find you 'cause y'all need to set up for my crew to run pipe."

My feelings must have showed on my face, because she looked me in the eye and said, "I might have asked if I'd had to, though. You're kinda cute." I grinned foolishly. "A little bit clumsy, though," she finished.

I couldn't take that, even off her. "If I'm so clumsy, how come I landed on top?" I asked.

She took my arm and led me towards Sprocket's front, where they were setting up to run pipe. "Maybe I wanted you on top," she said softly. Her fingers pressed into the muscle of my biceps, making it get hard in response. Then she walked off to get with her crew to help them set up the pipe derrick.

We started in the afternoon and set surface casing through the night. I took turns between paying attention to Sprocket's needs and helping with the pipe. I hadn't known that Star was the *segundo* on the crew, which meant that she did most of the supervising and a lot of the actual work, while her crew chief, lady name of Sabrina, kicked back and chatted with Doc while she kept an eye on the overall operation. Seems Doc and Sabrina had known each other off and on for some years and were real good friends.

Sprocket laid his tongue down for the first twenty-foot joining of casing to be snapped shut behind his drill-head. Then the casing gypsies with the epoxy pots mixed up some and spread it along the seam that ran lengthwise down the casing joint. It was a quick, thermosetting resin that hardened up in just a few minutes while they hoisted the joint up vertical in the air and ran most of its length in the hole. The joining narrowed slightly a couple of feet before the end, then flared out again. The next length of pipe was hoisted up in the derrick and snapped over the first one's nipple, epoxied, and let down in the hole itself. Then again. And again. We did that for almost eleven hours, putting a hundred and thirty joints of

sixteen-inch casing in the hole, averaging one every
five minutes.

Sprocket hummed and grunted and danced in place
while the crew played wild, high-energy music to
keep us moving that casing at a good clip. The casing
gypsies sang a clear, pure harmony while they yanked
joints off the pipe rack and hoisted them twisting and
spinning in the air, throwing capering shadows around
us, then stabbed them on the joint sticking out of the
hole. Somehow, whenever I looked at Star, she was
looking at me. Eventually, a billion bright night suns
came out in that infinite high-plains sky.

I ain't smart enough to really explain what it feels
like. All I know is, it's better than anything else I
ever run into. You go out onto locations in places
that God's forgot about. You put up with boredom
and hard weather and staying dirty and wet for days
on end and you do without sleep until the insides of
your bones hurt.

And it's worth it. No matter where you go, you got
family, you got friends. And I got Sprocket. I get to
be one of the gypsies that has the dangerous chore of
tearing into the Earth and, with heart and guts and
skill, ripping from its dark hiding places the petroleum that powers an entire civilization.

That evening, Big Red and his crew pulled onto
location and began to set up to cement when we got
all the pipe in the hole. This was the same bunch
that had done the cementing on the well on my
Papa's farm. They'd come to the field ahead of us,
and Doc was glad to see them. He told me cement
crews were all crazy people, and I should stay the
hell away from them socially if I planned to keep out
of jail. Earl the Pearl, the cementer on Big Red,

seemed to select his crew on their ability to party twice as hard and sleep twice as much as the average human being. But Doc said there wasn't nobody that could concrete like they could.

I was eating breakfast and watching Pearl release his top plug so Big Red could pump it downhole when Star wandered over and hunkered down in front of the fire. She poured herself a cup of coffee. She'd gotten cleaned up and put on a shiny new green jumpsuit. The zipper was in the usual place.

"Been a long night, Henry Lee,' she said, flashing those glowing blue eyes at me over the rim of her cup. "You about ready to go to bed?"

I nearly choked on my biscuit. She stretched like a cat and went on as if she hadn't noticed. "Myself, I ain't all that sleepy. Razer tells me you ain't spent much time around casing animals yet. Thought you might like a tour of Lady Jane."

Actually, I'd seen about as much as I wanted to of the insides of the Casing Critters when they was drilling the well on my Papa's farm, but it looked like Razer thought I needed more schooling on the subject, and who was I to argue?

So I said sure, gulped a last piece of ham down, and followed Star over to where Lady Jane stood. She looked a lot like Sprocket at first glance. I could understand how the fella at the filling station in town might have gotten confused. But if you looked careful, you could tell the difference. She had about twenty percent fewer legs, for instance, and her hide wasn't strictly black like a Driller's but more of a deep chocolaty color.

Star scratched her a bit and talked to her, introducing me, then we went inside through her mouth.

The differences inside were even more obvious. No drilling tongue, since she didn't drill. What she did was eat a lot of everything she could get her teeth on, especially gravel. Star led me down the center of the hallway that ran her length.

"When Lady Jane eats, the material is digested through a series of stomachs, then separated into two distinct bladders that run along her sides." She rubbed a toe along one of the two curbs that ran the length of Lady Jane just in front of the doors. "The bladders extrude processed material into these tubular sacs. She can produce four joints at a time on each side, for a total of eight joints of casing at a time, in two different sizes. Right now, for instance, she's working on some eleven and three-quarter stuff we'll be putting into a well up north of Notrees in a couple of days."

To tell the truth, I'd been so fascinated by Sprocket when he was drilling on the farm that I really hadn't found out that much about casing. "How can you control what size pipe she manufactures?"

"Same way you control Sprocket's drilling. She recognizes certain tunes as signals for certain kinds of casing. And we talk to her. Like Sprocket, she understands about two hundred words."

"Sounds pretty simple."

She gave a shake of her head, making her long hair swirl. "Wrong. The casing has to meet a lot of specifications. The length, weight, and outer diameter of each joint have to be uniform, with a specified maximum drift, to fit in the hole properly. Likewise with the inner diameter, for setting downhole tools inside. Depending on what quality of casing you're producing, from F-25 up to V-150, you got to come up to American Petrogypsy Institute standards on collapse and burst pressures, elasticity, and tensile strength, not to mention resistance to chemicals encountered in the well, especially acids and bases. The casing itself is a complex, bonded, multi-ply organometallic ceramic composite. Any impurities or inaccuracies in manufacture means it don't come up to API and makes great drainpipe in some town's sewer system."

I was impressed. "You're mighty serious about this, ain't you?"

She smiled, and it was a different Star, not the flirty mind-killing female I'd seen up to now. "I'm as serious about Lady Jane and casing as you are about Sprocket and drilling, Henry Lee." Then the smile changed and she was back to her other self.

She strolled down past a couple more curtains made of Lady Jane's flesh, coming to stop beside one. "I guess I fibbed a little, Henry Lee. Actually, I'm pretty tuckered out." She pried open the curtain, to show a room not unlike those inside Sprocket. A large, downy bed covered half its space. Embroidered, colorful rugs hung on the walls and covered the floor, and a ladder was bolted into Lady Jane's flesh, leading to a hole in the ceiling.

"You like my place?" She looked at me over her shoulder as she stepped in. I stood in the doorway. The temperature must have been going up quick. I felt like I was on fire. My tongue felt too thick and dry in my mouth to let me speak.

"I bet you're tired, too." She sat down on the bed. "Maybe not *too* tired, though?" She pulled the zipper all the way down on her jumpsuit and shrugged out of the top. It fell until it was stopped by the swell of her hips. Then she stood up and and swayed toward, me, lifting her arms to pull her hair back.

"You think you can help me get this the rest of the way off, darling?"

It was like somebody else took control of me. Whoever he was, he was an idiot. "I gotta go, Star."

She stopped a foot in front of me, amazed.

I looked at the floor. My mouth said more words without me willing them. " 'Scuse me. I, uh, I'll see you later on . . ." I stumbled back and the curtain slipped closed on her outraged, hurt expression.

When I could think again, I was outside. I saw Doc going toward the edge of the lease on the side toward where Uncle Foots was drilling. I figured he was going to do some visiting, and maybe it would be a good idea for me to get off location for awhile. Then I saw Razer and a couple other of the fellas running after him. Then I saw the look on Doc's face and my eyes swung to where he was going.

Tiny Small stood on the edge of the lease, with Uncle Foots' crew behind him, shifting back and forth on their feet, looking uncomfortable. Tiny towered over Mr. Mooney, who stood just on his side of the property line laid out by surveyor's stakes.

I was right behind Doc as he strode up beside Mr. Mooney.

"You know you're not welcome here, Mr. Small," Mr. Mooney was saying. "You step onto this lease and interfere with the drilling operation I've contracted for and I swear I'll have the Sheriff jail you for trespass and assault."

"Suits the hell out of me," Tiny said. He took a step, then looked at Doc. "Better yet, how about I invite your chicken-hearted pusher over to my side for a little, whatcha call it, Doc? A little dance?"

Doc growled and stepped forward. Mr. Mooney put a hand across Doc's chest. "Godammit, Doc!

That's just what he wants! We're already losing rig time!"

I looked over my shoulder and saw that he was right. Sprocket had stopped drilling and was watching us.

Doc looked at him. "Mr. Mooney, it won't take me more than a few minutes to step over there and rip off his head and piss down his neck."

"I don't give a damn what you do on your own time, but as long as Sprocket's on my location, you're on my time. If you can't live up to your contract, pull out of the hole and head on down the road. I don't need to worry every day whether somebody's gonna come along and distract you from taking care of business."

"He's right, Doc," Razer said. "We're here to make some hole. Everything else can wait."

Tiny raised a hand and picked his nose and flicked it at Doc. "If you had any balls you'd already be over here, fuckhead."

And it happened again, like it had the last time I saw Doc face Tiny in the tent. Suddenly he changed from hot as a pistol to cold, cold, cold. His voice went soft and deep. "No hurry, Tiny. You be in camp when we finish producing this well. We'll see who walks away and who gets carried away." He turned his back on Tiny. "Okay, people. Break's over. Time to get back to making hole." He raised his voice. "That means you too, Sprocket!" Sprocket made a wet, floppy, spluttering sound around his tongue and went back to drilling and marching.

The fun part of making this well was over, for awhile. The weather turned mean, cold and windy and usually wet. We didn't much party with the other crews for fear that Tiny might have us busted for trespassing or something. Just stayed on our lease and took care of Sprocket while he drilled.

We hit oil at around ninety-three hundred feet. Mr. Mooney got medium excited. Had a straddle packer with some test tools run in the open hole. It was a marginally producible zone. Way too much sulfur in it, among other things. When they flow-tested, it came in okay for awhile, then dropped off. Not much pressure, not much volume, not much quality. Not much worth messing with.

So we ran a string of thirteen and three-eighths pipe down and cemented over it. Star's crew came out to run it, and she mostly ignored the hell out of me. While they were on location, I kept rehearsing a speech inside my head about how I was sorry and wanted to be her friend and would she give me another chance. Somehow, I didn't ever get my nerve up enough to say it to her.

That evening, Razer wandered over and sat down beside me where I was staring into a camp fire I'd lit off by myself on the edge of the location.

"What's the matter with you, Henry Lee? You been acting like somebody shot your dog."

"Aw, I don't know, Razer."

"Uh-huh. You been getting a little insane over Star, ain't you? I noticed y'all not talking to each other. What happened, you come on too hard when you made your run at her?"

"I wish that was it! I didn't have a chance to make no moves, she was coming on to me so strong."

"Well, hey, that ain't nothing to be moping around about. That's one fine-looking little baby-doll."

"Except she's all bent out of shape and won't talk

to me no more." I felt more and more like an idiot as I told him what happened.

He was flabbergasted. "You mean this baby-doll asked you in for a visit—and you turned her down? You said 'No ma'am, I don't believe I want none of that fine stuff.' You—" Words failed him. The idea of turning her down was so strange that he just couldn't handle it.

"You don't understand, Razer. It's because I like her."

"Like her? Goddammit, Henry Lee, if you actually like her, you're even worse retarded to turn her down. The only ones you dump is the ones that make your stomach turn."

"It's just I didn't want her getting no wrong ideas—"

"Wrong ideas! She had the best goddam idea in the world! What is the matter with your head, son?"

We went around for a while, and I just couldn't make Razer see it, but I guess talking helped me understand a little more. Mostly, I guess it was that if I'd been chasing after her, I'd know what to do if I caught her. But she'd been chasing me, and I wasn't sure at all what would happen if she caught me. Razer and Doc had told me about casing gypsies. I wasn't afraid she'd think she owned me for life. I was afraid she'd jump me once and then be on her way to the next fella.

We figured there was some serious hydrocarbons somewhere down there, but didn't know where. Only that it looked like it was going to be deep. Doc kept an eye on where Uncle Foots and Munchkin were, but we couldn't trade well information with them any more, since Tiny declared them to be tight holes. Tight hole means no well information at all goes out.

We had to keep weighting up our mud as we got deeper, with more hydrostatic pressure, but it wasn't a scary deal, like with the well on the farm. Sprocket would come out of the hole when you needed him to, for working on his tongue, or whatever. But he *was* drilling hard as he could. Razer said Sprocket was having five-hundred-foot days, and if he kept it up all the way down, we just might beat Uncle Foots in the mating drill. I moped around, but I guess you get used to anything, so mostly it didn't show and didn't keep me from taking care of business.

We hung a nine and five-eighths-inch liner off the bottom of the thirteen and three-eighths down to fifteen thousand feet. We hadn't been having any problems with hole collapse or nothing, but Doc figured there wasn't no sense in pushing our luck. Big Red ran the cement, but the casing crew wasn't Lady Jane's.

The liner tested out fine; didn't have to squeeze the shoe or the top of it. Another high-class job from Big Red.

Sprocket drilled some more.

At seventeen thousand feet, the Gas Tankers quit arriving. Mr. Mooney drove his pickup into town to check it out. He didn't come back that day. Sprocket's gas reserves started getting low, due to the sincerity of his drilling.

The mud crew needed to go to camp to stock up on barite and a few other chemicals their engineer felt they were running low on, so me and Doc rode into town the next morning with them and their beast, leaving Razer in charge of the location. We found Mr. Mooney in one of the three beds in the infirmary right off the Notrees town square.

He was banged up bad. Couple of cracked ribs.

His face looked like somebody had broke a whole fistful of knuckles on it. Or maybe they just used a two-by-four.

He didn't talk so well, what with the way his mouth had been rearranged. "It was Tiny," he mumbled.

Doc just nodded. He'd already figured that part out.

Seems that Mr. Mooney had gone to the gas depot to see why we wasn't getting any, and was told that the bank had cut off his credit. He stormed over to talk to his banker, who wouldn't tell him much, just kept saying that they'd been keeping an eye on the situation and felt he had become a bad risk and they weren't throwing good money after bad. Mr. Mooney figured Tiny had gotten to the banker somehow. And when he'd gone to face Tiny about it in his office—"Dumbass move, there," Doc muttered—Tiny had put the hurt to him. A couple of the goons that hung around with Tiny told the Sheriff that Mr. Mooney started it. It was his word against theirs.

"Sorry, Doc," Mooney finished. "Guess Tiny's beat us."

Doc snorted. "Naw. He's just upped the ante a little bit."

"But I don't have no cash left. We were running on credit."

"Your credit's still good with me, Mooney, and we got enough money from that monster well that Sprocket drilled on Henry Lee's farm to bankroll the rest of this operation."

Outside, Doc squinted up at the sun and headed toward the camp. "That was real nice," I said. "Helping out Mr. Mooney that way."

He grunted. "Ain't no nice about it. The man owes

us money, and if we let Tiny bust him, we'll never see it. We stir a little of our own cash into the pot, I figure we got a pretty good chance of coming out ahead on the deal."

"How come Tiny gets away with all this stuff? If he's as rotten as he looks to be, somebody should have fixed his wagon a long time ago."

"I imagine some have tried. But he's big and mean, and in case you haven't figured, he don't fight real clean, either. And his sponsor happens to be the regional vice president of Hydroco."

"What's a sponsor?"

"Well, I guess I'm your sponsor, for instance. Your sponsor is the person that looks out for you, helps you on up the ladder, bails you out when you screw up. Now, the big oil companies, some of 'em, play heavy games that way. If you don't have a decent sponsor, you don't go nowhere in the company, no matter how good you are at your job. You have a good sponsor, he takes care of you, and you climb the ladder, even if your'e a asshole like Tiny.'

"How come somebody would be Tiny's sponsor?"

"Probably Tiny does dirty work for him that most folks wouldn't touch. Having a sponsor ain't a one way deal, it's one of those back-scratch affairs. Your sponsor helps you climb the ladder, you help him keep from falling off it. Nobody can survive by himself in a large corporation. You got to have troops backing you up, snitching for you, doing stuff to take out your competition."

"Well, if you're my sponsor, what am I supposed to do for you?"

"Work your butt off and take care of Sprocket. We don't play the sponsor game like the oil companies. I sponsored you onto the crew because I believe you have a natural aptitude for this business. You work hard without bitching too much, and I ain't never seen Sprocket take to anybody as quick as he did with you."

"Same here. Sprocket's great."

"Well, we'll see how you feel once the new wears off. Meantime, we got to go arrange for some juice for Sprocket."

Three days later, Sprocket was still drilling his gums off. Doc and Razer figured he was down close to nineteen thousand feet. We hadn't had him pull out of the hole to run wireline in and find out because there didn't seem no point to it. It would just cost time we couldn't afford, and nothing to be gained by the knowledge.

In the early afternoon, Big Red pulled up onto Munchkin's location, closely followed by a Casing Critter.

Doc took off his silver-metal hard hat and wiped his forehead with his bandanna. "That just don't make no sense. Why the hell are they out setting casing at this point? They sure as hell ain't TD'ed. We'd of seen that."

Razor pointed. "Doc, they ain't running pipe. Pearl's up on Big Red and they're mixing concrete."

Doc looked thoughtful for a second, then threw his hat down on the ground, hard. He booted it fifteen feet on the bounce. "That's goddam wonderful! It ain't like we're made out of money or nothing!"

I was confused. Which wasn't that out of the ordinary. Only thing to do was ask more stupid questions, like usual. I did and Doc finally calmed down enough to answer.

"Chances are real good that Munchkin has hit a

bad lost-circulation zone." He explained that if you hit a zone with a pressure lower than the hydrostatic pressure of your column of drilling fluid, it would drink the mud out of the hole until the pressures equalized. Some zones could suck up everything you could put in the hole for a month, and ask for more.

Big Red would be pumping down some cement to squeeze off the zone. It didn't look like they were planning on screwing around that way for too long, since they had casing coming on location. If you can't plug off, you just go down with casing and cement above and below the zone, isolating your hole from it.

"Well, can't we do something to keep from losing circulation in the first place?"

"Nope. Shallower, we'd maybe try some cellophane chips in the mud, but at this depth the bottom-hole temperature is so high they'd burn up before they got down."

Six hours later our hole lost circulation, and Sprocket wasn't real happy about it. He quickly went dry down to his drill head, and he wanted us to do something about it.

I stayed with him while Doc and Razer headed over to the edge of the lease in Munchkin's direction, and motioned for Pearl to wander over. I rubbed Sprocket's hide and sang to him, trying to get his eyeballs to slow their spin. He was coming out of the hole, after drilling dry for a couple dozen more feet. We hoped he hadn't messed up his drilling cones.

Doc and Razer came back looking discouraged. "Pearl says they'll be cementing casing on Munchkin's location soon as they can get it in the hole. They just tested and the thief zone won't squeeze off." He wandered over in front of the dinner pot cooking over the fire and lifted the lid, looking in without much real interest. "Looks like Tiny realized what was going on out here when the call came in for Big Red and got a corner on the market. Pearl says the other four Cementers in the field are out on Hydroco locations bouncing from well to well. Big Red moves over to Uncle Foots' location when he hits the thief zone, then he's got a couple other deals with Hydroco he's on standby for."

"Uncle Foots hasn't lost circulation yet?" I asked. "That means Sprocket was ahead of him."

Doc grunted. "Them zones don't necessarily run horizontal. But I like to think Sprocket was ahead. Don't matter, though. We ain't going to be making hole again until the mating drill's over. And probably not until Tiny figures a way to run us plumb out of the field. It's hard to fight all the money he's got behind him."

Razer looked over towards Munchkin. "Doc, seems to me that since Sprocket was deepest, and since him and Munchkin are both down to the same thief zone, they could maybe both go into the hole, and—"

Doc frowned and shook his head. Razer wouldn't meet his eyes. "It don't work that way, Razer."

Razer shuffled his feet. "Just a idea."

"Not the best one you ever had. I wouldn't ask it of Munchkin or of Sprocket. We won't say no more about it."

I opened my mouth to ask what they were talking about. Doc saw me and grinned for a second. He made the squiggly worm sign with his finger inching up his forearm. "Got to figure this one out for yourself, Henry Lee. It's got to do with the mating drill, boy."

I shut my mouth. I thought I had already figured out the mating drill. Looked like there was more to it.

Nobody spoke much through dinner. Afterwards, I was sitting around the fire with the tip of Sprocket's tongue in my lap. I'd pulled back the foreskin that normally covered it when he wasn't drilling. His cones hadn't been damaged, but the central spike's point had been somewhat blunted and scored, so I was working with a diamond-dust file, honing it back to gleaming obsidian sharpness. It would regenerate in time anyway, but Sprocket appreciated the attention, and it's always good to keep your equipment in shape. I'd just finished filing and was greasing its length when Spanky Blankenship slipped into the silent circle.

Without a word, Doc passed him the bottle. Spanky looked upset. He took a swig. "We didn't want Uncle Foots to win this way," he muttered. "It ain't right."

"Not your fault," Doc said. "Tiny—"

"Fuck Tiny and the horse he rode in on. I got a mind to tell him to shove the contract and head on down the road. Maybe collapse the goddam hole first."

"No reason to cut off your nose, Spanky," Doc said. "Uncle Foots'll make a fine daddy, and there ain't enough Drillers around that we can afford to waste a mating."

A couple or five drinks later, Earl the Pearl wavered in beside Spanky. He was a tall, lanky character, usually half loaded, always laughing and telling jokes. He wasn't laughing now. At least he brought his own bottle, although he'd already started it on its way to being empty.

"Your hands told me I might find you here, Spanky." He took a sip and passed his bottle to Doc. "It ain't right." He looked apologetically at Spanky. "Winner's supposed to take the prize. Sprocket was ahead."

Spanky shook his head indignantly. "No such thing. I figure that thief zone's on a slope."

"Maybe." Pearl shook his head. "Still ain't right, though."

"Yeah. Tiny shouldn't go interfering in a mating drill. It ain't right."

"Uh-huh. I wouldn't allow it if I was you, Spanky."

"Me?" Spanky looked outraged. The bottle got to me and I took another sip. The fog seemed to be coming in early tonight. Spanky struggled to his feet. "Me? All I'm trying to do is make a well! It's you that got them in a bind. Getting yourself put on standby by Hydroco for the next forty years."

Pearl looked guilty. "He offered a *bunch* of money to everybody back at the camp, Spanky. And nobody didn't know ol' Sprocket was up against the wall."

"Well, it ain't my fault you're greedy, is it?" Spanky said belligerently. "Why don't you tell Tiny to stick it, and come over here and cement Sprocket's well when you finish mine?"

"Can't do that, much as I'd like to," Pearl mourned. "A man's only as good as his word, and I promised as soon as I left your location, I'd head over to this well right outside of Goldsmith and do some block squeezing. Nothing in between. Now, if we could run some concrete for Sprocket while we're still on your location . . . Naw, that don't make no sense."

Him and Spanky stared at each other for a minute.

"How much steel hose you got to spare on the rig, Spanky?" Pearl asked.

"Don't know, but I can find out." Ignoring the rest of us, they stood up and staggered together into the darkness toward Uncle Foots' location. "We can flange up a bunch of connections if we need to use five-inch hose with three-inch, or whatever," Spanky said. "The lease boundary's about a hundred yards from Sprocket's wellhead. We move you over to the edge, and—" Their figures had been fading out of sight, when Pearl suddenly swung about.

"Damn! I almost forgot." He came back into the circle around the fire. "Y'all are a bunch of fine fellas, but I do believe somebody here is trying to keep my bottle."

I tossed it to him. It was practically empty.

Doc and Razer and the rest of us were staring at him, glassy-eyed. He caught the bottle, then shook the capped end at Doc. "Big Red's gonna run cement into your hole tomorrow. I was you, I'd get my butt in gear and hunt up some pipe to go with it." Then he vanished into the darkness.

Doc let me go with him to the camp. Schooling up the worm. I suspected once I lost my wormhood I'd do more real work and less running around, so I was thinking on how I could remain incompetent as long as possible without nobody noticing. We rode off in Mooney's pickup, which he'd let us have the use of as long as he was banged up in the infirmary.

The camp was quiet by the time we got in, around two in the morning. Lots of tents around, but not too many critters. Guess most of them were out on location. Doc cut the engine of the pickup right as we pulled off the Farm-and-Market, so as not to wake up anybody. We climbed out of the cab and threaded our way among the tents.

The casing crews pooled and coordinated their production, so we headed straight for the pipe rack on the far side of the camp. The camp was dark, but a full moon was out, and for a change the weather was good; a few high clouds motionless in the sky, so we didn't have much trouble finding our way.

When we got there, it looked deserted. Hundreds of casing joints of varying diameters were laid down, enclosed by a locked chain link fence. We climbed over it and started walking down the rows.

"Our last pipe was nine and five-eighths, down to fifteen thousand feet," Doc reminded me quietly. "So we have to hang about four thousand feet of seven-inch or smaller pipe off its bottom. We need an API rating of N-80 or better. I'd prefer some C-95, myself. Keep an eye out for a stack of that."

There didn't seem to be too much small pipe in stock, but it wasn't too long before we come up on a heap of just what we were looking for. The tag on the end of the center joint said the pile contained five thousand feet of pipe, and had been produced by a Casing Critter named Maniac.

"Looking good," Doc said, as we climbed back over the fence. "Now we need to see what Casing Critters are in the camp. If there ain't any, we'll wake up Zeke and see who's likely to be available next."

"Unless Tiny's got them sewed up, too," I said.

"Don't even think like that, Henry Lee. The son of a bitch can't stay ahead of us *all* the way."

There wasn't a single Cementer, or a Mud Mixer, or most importantly, a Casing Critter, around. We wandered around in the dark, and finally gave up.

Then we realized we didn't know which tent Zeke

slept in. We didn't want to wake up anybody if it could be helped. So we wandered around the camp some more, hoping to find some structure with his name on it, or directions, or something.

After a useless half-hour of that, we were near the entrance to the camp. Doc leaned on the fender of Mr. Mooney's pickup while he rolled a smoke and lit up.

"I give up, Henry Lee. Let's go wake up somebody and find out where the hell Zeke hangs his hard hat."

Right then, a Casing Critter came trudging up the road to the camp's entrance. Doc yelped and jumped out in front of it, waving his arms and shouting. It spooked and jumped around some, but managed to restrain itself from stomping him into strawberry preserves.

After a few seconds, a couple of heads stuck out on top of the Casing Critter. "You hit another cow, Lady Jane?" A sleepy voice came from near the front. "You know the rule—you kill it, you eat it."

"Star!" Doc shouted. "We'd like to do a little business!"

"Doc? We been up almost four days. Sabrina's about in a coma. You come back tomorrow afternoon."

"Can't wait, honey. We're in a bind. Lost circulation."

Her face was silhouetted in the light thrown by the headlights of a pickup coming down the Farm-and-Market. Made my heart hurt.

"Aw, damn." She turned to the others who'd woken. "Go back to bed, ladies. I'll dicker us a deal and line up some transport for the casing. We all ought be able to get a couple hours sleep before we gotta set up."

She slid down Lady Jane's side and strode over to

us. "Nothing personal, Doc, but this is gonna cost you." She must have been real tired, because her zipper was zipped all the way up.

"Hi, Star," I said.

"Howdy, Henry Lee," she said, without any expression. "Now, about this deal, Doc."

Doc opened his mouth just as the vehicle that had been coming down the road slowed and turned in. A shiny red pickup with a crew cab pulled around Lady Jane's side. The brights were in our eyes. All I could see was three figures climbing out.

"When it rains, it pours," Doc muttered beside me.

Yeah, it was Tiny and his goons.

"Well, well!" Tiny said. "Looks like we got a party here. Mind if we invite ourselves?"

"Just doing some business," Doc said.

"Me, too. I heard Lady Jane was done with that production string we sent her on, and come to put her on standby for another deal we got coming up."

"We was here first, Tiny." By this time, Tiny had come right up to us and was practically in Doc's face. He was a inch or so taller than me, so he towered over Doc. His goons weren't midgets either.

"Fine. I'll do some business with you tonight, too. 'Less you still got your usual case of the yellows."

"I'll take you up after the well gets made, Tiny. We just come in to get a Casing Critter lined out."

Tiny made his left hand into a fist. I tensed up, but Doc didn't move. "Too bad." Tiny cracked the knuckles on his left hand. "All the Casing Critters is on standby for Hydroco business."

"Lady Jane ain't on standby." The interruption came from Star. She moved to try to step in between

Doc and Tiny, but there wasn't room. Tiny put a hand on her shoulder.

"You don't do business with nobody but me, long as you're in this field. I been giving Mooney and Doc enough rope to hang themselves, and now I got 'em by the short and curlies. Mooney's hocked up to his eyebrows. In four days, his bank loan comes due. He ain't gonna get an extension, and without a producing well, he won't get no money anywhere else. Hydroco's gonna buy the note."

"Get your hand off me," Star said.

"Didn't you hear me?" Tiny growled. "You do business with Hydroco, you silly bitch!" He shook her roughly and I launched myself at him. Doc blocked me before I could get to him.

"You keep those two idiots of his off me, Henry Lee. This ol' boy here is mine."

The next few minutes was kinda confused. I been fighting since about the time I could stand up to get knocked down. I grew up with four brothers, none of 'em angels. And there's some rough boys lives back in the woods around Hemphill. For a couple of years, once I started getting my growth on me, it seemed like every one of them had to try a time or two to whittle me down to size after school. So I'd had some practice at this particular sport.

Most fellas lie when they tell about how they planned this strategy, or made that smooth move, or used a clever feint to sucker the guy they was fighting. Mostly all there is to it is moving as fast as you can, trying to hurt the other guy enough to stop him fighting and in the meantime keep him from hurting you more than you can handle.

Practice helps, though. And I was glad to have had it. 'Cause this wasn't no Marquis of Queensbury deal. It was the kind of fight that sometimes leaves people gimped for life, or maybe dead. If I'd have had time, I'd have been scared.

Both of them looked at Tiny. He nodded in my direction, and flat-footed, launched a kick at Doc's crotch. I saw Doc move back enough for it to miss, then I had problems of my own.

The first one to arrive got a fist in the face, then the other one was on me, ramming his shoulder hard into my chest. I staggered back, off balance, and he followed me. He got a knee in his belly when he closed again. Then the other one tackled me, and we all ended up scrambling around in the dirt.

I was not winning, truth to tell, until one of them quit strangling me long enough to scream. He twisted aside, trying to pull away the clawed hands of the long-haired angel that was ripping his face to ribbons. I still had a hand clutching the shirtfront of the one that was sitting on my chest. Star's help gave me the time to use that hand to yank his face close so I could pulverize it some with the other hand.

About the time he lost interest in his part of the fight, the first one was on me again. What I could see of his face as it twisted in and out of shadow didn't look too good.

After he got my elbow in the throat a couple seconds later, it looked worse. He started choking and coughing, so I punched him a half-a-dozen times in the short ribs to clear any obstructions. He started throwing up, so I let him go. The other one was lying nearby. When I poked him with the tip of my steel-toed boots he didn't move, so I relaxed enough to look around.

Casing gypsies were starting to slide down Lady Jane's side. Star sat up a few yards away, holding her jaw. I crawled toward her. "You okay?" I called out. "Thanks for keeping 'em from killing me."

She moved her jaw with her hand, testing to see if anything was broke, I guess. "Wanted the pleasure myself."

"Aww, Star, I'm sorry as all get-out."

"You hurt my feelings something terrible, Henry Lee."

"Last thing I ever want to do is hurt you." I put my hand on her knee. "I got scared. I wasn't sure how you'd feel about me after. I didn't just want a one-night stand." I hung my head.

The hand that wasn't still holding her jaw moved to cover mine. Her fingertips gently scratched my wrist. "Me neither, Henry Lee."

Our big reunion scene was interrupted by a couple of casing gypsies moving in to check out our health, and by Doc and Tiny shuffling back into sight around Lady Jane's side. Both of them was throwing punches, with Doc backing away from Tiny's longer reach, then stepping up quick to get his licks in.

"Want a little help, Doc?" I called out.

He blocked a punch with his forearm, then back-pedaled rapidly out of Tiny's reach. He looked at me. "You done entertaining Tiny's boys, huh?" He laughed. "Guess I better finish off this pus-bucket, too. We got some casing to set."

Tiny roared and charged him, which I believe is just what Doc wanted. Tiny bear hugged him up into the air. Doc snapped his forehead into Tiny's face. Broke Tiny's nose, I imagine. When Tiny's grip loosened from the pain, Doc wrapped his hands around Tiny's neck and started throttling him. At the same time, he was giving Tiny the knee where it hurt most. Tiny started driving punches into Doc's ribs, but Doc ignored them.

Then Tiny wrapped his own hands around Doc's throat. They stood in place that way, bathed in the headlights of Tiny's pickup, straining and grunting, each doing his best to throttle the other.

It seemed to go on for hours, but it couldn't have been more than a minute. Slowly, gradually, Tiny started to buckle. When he was on his knees, Doc brought a knee into his chest.

"That was for hurting Mooney."

He shrugged Tiny's hands off and dragged him over to prop him against the grill of the pickup.

"And this is for killing Cutbait Benton." He said it in that same dead voice I'd heard twice before.

Then he started to punish Tiny.

It wasn't my right to stop him, but the sounds of it made me sick after awhile, so I came up behind him and pulled him away.

The whole camp was up by the time Tiny's goons got well enough to load Tiny into the bed of the pickup and head back toward some serious medical attention in Notrees.

Doc and me were sitting on the tailgate of Mooney's pickup, passing a bottle of our own medicine back and forth, when Star approached with Zeke, both of them looking upset.

"We got a problem," Star said. "Tell him, Zeke."

"I can't sell you no casing," Zeke said. "Tiny bought everything we got in stock that's smaller than nine and five-eighths. I should have figured something funny was going on, but he offered thirty percent above book. I'm sorry, Doc. We shook hands on it."

Doc just sighed. "I wouldn't ask you to go back on a handshake, Zeke."

"Star tells me Lady Jane was already working on some five-and-a-half-inch pipe on the way in. I could get the word out to the rest of the Casing Critters in the field and have a string ready for you in five or six days."

"Ain't no other pipe around?"

Zeke shook his head.

"Guess it'll have to do, then."

Zeke hurried off to arrange it.

"That's too late, Doc," I said. "Even with Tiny off the scene, Hydroco will own Mooney Producing by then."

"Yeah. But I can't think of nothing else. Can you?"

I had to admit not. But it kept gnawing at me. We said good-bye to folks and headed back to location. I found out Star could say good-bye in a way that made your hair melt. That was in public. I figured her private one might kill a fella.

I guess I was light-headed from it on the way back, because I kept worrywarting on our problem.

"Maybe Big Red can pump down a hellacious bunch of cement and squeeze off the thief zone," I said.

"Yeah, just like on Munchkin and Uncle Foots' wells," Doc replied sourly. "Henry Lee, you can fill your entire hole with concrete, but you eventually got to drill it out. And if that zone ain't squeezed, you'll be right back where you started. We'll try it because we don't have no choice, but I suspect that a nineteen thousand-foot hole is gonna be undrillable because we can't get the casing to cover a damn twenty-or thirty-foot thief zone."

Something he said started me to thinking. And I got an idea. When I told it to Doc, he said it was the dumbest idea he'd ever heard. He said it was like playing baseball and skipping third base on your way to home plate. It hadn't never been done before. And it just might work.

He turned the pickup around and we screamed back to the camp and woke everybody up again. Lady Jane followed us out to location.

Big Red marched on the edge of Uncle Foots' location late that morning while we played music for him. Three hundred feet of miscellaneous-sized hose ran from his pump mouth to Sprocket. They'd cemented Munchkin's casing, then immediately bounced over to do Uncle Foots'. Three hours later, while that cement was setting up, we were ready for them to do us.

It took each casing crew on the other locations almost fifteen hours to trip their pipe in the hole. It took us two hours, much of that because Sprocket couldn't run in any faster.

I sat and nursed my bruises and let Star feed me breakfast while a couple of gypsies snapped casing around Sprocket's tongue. All four joints of it. My smart idea was actually pretty simple.

If you got a zone that you need to cover, and it's four thousand feet below your last casing, and you don't have four thousand feet of casing—why not just cover the problem zone?

Because you don't, that's all. If you're going to case a hole, you do it from the top down, not the bottom up. The thought wouldn't occur to anybody but a worm like me.

We had Sprocket take down four joints of that

five-and-a-half that Lady Jane made and land it on bottom. Just enough to make sure we covered that thief zone.

Early that afternoon, Spanky moseyed over. "Pearl told me he'll be ready to pressure up on your cement whenever you want."

Doc looked up from a new conductor's baton he was whittling. His last one got splintered in the fracas with Tiny. "Guess that means yours tested okay."

"Yeah. We're filling the hole with mud now."

"Good. I'd appreciate it if you could tell Pearl I'd like him to hook up and pressure-test in about an hour. Hate to hurry it, but I don't believe we can give Uncle Foots much more of a lead than that with any hope at all of winning."

Spanky squinted at a cloud that was moving to cover the afternoon sun. "My crew's been up all night and day, Doc. I figure after we get the hole full we might take a break. Catch a few zees. You can probably afford to let your cement set up proper, 'cause I don't believe we'll be ready to drill till after dinner."

"That's mighty decent, Spanky."

"Don't want you to have no excuses when Uncle Foots wins."

Spanky was good as his word. That evening, just as the sun was going down, Pearl stood on top of Big Red, visible to us all, and raised his bandanna high. Sprocket and Uncle Foots were both on bottom, waiting for the signal. Pearl whipped the bandanna down. Doc's baton led us into the first bar of "TD's A-coming," and Sprocket began to dance and drill.

Twenty-four hours later, they were still going at it,

when the first gypsies started coming from all directions across the scenery.

Zeke was first, riding on Lady Jane's nose section. Beside him sat Mr. Mooney. "Come to see the end of the mating drill!" Zeke shouted. "Maybe party some while we're waiting!"

They pulled up and Zeke helped Mr. Mooney climb down gingerly. He walked over and shook Doc's hand. "Hear you been taking care of business purty good while I was on vacation."

"Just making hole, Mr. Mooney. Just making hole."

"Uh-huh. I had to get out of the damn infirmary. Tiny's boys were bitching and moaning enough to drive a man crazy."

I hadn't thought about it, but I guess that was the closest place for them to have gone. "What about Tiny?" I asked. "He couldn't have been too happy, neither."

"Never saw him. They took him off in an ambulance to the hospital at Kermit. He needed more attention than the infirmary could provide."

"I guess we'll have finished up here and moved on down the road before he makes it back," Doc said.

Mooney looked surprised. "Nobody told you?" Doc shook his head. "Tiny ain't coming back."

"Just because he got whipped on a bit?"

"Nope. Seems like his sponsor got caught a couple months ago with his hand in the company's pocket. Tiny's goons told me. This was Tiny's last chance to hang on with Hydroco. If he managed to corner the field, they were gonna keep him on. But he screwed up royally, and Hydroco is gonna permanently run him off for it. They probably already got another fella on the way here to take his place. I don't see no reason you couldn't work with him." He hesitated. "After you finish drilling my other leases, of course."

"Of course," Doc said. "Soon as you pay your bills." He smiled. "I got a feeling we're gonna do all right on these wells, Mr. Mooney."

About then, Star stepped out of Lady Jane's mouth. She hip-swung over and linked her arm in mine. Her other hand reached across and slid inside my jumpsuit to scratch the hair on my chest. "Howdy, Henry Lee. Good to see you again."

"Pleasure's all mine, ma'am." It was.

"You figured out yet what a mating drill's about, Henry Lee?" Doc asked.

"I ain't sure. At first I thought it was just whoever drilled best. Now it seems it has to do with who can go deepest, soonest. I figure from the way y'all was talking that the one to first hit the producing formation gets to breed with Munchkin."

Doc just grinned. "Okay so far, Henry Lee. You tell me when you figure out the rest." Then he strolled off laughing to meet Sabrina as she was coming out of Lady Jane's mouth.

Later that night, after the partying had wound down, the walls of my room started to convulse. The bed began to jerk up and down spastically, damn near throwing me onto the rug-covered floor. It felt like an earthquake.

After a few seconds it settled down to a strong rhythmical pulsing and I managed to get to my feet. I staggered over to the ladder bolted into Sprocket's living flesh and climbed high enough to stick my head out the hole in the ceiling. I looked around. A dozen or so gypsies stood at the wellhead watching. "Is Sprocket first?" I called out.

Zeke looked up, his face split in a wide grin. "Sure is, boy. Was there ever any doubt?"

Sprocket had won the drilling contest. He was ahead of Uncle Foots in getting down to the deep producing zone. Sprocket didn't like nothing better than heavy crude, Doc told me on the farm. Now that he had hit he was sucking it up ecstatically. He was a drilling fool for sure.

Only— I'd seen him suck petroleum on the farm. And the rhythm was different. If I hadn't known better, I'd have thought he wasn't sucking oil up through his tongue. It felt more like—

Then Doc's head stuck out of the hole up front. A second later, Sabrina's appeared beside it. "You figured it out yet, worm?"

I figured I was about to make a fool of myself. "He ain't sucking oil up now, is he? He's pumping downhole instead." Sprocket's body rippled and trembled around us, and his high drilling hum had changed to another kind of howl entirely.

Doc nodded. "They don't mate after the drill," I said wonderingly. "They're mating right now."

Doc nodded again. "Not bad figuring, for a worm. Ol' Sprocket is pumping his seed to Munchkin right now. It'll fight its way through the cracks in the formation, till it reaches her well and she sucks it up to fertilize her eggs. We'll be seeing two or three baby Drillers about a year from now."

"Damnedest thing I ever heard of."

"Uh-huh." Sabrina whispered something in his ear. "Ah, Henry Lee, we'll talk about this some more later." Their heads disappeared back into his room.

I looked at the stars for a minute, feeling the strong, steady pulse of life around me, then climbed back down and rolled into bed.

"Henry Lee," Star murmured as the floor's heaving threw us together again. "Sprocket's taking care of his business. Now you come here and take care of yours."

In-Between

We worked the field around Notrees for eight months more before pulling up and heading on down the road. No real reason to go. Everybody got along fine with each other and with the Drilling Superintendant that Hydroco sent to replace Tiny Small. We all just started getting restless at being in one place too long. That's a gypsy for you. The camp had gotten big enough so's business went on as usual when we took off with Sprocket and Munchkin and Big Red and Lady Jane.

We headed down to the Gulf Coast and bounced around randomly, doing a little workover stuff at Chocolate Bayou, then moving over and drilling on a couple of government-sponsored reserve wells at Hoskins Mound. Probably should have stayed with that particular deal longer than we did. Those federal boys surely did know how to spend the money.

But Sprocket was a deep rig. All those shallow, easy wells didn't stretch him out at all, so we drifted along, pretty much staying together, running out of the same camps. Doc and Sabrina turned into a major item, so that explained Lady Jane staying with us. Me and Star spent as much time together as our jobs allowed. Razer went from one baby-doll to another. Big Red and his bulk cement holder, with his cementing crew headed up by Earl the Pearl, hung around because Pearl and Doc liked doing business together, I guess.

I practiced on my guitar a lot and got to where Doc would let me accompany the band on it.

And Sprocket and Munchkin, of course, waited for the blessed event.

Sprocket Goes Offshore

Sprocket and Lady Jane turned to the right when Broadway ended at the Galveston beach. Doc had me up top while him and the rest of the crew finished dressing. We followed the seawall for about a mile before I spotted the neon sign that told me we weren't as lost as I was beginning to think.

Just as the sun set behind us, Sprocket pulled into the parking lot beside the Bali Room's entrance. The high school kid parking cars for the rich folks tried not to look unhappy at the sight of Sprocket. He knew he wasn't going to get no tip, because he wasn't going to try to personally park a hundred and twelve feet of healthy young male Driller. Not that he particularly wanted a Driller in his high-class parking lot anyway.

"We'll find our own place, bubba," I told him. "Mr. Pickett invited us to drop by." He nodded and waved us in.

Sprocket and Lady Jane trundled to the back of the lot, where there was room to maneuver, and got properly situated side-by-side, being careful not to trample any nearby automobiles in the process. Normally I'd have climbed out of the hole in the ceiling in my room and slid down Sprocket's side, but I figured that wouldn't look too dignified wearing a coat and tie and brand-new ostrich skin boots.

I guess the rest of the crew figured similarly in their own cases, because when I ducked out of my room into the central hallway that ran Sprocket's length, a line had formed at his drilling mouth. Looked like a bunch of strangers, all duded up and slicked down. Not a patched jumpsuit or hard hat to be seen among them. One thing was normal—they were passing around a bottle of heart-starter to kick off the evening's festivities.

Doc came out of his room and faced them. Beside him, wearing a purple suit that seemed to glow and squirm, Razer pulled a small mirror out of his vest pocket and tried to comb his moustache into surrender.

"All right, men," Doc started. "Mr. T-Bone Pickett has invited us to his place tonight as his personal guests, free of charge. That *don't* mean you got permission to act like a bunch of wild animals. Don't start no fights. Don't spit on the carpet. Don't throw food, not even at each other. Don't fart loud nowhere but in the men's room. Those of y'all that ain't got a date—don't mess with the professional ladies in the bar. They cost more than you got, and they won't take kindly to you trying to dicker with 'em." You could tell he didn't count on his talk having much effect. Then he looked over at Razer and rolled his eyes. "Just try not to act like you was raised in a barn, okay?" he finished up.

Razer licked his moustache and combed it some more. "Doc, we wouldn't do nothing to embarrass you in front of Mr. Picket. I'll keep these boys to my own high standards of behavior and attitude. You can depend on me, boss."

"Aw, hell," Doc muttered, more to himself than to any of us. "At least I tried."

When we marched out Sprocket's mouth, we found that the ladies had already exited from Lady Jane's mouth. Casing gypsies are all women, and for some reason most of them are medium-wonderful to look at. About half of them paired up with hands on our crew. Star swayed toward me. Her shiny dark hair fell in numerous braids to hip-height. Instead of the usual half-zipped jumpsuit and steel-toed work boots, she wore high heels and a midnight-black dress that I immediately wanted to rub against. It was cut high up the sides and low down the front. The places that curved in on Star did it a few inches more than on most women. Likewise with the places that curved out.

Even after her being my main squeeze for almost a year, I still got seriously paralyzed at the sight of her. Not to mention the sound, and smell. And touch. And taste. And—

"Hey, sailor," she whispered as she slid against me and linked her arm through mine. "You looking for a good time tonight?"

"I could do with a little minor partying, honey. You available?"

She bit me on the earlobe, sending tingles down to my ostrich skin.

"Might be," she breathed.

Before we left the parking lot, we strolled over to Sprocket and Lady Jane. While Star chatted with Lady Jane, I scratched an area about five feet off the ground on Sprocket's hide. After a second he moaned in pleasure and a crease in his hide unfolded to reveal a deep green eyeball about twice the size of my head. He just loved being rubbed. Come to think of it, I kind of enjoyed it when Star rubbed me, too.

"We won't be gone too long, buddy," I said. "You and Lady Jane keep each other company."

I felt guilty, partying without him. But there wasn't no way he was going to get into the Bali Room. It was a coat-and-tie place, and they didn't make coats and ties his size.

I guess he didn't mind. He just purred and leaned a little harder into the hand that rubbed him.

The Bali Room was actually a bunch of rooms, strung out along a pier that ran out from the seawall for almost a quarter of a mile into the Gulf. We went through several rooms before we come to the main restaurant one. The maitre-guy told us Mr. Pickett had been delayed by some other business of his, but had left a message with his people to take care of us. The waiters was all nice to us, although the guy with the big key around his neck, what Doc called the wine steward, almost showed some surprise when Doc spent ten minutes grilling him about the contents of the wine basement before ordering several kinds of wine for before, during, and after dinner. Doc never talked about it much, but he spent a couple of years on the other side of the Gulf near the end of Number Two, and he got knowledgeable about all them fancy wines, since Beam and branch water was in short supply over there.

We finished up with brandy and cigars in a private drawing room for VIPs like us. I don't smoke, myself, but Star can appreciate a fine Havana, given the chance.

After that, Doc cut us loose. Reluctantly. Most of us headed for the casino, which was situated farthest out on the pier. Me and Star sat in on a couple of card games. Separate tables, of course. I been playing penny-ante since I was knee-high to a coon, so I pretty much stayed even. Star, on the other hand, is a barracuda. Lucky, too. I played strip poker with her once. Ended up in my skivvies before she had her socks off.

She wouldn't tell me how much she victimized the gentlemen at her table, but after we wandered into the main bar, she nudged me.

"Henry Lee, I could afford to treat you to one of those professional ladies in the booths off to the side, if you want."

"I believe I already got an extremely talented amateur lady lined out for later on, thank you very much anyhow." I may not be a genius, but I'm a survivor.

It was a good bar. Real dark. We danced a little bit to the music from the band that was sweating under the red-and-blue spotlights. That velvety black dress felt as good under my hands as I had thought it would.

Everybody seemed to be having a fine time. Most of the crew drifted in after awhile, walking loose and feeling spruce.

The last drilling we did was a shallow injection well at Freddieville, just a couple miles up the road from the coast. It was contracted by Mesh Petroleum, which was one of the companies owned by Mr. T-Bone Pickett, an old-time wildcatter who had made it good and diversified into all sorts of other enterprises. Including high-class nightculbs on the island. Doc and him knew each other from back when Doc was a kid and T-Bone was rubbing two dollar bills together to try to grow a third one. Doc said T-Bone liked to collect businesses, like some people collect baseball cards or china figurines. He visited us out on location a couple times. Mostly for nostalgia, I had figured. For the last twenty years, nobody'd been in a position to make the man get mud on his boots unless he wanted to.

However, it seemed like he'd been mulling over offering us some kind of mystery deal, which he invited us to discuss this evening at one of his clubs on the island.

So I recognized him when he came striding through the bar, with about a dozen men following him. He was a compact, solid man with brush-cut white hair who somehow reminded you of a lion. Not from the way he moved. Just from his eyes. He nodded and smiled when he saw us. Razer yelled over the music that Doc and Sabrina was still back in the casino someplace. T-Bone waved to indicate that he'd heard, then said something to the men with him. The tallest, skinniest one of them left with him and the rest drifted into the bar. I figured they were business associates of his.

We did some more dancing and drinking. About three or four songs later, one of the men that had been with T-Bone approached our table. He looked like a rough character. Had black patch over his left eye.

I could tell he was stoked, but he seemed to be handling it okay. "Mind if I ask your friend for a dance, mate?" he asked.

I looked at Star. She shrugged. "No problem with me, mister," I said.

They got out on the floor and fast-danced. I kind of
kept an eye on them. Not jealous or nothing, mind
you. When the first song finished, she turned to
come back to the table, but he said something to
her, and, after a little hesitation, she started a slow
dance with him. I kept a sharper eye on them now,
especially on where he put his hands while he held
her. She had to move his hands twice, and about
halfway through the song he whispered something in
her ear.

She broke away from him and came back toward
the table me and Razer and his baby-doll was sitting
at. He followed her and caught her by the arm, just
as she reached her chair.

"What's the matter, missy? Fifty dollars not enough?
We can negotiate."

I scraped my chair away from the table, but Star
waved me back. "Nothing to talk about, mister. You
made a mistake, that's all." She pulled her arm loose.

He laughed, real ugly-like. "Not likely, missy. I
know a high-tone whore when I see one."

I stood up. She put a hand on my chest. "Take it
easy, Henry Lee. He's a whole lot more fried than
he looks."

"How does a hundred dollars sound, whore? That
has to be more than this lubber is paying."

That did it. "Mister, maybe you better take your
self and your money someplace else before your
whole evenin' gets ruint," I said.

He swung on me. Didn't hit nothing but my shoulder, and he nearly fell down in the process. *Real*
drunk, he was. I stepped forward and grabbed him
by the shirtfront and lifted. He was a normal size
fella, almost a foot shorter than me. Not much takes
the fight out of a man like being picked up one-

handed and just held in place for a minute or two, maybe with an occasional shake.

Only, he pulled a knife out of his back pocket and slashed my arm. Barely nicked me. I dropped him on his butt. He started cussing and screaming about how he was going to spread my guts out on the deck and then tromple on them. He tried to get up and come at me, so I gently kicked him in the face. The knife went flying.

About that time three of his friends jumped me from out of nowhere.

They crawled all over me, but I was still standing when two of them got snatched off of me suddenly. Razer put one in a hammerlock and throat-clutch. Big Mac carried the other one over his head and tossed him out through the entrance door, which was closed at the time. Big Mac's a wrestling fan and likes dramatic stuff such as that.

Everybody in the room started fighting everybody else. Women screamed and furniture broke and glasses flew through the air. Fortunately nobody got chucked out a window, since it was twenty feet down to the surf and they might have drowned. It was fun for a few mintues, though. Me and Star fought mostly back to back, me bare-handed and her with a chair leg in her right hand.

The party had started to naturally wind down, everybody a little battered and getting cautious, with most of the breakables already broke, when Doc and Sabrina and T-Bone and the tall, skinny fella that had earlier been with T-Bone appeared at the door. None of them said a word, but the fighting stopped immediately as they was noticed.

Beside me a fella and his date crawled out from

under one of the few tables that hadn't been over-turned and started to brush each other off.

"Perhaps we should cease giving our trade to the Bali Room, Sandra," he said. "It looks as though they're admitting the lowest sort of trash these days." He looked at *me*! I didn't start the damn fight!

He must have seen something in my face that he didn't like, because they scurried on out of the room.

A few minutes later, the crew gathered in a room built on top of the gambling casino at the end of the pier. Nobody had taken any serious damage. Your typical recreational bar fight. The man with T-Bone had remained with his hands in the bar while we was conducted out by Doc and T-Bone. Sabrina took her crew to the ladies' lounge to tidy up.

Eventually the casing gypsies rejoined us, followed by the strangers we'd tangled with. They looked more racked up than us, of course, but not by much. Most of them grinned at us and we smiled back. No hard feelings. I didn't see the fella with the eye patch among them. We all settled down into a bunch of overstuffed couches and chairs that mostly looked out of a big floor-to-ceiling window onto the ocean. You could see lights scattered off along the bay, mostly ships at anchor, and close below the window, a small Driller making hole on a platform at the end of a granite jetty.

Mr. Pickett saw to it that we was all comfortable, then poured himself a dose of heart-starter into one of those big snifter glasses. He swirled it around and took a sip. Then he wandered over to the big window and pointed at the jetty rig.

"All the oil on this planet didn't get buried under dry land," he said. "But all of it that did, at least on this continent, and for fifty miles out from the coast,

is under the stewardship of the goddamndest, greed-
iest, most incompetent bunch of bureaucrats since
the fall of the Roman Empire.

"And it ain't much better in any other country.
Everybody taxes and regulates the oil producers,
especially the independents, until it ain't hardly possible to do business any more. Then they bitch about
prices bein' too high to suit 'em. Me and the rest of
the board of Mesh Petroleum believe we've come up
with a way to get outside the jurisdiciton of the
bureaucrats. A way to acquire some hydrocarbons
without getting crippled by the regulations and taxes
they impose. They've made it damn near impossible
to play the game in their yard. So we're gonna take
our ball and play somewhere else."

He took another sip of heart-starter. "Somebody's
got to be first to drill further offshore than we can
run these jetties. About fifty miles offshore, beyond
the reach of the bureaucrats. How'd you folks like to
help make oilpatch history?"

We left an hour and a half later. We'd made up
with the sailors and had a time visiting with them
and talking about their boat. We all voted to take
T-Bone up on his proposition and I looked forward to
doing business with him. The tide was running in,
and the crash of the surf sounded loud and clean.
The salt air was plumb invigorating. The valet guy's
stool sat empty beside his booth when we went by.

"Just a second, sweetheart," I said to Star. I checked
my pocket and found a silver dollar.

I cast around and spotted him over in a corner of
the lot beside a fancy car with its hood up. A Bugliosi,
or Masturbatto, or some other kind of low-slung
mafia car that would fall apart after thirty seconds off

a paved road. This one apparently even had trouble in parking lots. The fella that had made the crack about me in the bar was bent over beside the valet guy, looking at the engine, while his date ground on the starter. It growled and whirred real healthy, but the engine wouldn't kick over.

Me and Star moseyed over. I tossed the silver dollar to the valet guy when he straightened up. "That's for being a sport about Sprocket and Lady Jane." I looked at the guy who owned the car. "Need any help, mister?" Bygones, and all that.

"We'll have it fixed in a minute," he said, cold as a Baptist talking to a bootlegger. His date punched the starter again.

"Fine." I took Star's hand and we started to walk away. "I was you, though, I'd see if there was any gas in the tank before I run the battery all the way down."

We caught up with the rest of the crew about halfway to the back of the lot. Star was still giggling at the look on the guy's face when he found that his gas cap was gone. We figured some J.D. had sneaked in after it got full dark and siphoned his tank.

My attention got drawn off to the side when I saw something light-colored moving close to the ground in the dimness at the side of the lot. For a second I figured it was the J.D. But it didn't really look that much like a person. I touched Doc on the shoulder.

We veered over to the side of the lot to give it a closer examination. It was a gleaming white length of Sprocket's drilling tongue, sliding along the asphalt like a albino anaconda. It shouldn't have been where it was because Sprocket had parked more than two hundred feet further toward the back. In the dark, we couldn't even see him from where we stood.

We traced the length of tongue, being careful not to step on it. It ran toward the entrance of the lot, passing in front of the noses of half-a-dozen cars. We got to the tongue-tip just as it turned in and ran beside a Packard convertible. The point of the main drill spear extruded from the tongue's foreskin. The tip snuffled along the ground, like a bloodhound on the trail of a fella that had left the obedience training school at Huntsville without graduating.

When it got near the rear of the car it lifted the last few feet of itself into the air and began to feel along the fender.

Doc and me bent over close to watch what happened next. Sprocket's tongue found the rectangular crack of the gas tank cover. The tip carefully positioned perpendicular to it, then slipped into the crack and pried the lid up on its hinge. Then the tip receded inside the foreskin. The foreskin contracted into a sucker and tightly encircled the gas cap. Slowly, it flexed and twisted and rotated, unscrewing the cap. After a few seconds the gas cap came loose and vanished, sucked inside the drill-stem.

The foreskin elongated and contracted in diameter. When it was about an inch across it inserted into the gas tank. Shortly, the tongue silently began to pulse as fluid passed through it.

Doc straightened up. "The son of a bitch is sucking the tank dry! He's a goddam vehicular vampire!" He looked wildly around the lot. "Jesus, Son of God! How many cars has he drained tonight?"

Me and Star and Sabrina about fell on the ground. Doc slammed the lid and Sprocket's tongue jumped out right quickly, spewing gasoline all over Doc's new suit.

When Sprocket danced past the little valet guy,

every one of us on the crew poked out of our holes up top and tossed him a silver dollar apiece. We figured he had a long night ahead of him.

The best part of the evening had just started to start when Star pulled away from me. The camp lay quiet around us and the hole in the ceiling of Star's room perfectly framed the full moon. She threw the cover back and reached to the table bolted down beside the bed. A second later a phosphorus match flared and she slowly sucked into life the last of the Havanas she'd gotten at the Bali Room.

She rolled it back and forth between her fingers, staring at the glowing tip. "Henry Lee, do I act like a whore?"

Before I could say anything, she went on quickly. "I mean, this ain't the first time a man's called me names. I know I flirt around—" She blew out the match, but not before I saw tears tracing down her cheeks in the moonlight.

"Star . . ." I wasn't sure what to say. "The problem is, you're so much of a woman that it shines through every move you make. I think most fellas are blinded from the brightness of it. Maybe even scared by it, like I was for a while. And some of the stupid ones can't tell the difference between a real woman like you, and a whore, which is nothing but a empty woman-shaped machine made for separating a man from money."

She wiped one cheek with the hand that wasn't holding the cigar. "Can *you* tell the difference, Henry Lee?"

I reached over and wiped the other cheek. "You still make me blind and crazy both, but I've known for a long time that you're the finest lady I'm likely to meet."

"Aw, damn." She put down her cigar and kissed me. "You're so sweet. You sure make it hard for a girl to feel bad. Hold me awhile?"

About ten minutes later, she stirred from cuddling and straddled my chest. "You been so sweet, Henry Lee," she said. "For you, tonight only, I'm gonna cut the price in half."

Then, before I could quit laughing, she began to show me once more what a loving, real woman she was.

We loaded out on Mr. Pickett's boat three mornings later. It had been dry-docked in Todd Shipyards for almost three months while they modified it to become the world's first deep-sea drillship.

Sprocket went on board easier than any of us thought he would. It only took an hour of coaxing and music before he placed the first foot on the specially made, heavy-duty gangplank that had been laid from the dock to the deck of the *Belle Butange* for his benefit. The sailors leaned over the rails and hooted while we cajoled him. Finally he trudged up it, grumbling in low C.

I got hung up with saying good-bye to Star, who'd come down with the rest of Lady Jane's crew to see us off, so I didn't ride on board with him.

When I did go up the gangplank, the action had moved mostly forward. Sprocket had been led to stand lengthwise along the keel of the ship, right behind this tower that jutted up about a third of the way back from the prow. Later on, I learned the tower was called the foc'sle, and contained inside it, split into four levels, the galley and the crew's bunkrooms, among other things. The Captain and his officers steered the ship in a big room at the top of the foc'sle, what they called the wheelhouse. It had thick glass all the way around, so they could see icebergs and other boats coming at them from any direction.

A couple of sailors still lounged on the rail near the gangplank, and waved back when I waved at them. One of them had a big purple bruise on his cheek. T-Bone had wanted us all to get acquainted before the cruise. I guess we did.

Another sailor headed my way carrying a heavy coil of rope. He was looking back over his shoulder shouting something at somebody back beside Sprocket. It wasn't until he faced in my direction that I saw the black patch that covered his left eye.

He'd left the Bali Room right after the fight, so I hadn't had a chance to get straight with him. I angled so as to cross his path. He was already frowning when he turned, and it just got more sincere when he spotted me.

When we got within a few steps of each other, I stuck out my hand. "I'm Henry Lee MacFarland, sir. I'd like to apologize for my part in the goings-on at the Bali Room the other night."

I figured the fight had been mostly his fault, but I could have been a little less quick on the trigger myself.

He dropped the coil of rope to one side and scowled ferociously at me. "I don't care if you're Jesus's bastard brother, lubber. You and me still have some settling to do."

The four or five sailors lounging against the rail perked up and started paying attention to us.

I didn't try to keep the smile on my face, but I

spoke as evenly as I knew how. "Bad feelings won't do neither of us any good, mister."

He stepped up and prodded my chest with a forefinger and stared at me with one cold gray eye. "You better stay tight with your oilfield trash friends as long as you're on my ship, lubber. I catch you alone some evening, you'll be found scattered in pieces all over the Gulf." While I watched his finger draw back for a last prod, he sucker-punched me in the gut, hard, with his other fist. It bent me over and he hit me in the mouth while I was down. The ring on his hand tore my lip.

Before I could react, a burly, bald-headed man stepped up and shoved us apart. The one-eyed sailor stumbled back and tripped over the coil of rope that he'd dropped.

"We'll have none of that on board my ship," the bald-headed fella said. The look on the sailor's face indicated that he didn't agree. The bald-headed man saw the look, too. "You have any doubt about it, the purser will pay you off right now and you can be on your way."

The one-eyed sailor glared at me one more time and then looked away. "No problem, Chief," he said.

"Glad to hear it. You two shake hands now, and then you go about your business, Pegleg."

Pegleg shook my hand, but I don't believe he meant it. After he had picked up his rope and vanished belowdecks down a nearby stairwell, the bald-headed man grinned at me.

"Don't mind Pegleg," he said. "He's hard to get along with only when he's drunk or hungover." He stuck out his own hand to be shook. "Of course, he's always one or the other. So I guess it's up to me to welcome you aboard the *Belle Butange*. Or *Miz*

Bellybutton, as we call her. Sorry I missed meeting you people the other night. I hear that a good time was had by all. I'm Chief Hightower. Head of the engine room crew on this tub."

I shook his hand. "Pleased to meet you, sir. Uh . . . that sailor. His name's Pegleg?"

"That's what everybody calls him."

"But he ain't *got* a pegleg. He's got—"

"He's got only one eye. And it would be terribly rude for anybody to draw attention to that fact." The Chief laughed. "So we call him Pegleg."

The day stayed sunny and the ocean stayed smooth. It took *Miz Bellybutton* six and a-half-hours to get to location, which turned out to be nothing more than a stretch of water identical to the rest. It was fifty-four miles from the nearest dry land. None of Mr. Pickett's bureaucrats had a call to a penny's worth of any hydrocarbons we might chance to discover out there.

The jetty rigs near the beach all had a circular hole cut into the center of the platform, through which their Driller could run his tongue to the well-head. They called it the moon-pool. I didn't understand why until I looked down at one on a clear full-moon night.

Todd Shipyards had cut the moon-pool right behind *Miz Bellybutton*'s foc'sle—run it right through the body of the ship, by sealing one of the cargo holds and removing a couple of plates from the bottom of the hull and the top of the deck. Then they welded a full derrick in place above it.

An hour after we anchored on location, we set up around the moon-pool and started tuning up our instruments. Sprocket looked dubious about the whole idea.

After he'd let Doc check out his drill-head one last time, he meandered up the ramp that led to the moon-pool, until his mouth hung right at the edge. He stuck his tongue out and dropped it into the water, then pulled it out again. Not too enthusiastic.

Finally, everybody was ready. The whole ship's crew seemed to have gathered behind the balcony railing that circled the third and fourth levels of the foc'sle. Captain Johnson and his officers peered through the wheelhouse's windows. I personally hooked Sprocket to a cargo hold full of lead-free gasoline, so he couldn't gripe about being too thirsty to work.

Doc pulled his baton out of the long slender pocket that ran down the right leg of his gray, patched jumpsuit. He tapped it on the podium in front of him and everybody quieted.

He raised the baton for a long second, then brought it down in a graceful arc that kicked the band into "Spuddin' on a Wildcat."

Sprocket shuffled uncomfortably at the lip of the moon-pool, but he knew what was expected of him, and Drillers gotta drill. His tongue dropped free and headed for the bottom of the ocean.

A minute later, he got there and his tongue began to rotate. The furrows of doubt between his eyes smoothed and vanished. He began to hum along with the song while he spudded in on the first deep-water, offshore, exploratory oil well. Making oilpatch history, we were.

The next day we ran thirty-inch diameter drivepipe down. In case we ran into problems later and had to set casing more often than planned, Doc and T-Bone had decided Sprocket should make the widest hole possible all the way down. The ocean floor had checked to be about five hundred and thirty feet below, and Sprocket had drilled two hundred feet, so we ran twenty-six joints, each thirty feet long.

Usually, Lady Jane and her crew would come on location to set the pipe that she had made, but it wasn't practical at sea to do it the traditional way. Instead, the sailors had used the half-dozen cranes on board to cover a sizable portion of the deck with stands of pipe in various sizes. I thought about Star and missed her the whole time we ran the drivepipe in the hole. Big Red had been towed out on a barge. He didn't look like he was any more enthusiastic about the experience than Sprocket had been, but he was a pro. We hooked lines from the barge to the wellhead, and the cement job was perfect, as usual.

The Chief sauntered up cleaning his hands on a shop rag, as we finished. He stepped to the edge of the moon-pool and shouted up at me. I had stationed myself at the top of the draw-works to keep the lines clear as we ran in.

"Afternoon, Henry Lee! Thought I'd see how you're coming along."

"Doing just fine, Chief," I answered. "Hooking up the telescoping riser pipe on top of the string."

The Chief shook his head. "Ah, excuse me. I thought we all spoke English on *Miz Bellybutton*. I was mistaken."

I laughed. I patted the joint in front of me. "This particular piece is new to me, too. You know how y'all set anchors in the four directions of the compass to prevent the ship from drifting away from the hole?"

He nodded. I turned the pipe slightly. I looked down at Razer on a platform below the moon-pool

opening, just above the water level in the hold. He
signalled for me to turn the pipe just a hair more.
"Well, the ship still rides up and down a bit. Mr.
Pickett's engineers anticipated that, so they designed
and fabricated a special piece of pipe to be the top
one. It's actually two pieces, one slightly smaller in
diameter than the other. The bottom part is epoxied
to the top of the normal string of casing we're running in the hole. The top part will be attached to that
framework beside you, in the center of the moon-
pool. The two parts are sealed and greased, so they
can slide fairly freely, like a piston, when the ship
rides the waves. That way the top of the hole stays
stable, allowing us to work more easily through it."

Razer signalled me to let the pipe ride down the
last crucial couple of feet. I did so and he nippled it
onto the joint below it and slopped epoxy all over it.
One of the holds next to the moon-pool had been
converted to a mud pit. He hooked the mud lines
that led from it to a tee that had been welded to the
side of the pipe.

"Hold on," the Chief said. "The top of that thing,
that, ah, *joint* is twenty feet in the air. How can
Sprocket drill that way? I'd think you'd want it flush
with the deck, or a bit lower."

"You're right." I started climbing down from the
draw-works. "After that epoxy dries, we'll punch the
string down another thirty feet. The clever part, is
that when time comes to move the ship off the hole,
we just set a bridge plug, yank the top section of the
riser pipe out, leaving the bottom part below the
ship's hull, and steam away."

"Uh . . . right."

Sprocket woke up. His drill-head poked out of his
mouth, then fell to the deck as his eyes widened and

began to vibrate horizontally. The drill-head glided toward the moon-pool, snuffling loudly. It raised up off the deck like a cobra and turned in the Chief's direction, still snuffling.

Sprocket started to tremble and hum. The Chief drew back a step. "What did I do? Is he mad at me?"

Before either me or the Chief could move again, the drill-head darted forward and sucked the shop rag out of the Chief's hand. Then it swallowed his forearm.

The Chief tried to pull away. "That tickles!"

"What's he doing?" I asked.

"Feels like he's licking my whole arm."

Abruptly, Sprocket's tongue withdrew and slumped back to the deck, then raised up and started snuffling again.

"He's been known to be rude on occasion," I said. "But that's the first time I ever saw him do *that*. What was on that rag, anyway?"

The Chief raised his hand and looked at it. Sprocket had even managed to clean the dark from under his fingernails somehow. He could do delicate work if he had to. "Ah . . . let's see. . . . I was working in my Goody Room on some bearings. Greasing them."

Sprocket's eyes squinched shut in concentration. His tongue shot away in a loop around and behind him.

"Uh-oh," I said. "Chief, was there anything unusual about this grease?"

"Hmmmm. Maybe. It's called Muracon-E. We don't use it except for three small, delicate bearings deep inside each engine train. It contains special anti-corrosion and de-viscosifying additives."

I picked up a nearby valve handle and pounded on Sprocket with it until he opened an eye. "You better not break anything!" I said to him. "That stuff ain't your anyways."

He closed his eye again. I pounded on him some more, but he ignored me.

"Chief, you and me better head for your Goody Room right now! Sprocket's trying to get to that special grease!"

"The Goody Room is locked," the Chief said. "I'm the only one with a key."

"Even worse. Sprocket ain't got much moral character where petroleum derivatives are concerned. I'd be real embarrassed if he tore down your door getting to this Muracon-E."

The Goody Room was a couple of dozen feet from the entrance to the engine room proper. Sprocket hadn't yet lost his patience when we got there, both of us out of breath from the run. His drill-head still snuffled around the area, looking for an opening to sneak in, rather than battering through.

"That's remarkable," the Chief said. "How he found it so quickly."

"What's remarkable is he didn't sniff it out sooner. His foreskin can sense hydrocarbon molecules in parts-per-billion concentrations. And it looks like he considers this Muracon-E to be a genuine gourmet item."

The Chief took a ring of keys from his pocket. "Well, no reason to let things get out of hand." He turned to unlock the door to this Goody Room.

"No call to give in to him that way," I said. "Let's find us a couple of crowbars. If we knock his drill-head away from the door for fifteen minutes or so, he'll understand the Muracon-E is off-limits."

"I don't mind. It's not particularly expensive, and I have three unopened cans left, enough to last for years. I'll feed him the can I opened today."

He opened the door and Sprocket's tongue tried to dart inside. I grabbed ahold of it and wrestled it while the Chief got a five-gallon can off a workbench that was welded to the bulkhead next to the door.

"He probably can't smell the stuff that's still sealed," I said. "But if your Goody Room gets broken into in the middle of the night, you'll know who did it."

The Chief wanted to watch him drink it, so I captured Sprocket's drill-head and followed the Chief topside and across the deck with it, until we stood in front of Sprocket again. Both Sprocket's eyes tracked us as the Chief deposited the five-gallon can on the deck and pried the top up.

Usually, when Sprocket got excited, his deep green eyes sprung clockwise. But this time, they held wide open and vibrated rapidly sideways, just like when he'd first smelled it.

I let go of his tongue. It thumped to the deck and slid sidewise until it trapped the can inside a circle about three feet in diameter. The drill-head lifted off the deck and, snuffling more slowly now, cautiously peered over the top of the open pail. It dipped in delicately, then withdrew, only the first couple of inches of his drill spear dripping a chewy, glistening black liquid. Then his foreskin puckered and vacuumed the Muracon-E inside his drill-stem.

He repeated the process, even more slowly. He moaned with delight.

"I don't know what that stuff's got in it," I said. "But if I saw a human being acting that way around it, I'd know for sure it was illegal."

The Chief was fascinated. He watched while Sprocket took almost an hour to lovingly, agonizingly devour his treat.

Then Sprocket ate the can. And the lid.

*   *   *

A week after we got to location, Sparks reported
that ships at sea were warning of a storm brewing out
in the Atlantic. It looked like it would be blown into
the Gulf if the prevailing winds continued to prevail.

He kept us on top of the situation as the storm
came right at us, getting stronger as it went. It hit
three days after the first report. According to the
sailors we talked with, it wasn't much of a storm,
really. More like a heavy collection of gusty rain
clouds. We decided to keep on drilling through it if
we could. You don't stop making a well just because
it rains or snows a little bit. This is one of the less
wonderful facts about working the oilpatch. Sometimes it almost makes up for the good stuff. Setting
pipe in the midst of a freezing sleet storm, for instance, can get old, awful fast.

The skies were clear and the sunset was unusually
glorious the evening before the storm hit. I worked
the afternoon tower, from three to eleven. Naturally,
I got woke up by the ship rolling from side to side.
The sphincter ring muscle had clamped shut the
hole in my ceiling. Sprocket usually only does that
when the weather outside has gone to hell, or in the
dead of winter to make it easier to maintain internal
thermal equilibrium.

"How about a light?" I yelled. After a second, the
wart over my bed brightened enough for me to see
my clock. It was a little after midnight.

"Open the hole for a second?"

The sphincter muscle relaxed until the hole
spanned a foot, about a third of its usual diameter.
The rain poured in and the wind screamed. The
lighting set up in the area of the wellhead illuminated the sky enough for me to see the low-slung

clouds racing by overhead. The rocking of the boat, that had until now been vaguely comforting, took on a new aspect. If the waves were high enough to make *Miz Bellybutton* bounce around so much, this landlubber ought to maybe worry some.

"Close the hole! Thanks." I tried to go back to sleep and had succeeded by the time Razer scratched on my curtain. I sighed and told Sprocket to let him in.

I reached for my coveralls and steel-toes even before he started talking.

"We had to pull out of the hole, hoss," he said. His coveralls were plastered to his body and his hard hat still dripped freely. "Just too much lateral movement, not to mention the vertical. Looks like we're gonna have to move off entirely. Need all the hands to break down and button up."

"Great," I said. "Gimme five minutes." He nodded and headed down the hall to wake up the rest of the hands. Another rotten fact about working the oilpatch. In the middle of a crisis, which usually happens half-a-dozen times per well, sleep breaks become as scarce as chicken teeth. You get used to it.

If you got a good tool-pusher, like Doc, you don't mind so much, because he lets you make it up as soon as possible. Some pushers mickey-mouse their hands to death, making them do maintenance chores after they been up forty or fifty hours. They tend to have a high crew turnover. They also tend to lose their teeth young. Not one hand had quit Sprocket's crew since I had hired on. Nor had Doc needed to protect his teeth from anybody but Tiny Small.

Outside was as bad as I had feared. Sprocket had moved a couple dozen steps back from the wellhead to give everybody room to work. The rain-slick deck pitched erratically as the waves battered the ship. When we anchored *Miz Bellybutton* before spudding in, her nose had been aimed out into the Gulf. That was the direction the storm was blowing from, so we had left her as-is. Only, the storm had curved around and hit us from the north. Until we got off the hole, *Miz Bellybutton* would have to take the wind-driven waves broadside.

Sailors scurried into and out of the foc's'le, battening down hatches and cranes and lifeboats.

Razer yelled at me from the platform on the derrick and waved me to him. The riser pipe spun and twisted below the hay pulley.

I sighed again and headed toward the hole.

A sailor in a yellow slicker staggered into me when the deck rolled again. He grabbed me by the arm and hissed, "You son of a bitch! Watch where you're going!"

His one good eye squinted angrily at me. I was still sleepy and not too excited at the prospect of working all night in a storm on a moving surface, so I didn't say anything. I just jerked my arm loose and moved to go around him.

I got past him and he kicked me in the butt. When I turned to face him, he swung at me again. The deck rolled and he lurched into me.

I put a hand on his chest and shoved him away. His breath reeked of sour beer. He started cussing at me in a loud voice. Half-a-dozen hands stopped to watch. About then I got tired of being the center of attention with Pegleg.

"I don't know what your problem is, mister," I said. "I've stayed clear of you as best I could. But I've about had it. You keep screwin' with me, I'm gonna straighten out your attitude once and for all."

Of course, that didn't help a bit. He swung again, and I decked him. I never thought about where that word came from before, but now it made sense. He landed on his back and bounced once.

Right then, all the lights went out. The rain had shorted out the lines. Sprocket immediately brought all his external running lights up to maximum illumination, but they didn't make much difference.

I watched Pegleg's shadow on the deck for a second, but he didn't seem to be in a hurry to make another try for me, so I headed off toward the derrick.

We worked all night. The most fun happened when the hold-downs on a stand of ten and three-fourth inch casing came loose, and the pipe skittered all over the deck, knocking three other stands loose. This happened before we got off the hole and nosed into the wind. The deck was barely stable enough for us to unship one of the cranes and spend a dangerous hour corralling and securing the pipe again, before it did more damage. In the dark. They didn't get the lights back on for hours. Sprocket helped by using his body as a barrier to keep the wild pipe confined to the rear of the ship.

After we finished with the pipe, we carefully moved back onto the hole and anchored with the nose of the ship into the wind, but when we tried to reattach the riser pipe, the ship was still tossing too much. We decided to wait until the storm finished blowing. Far as I was concerned, we should have chugged back to shore and docked for a couple of days.

The only other event of note, and one that came to haunt me later, because it led to me being out of everybody's sight for more than an hour, was when Sprocket and me lost it at the same time, right after we gave up on the riser pipe. My stomach finally couldn't take the strain any more and I leaned over the rail and fed the fish.

As I completed the first series of spasms, Sprocket moved up beside me and began to empty his stomachs with one mouth and his bladders with the others. Not a pretty sight.

I staggered in the dark to the nearest stairwell that led below. I managed to stumbled through the deserted corridor until I found a head, and spent the next eternity on my knees squeezing porcelain.

Sprocket had managed to reach twenty-five hundred feet before the storm hit, so we decided to go ahead and set surface casing before we resumed drilling. Right after we hooked the riser pipe joint into the string, while it still bounced up and down on spring-loaded bearings, Sprocket stepped up and peered into the moon-pool. His tongue slipped into the top of the riser, then back out, dripping seawater. His eyes popped wide open and began to vibrate from side to side, then squeezed shut. His tongue dropped back into the hole and started running in rapidly.

Doc walked over and tapped him with a thirty-six-inch crescent wrench. "Hey, Sprocket! Get alert, boy. We ain't drillin' today. We're settin' surface pipe."

Sprocket ignored him.

Five minutes later, his entire body recoiled convulsively from the hole. The whole front end of his body clenched up in a way I had never seen before. As we all stared at him, he slowly re-approached the moon-pool. His tongue played into the hole again.

When he stopped this time, his tongue started to twist and twitch delicately.

"Looks like he's fishing," Doc said. "But we ain't got a fish in the hole."

Which was true. Every now and then a tool breaks up on you downhole, or the wireline snaps, or some idiot drops a valve handle in, and you have to fish for the pieces before you can get back to business, but this hole shouldn't contain anything other than the seawater we were using for drilling mud.

After a minute, Sprocket caught whatever he'd been fishing for and started back out of the hole. Typically, he'd just suck a fish up inside his drill-stem and grip it with his foreskin, but that's not what he did this time. I wouldn't have either, if I'd been him.

He backed away from the moon-pool while he pulled his tongue up the last few yards. At first, I didn't recognize what he had retrieved from the hole and dropped on the ramp. His tongue quickly slithered away from the shapeless mass of clothing on the deck. It smelled real bad. Then I realized what it was.

Sprocket had pulled a dead man out of the hole. He lay facedown in front of us. Fish had eaten parts of him. Sprocket's tongue had been wrapped around his legs. He must have been floating head-down near the bottom of the hole.

Nobody moved for a long couple of breaths. Doc went up the ramp, bent over, and turned the man on his back. The face was chewed up so much you couldn't identify him by it. But the eyepatch had stayed in place.

Every head on deck turned in my direction.

I found myself blurting out, "I didn't kill him!" Sounded guilty as hell.

Nobody looked completely sure they believed me. I wouldn't have believed me, either.

Doc came over and put his hand on my shoulder. "He probably fell in the hole accidentally, Henry Lee." In a lower voice he went on. "But if not—if say, he come at you last night and you had to defend yourself and maybe panicked afterwards, it ain't too late to come clean. Nobody would blame you for defending yourself, Henry Lee."

"I didn't kill him, Doc," I said. "Swear to God."

He looked at me for a long second. Then he squeezed me on the shoulder. "I believe you, Henry Lee. Now all we got to do is convince everybody else."

I heard somewhere that the captain of a ship is the final law aboard it, and I halfway expected Captain Johnson to have me thrown in the brig, if they had one, and fed bread and water till they keelhauled me or whatever they do at sea. However, it turned out that the Coast Guard had jurisdiction of all ocean-going crimes, even outside territorial waters, when the U.S. was the country nearest to their occurrence.

Sparks radioed ashore, and a Coast Guard cutter met *Miz Bellybutton* as we passed Point Bolivar. They escorted us to their station beside the ferry landing.

Their place looked fancier than some of the yacht clubs along the coast, until you noticed that most of the yachts nosed into the docks had artillery bolted onto their decks.

The main building resembled a tropical plantation house. Inside was the same rich look, with the place all carpeted and low-key, furnished in wicker and chrome. I got interviewed by some fella dressed like an admiral. Seemed like a nice guy, asked friendly questions, listened to my side of the story, then showed me another reason the place wasn't a yacht club by throwing me into their own personal jail while he interviewed everybody else on the ship that he figured might have anything to contribute.

They fed me bread and water. Plus big helpings of chicken with mashed potatoes, and hot rolls, and green beans, and iced tea. It was a sad waste. For the first time in my entire life, I couldn't empty the plate.

Not that their bunk was so uncomfortable, but I didn't sleep worth a damn that night, either. What mostly kept me awake, was I couldn't remember whether in Huntsville they still hung people or had moved up to the hot squat.

In the morning they let me go. The admiral hadn't decided I was innocent. Doc had gotten some judge to remind them that they didn't really have enough evidence to charge me, and until they did, maybe I better not be locked up. A preliminary examination had been done on Pegleg and it showed that he had been bashed on the head. It also showed that he was pretty drunk when he died, and there was no way to say he hadn't fallen in on his own and banged his head inside the pipe, or on the way down to it.

Star waited outside the Coast Guard station's fence for me. As well as Sprocket and Lady Jane and both our crews.

I stopped a few feet away from her. "I didn't kill Pegleg, Star."

Her face crumpled and she rushed forward and held me. "Goddammit, Henry Lee. This is *me*! I never thought you was anything but innocent!"

We stayed ashore for another day, with me and Star spending the night in Lady Jane. Nobody acted any way other than decent to me, but every time I talked to somebody, I could almost see the thought going through their heads.

Did he or didn't he?

Maybe I was too sensitive about the whole thing. Maybe not everybody thought that. But I realized that if somebody asked me the question out loud, I couldn't do nothing but deny the charge. Just like the Coast Guard didn't have no way of proving I had murdered Pegleg, I didn't have no way of proving I was innocent. And maybe never would. That's a hell of a thing to carry around with you. Because, crazy as it sounds, even though I knew I was innocent, I started wondering if I was acting like I was guilty. How do you act if you're innocent? Do you talk about the whole thing, or do you stay silent? Do you act angry that you could even be suspected, or relieved that they let you go?

And how do you make yourself believe that somebody believes you're innocent when they tell you so? How do you handle people who pretend like nothing has happened and their dealings with you are business as usual?

I guess I knew Star and Doc and Razer believed me to be innocent. But I still felt guilty of something somehow.

That Friday we got ready to go back out. Would a guilty man want to go, or would he stay ashore? I didn't know, so I didn't make no fuss either way, and Doc didn't ask me to stay back at the camp.

Sprocket marched up the gangplank like he'd been doing it all his life, and we followed. Captain Johnson waited for us behind the foc'sle. He looked more like a depressed stork than ever. When me and Doc reached him, he held up his hand.

"Mr. Miller, I'd like a word with you."

"Fine. Start talkin'."

"Privately, if we could."

"This about Henry Lee?"

The Captain nodded.

"Then I don't believe there's no reason to talk about the man behind his back."

"As you wish. I don't want Mr. MacFarland aboard my ship."

"How come?"

"Don't be difficult, Mr. Miller. You know why."

"No, sir, I don't. You can enlighten me."

I had to give Captain Johnson credit. Doc wasn't helping him at all, but he stood his ground. "Very well, sir." He looked at me. "I don't want Mr. MacFarland aboard my ship because he may have murdered one of my crew."

Doc brought his face close to the Captain's. "Two things. First—in this country a man's considered innocent till proved guilty, and Henry Lee ain't even charged with a crime. Second—you don't tell me who works for me, just like I don't tell you who works for you. We both contracted to drill a well for Mr. Pickett, and I plan to keep up my end of the deal, with the crew that I picked for it. You run your crew and I'll run mine, and we'll both stay happy."

The Captain didn't turn red or nothing. His face just got a little stiffer. After a second, he nodded and turned to go.

Doc caught him by the elbow. "Captain, it ever occur to you that Henry Lee might be innocent? I've known the boy for some time, and I believe he is. If I'm right, there was either a terrible accident a couple of days ago or somebody else on board your ship killed Pegleg. Maybe one of your own crew. Until we learn more, don't be so quick to point a finger."

I got to stay on board, but it wasn't like I got your returning hero's welcome by the ship's crew. Most of them leaned on the rail, watching us blank-faced, while we steamed back out into the Gulf. One of them caught my eye and silently mouthed one word.

Killer.

For the rest of the drilling program, Sprocket was reluctant to go into the hole. We had to coax him and play extra-sweet to him. I couldn't blame him for it. If I had found Pegleg's body the way he had, I might have wanted to keep my tongue in my mouth, too. Once he got to drilling, he was fine, though. Three weeks later, Big Red came out on the barge and cemented a thirteen and three-eighths-inch long string for us. We fed lunch to Pearl and his hands, then they headed back to shore.

After supper, Doc called me into his room. His desk and his bed were covered with piles of musical notation paper. A couple of days before, he'd started working on another composition. Crumpled sheets littered the floor.

He leaned back in his chair, rubbed his eyes tiredly, and motioned for me to clear a space on his bed and have a sit.

"How's the new piece going?" I asked.

"It's gonna be longer than I thought. I figured I had an idea for a nice ten or fifteen minutes of structured noise, and it's turning into a goddam major composition right in front of me."

"Tough," I said.

"Yeah." He smiled.

He stretched and his face got serious. "I talked some with Pearl today."

"Yeah?"

"He told me the county coroner finished a detailed autopsy on Pegleg. Kept the results quiet for almost two weeks while the D.A. decided what to do."

That could only mean one thing. "They figure it wasn't an accident."

"Uh-huh. He was dead before he went in the hole. No water in his lungs, for one thing. His clothes were drenched with a couple of different kinds of oil, none of which were present in the mud we were running. He had abrasions and cuts on his hands and face, and the way the oils were present in most of them indicated that they'd been smeared in during some kind of scuffle, not by him banging around in the casing after he died. And his skull was cracked."

"They think somebody killed him and dumped him in the well. They gonna charge me with murder?"

"No. The D.A. decided that he couldn't get a conviction without more evidence directly implicating you."

I let out a breath I didn't know I'd been holding. "Thanks, Doc."

"Just wanted you to know as soon as possible."

I stood up and headed for the door. Then I realized what he had really meant. "They're gonna try to get more evidence aren't they? They still think I did it."

He rubbed his eyes again. "Hell, I don't know what they think, boy. Just be careful."

I climbed out of the hole on top of Sprocket, with my Epiphone strapped to my back and the little battery-powered Pignose amplifier clipped to my guitar strap and plugged in.

It had just got too close inside Sprocket. That didn't happen too often for me, but after talking with Doc I was wondering about Pegleg's death and if it was going to follow me around for the rest of my days.

I patted Sprocket halfheartedly and wandered down his length toward the rear of the ship. I brought the Epiphone around and strummed on it lightly as I walked. If anything, it made me feel worse. The notes sounded wrong, boring, stupid.

After awhile I ended up on the fantail at the very rear of *Miz Bellybutton*.

I sat down and played for half-an-hour, staring at the three-quarters full moon, cranking up the Pignose as loud as it would go, and getting more and more depressed.

"Say, you're pretty good," said a voice behind me. I turned. It was Chief Hightower.

"Thanks."

He pulled a mouth harp out of his shirt pocket and blew into it experimentally. "You mind a little accompaniment?"

I was still surprised that any of the ship's crew was actually talking to me. I'd seen the Chief once or twice since Pegleg's body turned up, and he'd nodded politely at me, but he always seemed to be on his way someplace else at the time.

"Couldn't make it worse, anyhow," I said.

He nodded. "I guess. You were sounding awful depressed on that thing. What's the matter?"

I still didn't quite trust that he wasn't setting me up to say something nasty to me. "What you think?"

He blew into the mouth harp again, doing a blurred

upward chromatic run. Sounded like he would prob- ably he competent on it. "Hmmm . . . I suspect you got the news today about the autopsy."

"How'd you know about that?"

"Man from the D.A.'s office had a long chat on the radio with me and Captain Johnson day before yes- terday. Asked us to reinterview the crew for any more details that might link you to Pegleg's murder."

"Great."

"Johnson asked Mr. Miller again to remove you from the ship this afternoon."

"And?"

"You're still here." He tapped the harp against his palm. "Don't worry about the Captain. He's edgy because this is his first time out on *Miz Bellybutton*. He's trying to get along with a crew new to him, most of which don't like you a bit."

"I noticed."

The Chief grinned. "He's caught between a rock and a hard place, because Mr. Pickett backed Mr. Miller up on this matter. Axis Ortell, our old captain, would have told Mr. Pickett to take a flying leap and then tossed you over the side if you pissed him off. Better for you to have to handle Johnson."

"I'm so relieved."

The smile faded off his face. "Hey, it's not that bad. You didn't do it. You'll be cleared eventually."

"How do you know I didn't do it?"

He leaned against the rail and looked somberly at me for a long minute. Moonlight gleamed on his bald head. "I'm a good judge of character," he said finally. "I've been around a while, and I know very well what kind of person it takes to kill. You don't qualify. I'm sorry for the way my boys have treated you.

They simply don't want to think it might have been one of them."

For some reason, I believed him. It made me feel less guilty.

He blew into the mouth harp again. "I was listening to you," he said. "Your problem is, you got the blues."

"You got that right."

"Best thing to do is *play* the blues when you got them." A long wail like a lonesome train in the distance came out of the mouth harp. He followed it with an involved riff that sounded so sweetly aching that I shivered.

He broke off and grinned. "See?"

"How did you *do* that?"

"It's the blues. I've been a fan since I was a boy."

"What scale is that? The note intervals sounded almost like an incomplete Major, but your phrasing was—"

He blew a descending six-note scale. "This is a G harp, so it plays blues in D," he said. "I don't know anything about scales, but that's the notes I was taught."

I echoed the notes and we worked it out over the next half-hour. It was exactly the sound I'd been trying to find. It was so lonesome that it was perfect for how I felt. The band played jazz blues on occasion, but this was different. The progressions were simpler, more elemental. And somehow harder. The scale was a pentatonic minor with an added flat-5, and I figured out that the song structure was a I-IV-V chordal progression in twelve bars, twelve/eight time.

I started getting excited. "How come I never heard of this stuff before? This is great."

"It's Negro folk music," the Chief said. "From the

way you've been talking, your bunch comes from a more classical orientation. I don't know much about that sort of music. I just know what I've learned about the blues from a life spent hanging out on the wrong side of the tracks."

We played for another hour, me mostly accompanying with chords while he wailed. He showed me some variations on it, including minor blues, which sounded positively suicidal. It was wonderful.

Eventually, we went back to his stateroom, where he cranked up his record player and put on one of the hundreds of blues records arranged neatly in three cases beside his bed. I realized we hadn't even scratched the surface. I managed to pick clumsily along with a few of the easier tunes.

Finally, exhausted, I headed back for Sprocket.

The Chief escorted me to the bulkhead and shook my hand. "Thanks, Henry Lee. I haven't had so much fun in a long time."

"Me, neither. Mind if I come listen to more of those records some other time?"

"Sure. Any time at all." He clapped me on the shoulder. "I believe in you. You're going to be all right."

I was grateful as a puppy given a new bone.

Me and the Chief hung out a lot together after that. I'd go to his room for hours and listen to his records and play along with them. A couple of the hands on Sprocket's crew knew a little about the blues, but said they didn't much care for them. Preferred the more technically demanding forms of jazz or classical music. Doc pulled a couple of instruction books about the blues from out of the file cabinet for me, but otherwise seemed less than interested. His

new composition was keeping him up at all hours,
anyway.

The Chief would talk to me when I visited, and he
showed me around the ship and the engine room. I
think he tried to get a couple of the sailors to party
with us in his room, but I ain't sure. Nobody ever
showed up. He visited with us and Sprocket during
his off-time, for dinner and the like. Seemed to get
along with everybody. I showed him around the
drilling operation, explaining the ins and outs of
making a well as best I could.

He made me feel better, but I still got depressed
about most of the ship's crew thinking I was a mur-
derer. Life went on.

Sprocket was down around twelve thousand feet
when he hit a pocket of high-pressure sour gas. It
was the middle of a lazy afternoon. Most of the crew
was taking a nap while me and Big Mac watched the
drilling. Mac had gotten bored and was face down on
the deck doing one-handed push-ups. A couple of
sailors leaned over the balcony rail that ran around
the back of the foc's'le, smoking hand-rolls. They still
hadn't thawed to us much, but some of them seemed
to enjoy listening to Sprocket's soothing hum while
he made hole.

Sprocket had been in the hole for about a day and
a half, drilling steady. Suddenly, his low, relaxed
purr got louder and higher. His eyes began to blink
open and shut rapidly. Then he stopped drilling and
marching. He took a couple of steps forward and
clamped his mouth over the wellhead. The wrinkles
on his face deepened as he pressured up on the hole.

"Doc!" I yelled. "We got a problem!"

After a couple of seconds Doc's head poked out of
the hole in the top of his room. He yawned and dug

sleep-crackles out of his eyes. Then he climbed out and crawled forward on his knees until he could see the way Sprocket's mouth covered the wellhead.

"Drilled into a high-pressure formation," he said. "Get the mud weighted up."

"Believe it's more than that." Sprocket started to march in a different cadence, driving his legs down in triplets hard against the ship's surface. It wasn't the signal he usually made when he hit a high-pressure zone. I'd seen another Driller march in this cadence only once before. "Believe he's got into some sour gas."

"Aw, crap," Doc said. Then he looked at me speculatively. "You're on tower, Henry Lee. Handle it."

"Are you out of your mind?" I looked over my shoulder at the sailors in the foc'sle. They'd clumped together in a bunch and were watching us intently. I moved closer to where Doc sprawled. I spoke as soft as I could and still be heard by him. "I could kill everybody on this ship if I screw up."

Doc nodded. "Uh-huh. But you been around the oilpatch almost two years now, Henry Lee. You been standing tower by yourself for half of that. You can't handle the pressure, I'd just as soon find out now."

"But——"

Doc frowned at me. "Don't but me no buts, boy. You're in charge. What you gonna do?"

A couple of other heads had popped up along Sprocket's top. They all stared at me, waiting. Well, it wasn't as if I hadn't been schooled up on how to handle sour gas. I took a deep breath.

"Sour gas! Get your asses below, worms! Now! I don't want to see any of you again without a respirator on your face!"

I gestured at Big Mac. "Bring me a mask and get one on your own self." He gave me a mock salute and double-timed away.

I licked a finger and tested the wind with it. We were lucky. The wind blew from the nose of the ship. The foc'sle was upwind. But the engine room wasn't. I moved myself upwind of the hole, just in case.

"Razer!" I yelled. His head popped up out of his hole. The respirator covered his entire face, with the oxygen cannister hanging down on his chest. He yanked the straps down tighter where they met at the back of his head. He goggled at me through the faceplate. "We got spare masks in the iron room. Get 'em to the engine room ASAP. Along with a detector. Explain to the Chief. Show him and his boys how to use 'em."

He gave me a thumbs-up and ducked below again. As a couple of the crew, all wearing masks, popped out of holes atop Sprocket, I turned to the sailors that were gawking at the goings-on. "One of you, please get the Captain for me. The rest, stay upwind of the hole."

"What's the big deal, lubber?" one of them shouted.

"No big deal. Just kindly stay away from the well-head till we say otherwise."

I turned again and saw Doc had climbed out of his room and was getting ready to slide down Sprocket's side.

"Hold up there, Mr. Miller!" I said. "You get upwind with your shaving kit and take that beard off right now." The hair on his face would keep the mask from making a perfect seal. And around sour gas, perfect is the only way to be.

"Aw, Henry Lee," his words came muffled through

the respirator. "I got positive pressure blowing on this thing. I even smeared Vaseline all over my face."

"Fine for you. You get killed on your own tower. Long as I'm in charge, we do it API." My voice rose again. He wasn't the only one on the crew that sported a beard. "You hear that, people? Shave it off. Right now! That means sideburns, too!"

If there's one thing a gypsy hates most, it's taking the hair off his face.

One of the hands, I couldn't tell who with the mask on, slid down Sprocket's side and started setting up a sour gas detector. They'd be deposited in various places around the location, especially by the reserve pits. Sometimes sour gas could percolate through the mud undetected until it released there. Also around the pipe joints all over the location.

"Set the low-level screamer to go off at 20 ppm," I said. "High-level at 50 ppm."

He glanced over his shoulder. "Teach granny to suck eggs, Henry Lee," he said. Never hurts to remind somebody in a situation like this. He turned on the detector. It didn't start screaming.

Mac popped out of a hole on top and tossed me a respirator. I snatched it out of the air and had it loose around my neck when Captain Johnson showed up on the balcony.

"Where's Mr. Miller?"

"He's busy," I said. "I'm in charge right now. You and me need to talk."

He didn't look happy at that. He got even less happy shortly.

"Captain, we've drilled into a pocket of hydrogen sulfide gas. I don't know how much of it there is, but until we get it taken care of, I'd like you to keep your hands away from the hole as far as possible, preferably upwind of it."

"Why?"

I felt like screaming, but I explained patiently. "Because it's poisonous as hell. A concentration of two hundred parts per million in the air will kill you dead as a mackerel on a mountaintop. You can't see it because it's transparent, and the first whiff numbs your sense of smell, so you don't know you're breathing it until you drop over. Then you're in real trouble, since it's heavier than air and tends to pool near the ground."

"My God!"

I nodded. "Uh-huh. It's scary stuff. Good news is, Sprocket caught it before it did any damage, and we know how to handle it. Give us a day or so, you and your crew can get back to business as usual."

"Mr. Pickett never said a word about my crew facing this sort of hazard when we made our agreement."

"It's not all that common. He probably didn't think of it."

One of the sailors on the railing behind us said loudly, "You gypsies aren't satisfied with Pegleg, huh? Gonna kill us all!"

Captain Johnson wheeled on him. He looked angry for the first time since I'd seen him. "That'll be enough, mister!"

The sailor looked at us both stonily and took another drag on his pipe.

The Captain turned back to me. "Have Mr. Miller meet me in the radio shack when he's free," he said. Then he left.

The Chief patted the derrick strut. "Nice. This little episode is getting us all a twenty-five percent raise." We both had backpack respirators on, but I'd have enough practice in the last day and a half that I didn't have any problem understanding his words.

Sprocket still sealed the hole. Right beneath his mouth, I hammered some more on the knocker-half that connected the relief line to the riser pipe, tightening it.

"I figured it took something like that to quiet Captain Johnson down," I said. "Nobody offered us a raise, though."

"Way I heard it, Doc didn't ask for one. Said you boys already knew what you were getting into. Mr. Pickett apparently agreed."

"Everybody is staying?"

"Mr. Pickett offered to send a speedboat out to ferry anybody who wanted it. Nobody's quit just yet. If this burn-off looks good, I imagine the whole crew will hang on. It's good money."

Sprocket blinked beside us, and banged his drillhead against the pipe beside me. He was almost out of the hole. I gave him another few seconds to get completely clear, then pointed at the valve on the other side of the pipe and a few yards above my head.

"How about turning that wheel for me?" I said to the Chief. "Clockwise, to shut it."

"Sure thing." He leaned over and closed it.

Sprocket backed down the ramp away from the hole. "Make sure it's snug," I said. "That's the blowout valve. We don't want no sour gas escaping through it."

He put a bind on the wheel. "I thought Sprocket was your blowout preventer."

"Sometimes he has to be out of the hole even when there's a kick, like now. That valve has special teflon lined inserts for sour gas service. It'll hold against a twenty thousand psi pressure differential. So will this one." I touched the wheel on the valve beside me.

"I'm impressed."

"You should be. They cost about five thousand bucks apiece."

I looked up at Razer at the top of the derrick. I pumped my fist up and down a couple of times. He looked toward the bow and repeated the motion. A couple of seconds later, he pointed at me and moved his finger in a circle. I twisted the relief valve open and climbed out of the hole.

The sun had gone down a couple of hours ago. I went with the Chief to the bow rail and watched along with the rest of the hands.

Just as we arrived, Doc triggered the electric ignitor. A couple of hundred feet away from the ship, bright orange suddenly glared into the sky.

We'd coupled lengths of steel hose to make a long boom out over the water. The end of the boom rested squarely across one of *Miz Bellybutton's* lifeboats. It rose lazily in the gentle swells, slowly shifting the shadows thrown by the billowing, burning, sour gas.

The fire burned all night, dangerous and beautiful.

Sprocket drilled another thousand feet to make sure that was all the sour gas we were likely to run into for the time being, then we invited Pearl and Big Red out to cement a liner over it all.

After it tested, Sprocket went back to business as usual. He still had to be coaxed into the hole, and I could see a worried look clouding Doc's face every time it happened. Nobody quit *Miz Bellybutton,* but only the Chief thanked us for the pay raise.

We completed the drilling program fifty-eight days after we first anchored on location. Sprocket TD'ed at twenty thousand feet, exactly as planned.

T-Bone's drilling venture had got lucky first time out. As far as the well itself was concerned, it went perfect after we disposed of the sour gas. No hole degradation, no more unwanted fluids or gases infiltrating, no thief zones. But we did hit three good zones on the way to TD: producible amounts of light crude at eighty-eight hundred feet and twelve thousand two hundred feet, and as a bonus, a high-pressure reservoir of clean, non-stinky natural gas at fifteen thousand seven hundred feet.

T-Bone sent out a couple of perf-gun operators on his speedboat. We perforated the casing for the oil zone at twelve-two and ran in a production packer on a string of two-inch tubing. Then we sealed off the hole as quickly as we could, pulled the riser pipe up, weighed anchor and steamed for shore. The perf-gun operators and the speedboat driver decided to stay aboard and ride in with us, since the water was getting a little too rough for their preferences.

We were in a hurry because a hurricane had brewed in the Gulf south of Cuba for the last week that we drilled. We had been afraid that we'd have to pull off before setting our production string, but the storm had dithered around instead, gaining strength, until it decided to charge straight at us. Dark clouds scudded high in the atmosphere behind us, looking like torn ribbons, as we turned for shore.

A half-an-hour after we moved off location, I wandered around the deck and came upon the Chief fishing over the rail.

He looked up and gestured me to come over.

"Catching anything?"

"Nope." He pointed to an area a couple of hundred feet off the bow. "See that?" I looked. After a second I saw half-a-dozen fins cutting through the still water. "Sharks. Imagine they're scaring everything off."

Beside him another pole reposed on the deck. He handed it to me. "Here. Third Mate was going to join me, but he decided at the last minute to catch a few winks instead. This may be our last chance to fish for awhile."

I generally preferred to use live bait, but I realized there wasn't many worms aboard ship, and no convenient bait houses nearby, so I made do with the spoon he'd already attached. After about fifteen minutes I hadn't had much luck either, when I felt eyes on my back. I twisted around. Sprocket loomed over both of us, green eyes blinking slowly. Jokingly, I held out the rod to him. "Here you go, Sprocket. Maybe you'll have better luck than us." I swung the tip back and cast out with the weighted spinner. "See, it ain't too hard once you get the hang of it."

His eyes spun for a second, then steadied. He hummed for a minute. His mouth shot open and his drilling tongue arched over the rail and splashed into the water hundreds of feet away. The Chief guffawed and slapped his knee.

"Guess he brought his own equipment, Henry Lee. Doubt he'll catch much using his drill-head for a lure, though."

Sprocket's hum changed in pitch. I looked and saw

the length of his tongue rapidly playing out through his mouth.

"Damn, he's got a bite! Must be a big 'un!" the Chief exclaimed. "Don't let him get away, boy!" He dropped his pole and started shouting advice to Sprocket. "You got to let him run awhile, then draw in when he slows. Don't jerk, he might pull loose; just reel him in smoothly. Then let him run some more, only make it harder for him. He's got to fight the line. After awhile, it'll tire him and you can pull him aboard."

Sprocket seemed to be listening. His tongue reeled out for about five minutes, then drew in some, then reeled out some more. This repeated three or four times.

Beside me, the Chief stayed excited. "Damn, that's a big one he's got. Say, doesn't this hurt his tongue?"

"Nope," I said. "That drill tongue's tougher than steel cable. Stands up to heat and acid and all sorts of horrible conditions downhole."

Finally Sprocket started to reel his catch in. It took him more than ten minutes. Whatever he had caught still had some fight in it. The Chief leaned over the side with a gaff, but Sprocket yanked it right up the side of the ship without any help.

I didn't know what he had, not being all that familiar with sea fish. But it looked mean as hell. The Chief recognized it though, and motioned for me to back away. "Son of a gun! He's hooked a white shark."

The damn thing looked to be fifteen feet long. Finally, Sprocket pulled it over the rail and flopped it on the deck.

"Shark fin makes a tasty soup," the Chief said. "If you have a taste for it."

The shark lay still. One eye stared at me. Most fish, you look them in the eye, all you get back is a fishy look. This white shark was different. It looked seriously pissed off.

Suddenly, its mouth released from Sprocket's tongue. The flippers spasmed into furious activity and, before anybody realized what was happening, a whole mouthful of teeth was coming at the Chief like a freight train. The jaws were big enough to chomp him in half, and that's what they intended to do. The mouth had begun to close around the Chief's waist, when it was jerked back like magic. The Chief had raised his arm to try to fend it off. The shark's snout barely touched his elbow as it was whisked away.

Sprocket had whipped his tongue around the shark's tail and pulled it off just in time. Weakly, we both leaned against the rail and watched. The shark struggled furiously.

I don't think it realized the truth, even at the end. All its life, everything it had ever run into was dinner. Except Sprocket. Sprocket liked hydrocarbons best of all. But everything else, including sharks, was okay by him.

Sprocket stuffed that shark, fighting all the way, into his eating mouth. Then came a couple of meaty crunches and the show was over. One less white shark. One more taste treat for Sprocket.

The Chief kissed Sprocket's hide, then went below, still visibly trembling. Said he needed to change his underwear. I figured he was joking, but I wouldn't have blamed him if he wasn't.

Sprocket went back to fishing. The hands that

were loose gathered at the rail and encouraged him. A couple of sailors joined us and patted Sprocket's hide. For the first time since Pegleg's death, they mixed freely with the crew. None of them scowled when they glanced at me.

But none of them came up and shook my hand, either.

Sprocket's first couple of casts came back bare, but on his third try, he hooked something again. Something that seemed as big as the deceased shark. As we egged him on again, his tongue ran out smoothly. After five minutes, he took up the tension on it and his catch started to fight. His eyes gleamed with excitement. And with the anticipation of another snack.

He played his tongue out again, then pulled in. That's when the program changed.

His tongue abruptly jerked downward so rapidly that he stumbled forward into the rail. He grunted with the effort and reeled on it. His tongue drew taut, then went slack.

As he brought it in, we figured that the fish had pulled itself loose, but we were wrong. His drill-head came up the side of the ship with something still attached to it.

It had been another white shark, a huge one, maybe twenty feet long. It had been torn in half. The jaws were still clenched around Sprocket's drill-head, but everything a foot past the gills was simply gone.

Behind me, Doc whistled. "What the hell could have done that?"

Over where Sprocket had made his last cast, where the fins cut across the surface, the water boiled white.

Sprocket stuffed the half-a-shark into his eating mouth and began to chew.

As he finished the last gulp, the Chief appeared around his flank. Sprocket bemusedly smacked his lips as the Chief set down the five-gallon can he was lugging.

"I figured out how I could reward Sprocket," he said. He pulled a big screwdriver out of his back pocket and bean to pry the lid off.

"Here you go, Sprocket." The Chief stepped back from the can of Muracon-E. "Have a ball. Thanks for saving my life."

Sprocket's drill-head poked tentatively out of his mouth and snuffled once. His eyes popped open and spun alarmingly, then he croaked in panic and backed rapidly away from the can.

"What's the matter with him?" the Chief said. We both looked at the can at the same time, but it was really Muracon-E, not something else.

"Hey, Sprocket, calm down," Doc called out. Sprocket continued to back across the deck. His whole front end clenched up.

"What's happening?" I asked nobody in particular. "He loves that stuff. He's acting like—"

Then I glanced over at the Chief. "He's acting," I finished slowly, "exactly like he did when he pulled Pegleg out of the hole."

The blood drained out of the Chief's face. I knew and he knew that I knew.

"Aww, Chief." He wouldn't meet my eyes.

"The stuff that was smeared in Pegleg's clothes," I went on. "Some of it must have been Muracon-E. That's why Sprocket don't like it any more. The only place it could have come from is your Goody Room. And you're the only person with a key to it."

The Chief started to recover. "No, that's—"

Behind me, Doc spoke. "I bet somewhere in that

police investigation of Pegleg's murder is an analysis of the stuff in his wounds."

"There's no evidence—"

"When you know where to look, there's always evidence," Doc said. "There's probably still traces in the Goody Room, blood and hair and such."

"Aww, Chief," I said again. "Why?"

The Chief's hand dipped into his pocket and came out with a small-caliber revolver.

For a long minute, the Chief faced us. The gun swung slowly back and forth as if he wasn't sure who to point it at. Nobody moved. Maybe fifteen of us stood in a semicircle around him, with another half-dozen staring down from the balcony. He had six bullets at the most in his pistol, but nobody wanted to be the first to help him use them up.

"What you gonna do now?" I finally asked. "We're out in the middle of the damn ocean. There's no place to go. Even if you hold us up till we get to shore, then jump ship, you can't get much of a head start."

He still looked uncertain. I started to hope that I could plain talk him out of the gun.

"Look, this is crazy," I said. "You and me are friends, Chief. Believe me. You ain't gonna do nothing but get in deeper from here on. Unless you call it off right now."

"It was self-defense, Henry Lee," he said.

"I believe you."

Behind him, Sprocket growled and his tongue poked out of his mouth. He may not have understood what was going on, but the sensed that we were all sure unhappy with the Chief at the moment.

The Chief turned at the sound and eyed Sprocket.

Then I made a stupid move. I stepped forward and reached for the gun, but the Chief slid aside and pointed it at my face before my hand could close on it.

"I can't trust you either, can I, Henry Lee?" he said. "You don't give a damn about me. Nobody does. Nobody ever did." The gun was pointed at me now, not waving from person to person.

"Everything I been saying is true, Chief. You're just making it worse on yourself. If it was self-defense—"

"Shut up. Let me think." He moved so he could see all of us and Sprocket at the same time. While he pondered, the breeze freshened from the dead calm it had been.

"Okay," he said after a minute. "I think I've got it worked out." He gestured toward the second mate. "You, Mr. Atkins. Get the engine room gang up here." He searched the faces on the balcony. "Sparks, you stay in sight. Nobody but you knows how to run that radio of yours. I'd just as soon no transmissions were made right now. Marvin, you get the wheel-house crew down here. I want every hand on this ship assembled on deck in five minutes. If anyone comes up missing—you won't like it."

"But that'll leave the ship adrift!" the second mate protested.

"That's an order, mister!" He pointed the gun at the mate.

The mate nodded and left.

The Chief turned back to me. "Okay, Henry Lee. Come here a minute. Don't worry," he said, when I hesitated. "Everything will work out fine. I just need to set things up properly."

He took me by the arm and led me over to stand with him next to the wellhead. "I need to simplify things. So I can get away without anybody getting hurt in the process. First, let's make sure I don't have to worry about Sprocket any more." He smiled at me, just like we were still buddies, then stuck the pistol barrel into my ear.

"Doc, Razer, you bring Sprocket's tongue over here."

"How come?" Razer asked.

The Chief smiled again. "Don't fuck with me. Just do it. Now!"

Sprocket stared at us while his drill-head was brought up the ramp. The works around the drilling area had been partially disassembled. "Open that valve," the Chief said to me, pointing with the gun at the shut-off valve that led to the mud tank.

"All right," he went on when I had finished. "Now, let's run his tongue in through it. Thirty or forty feet's worth. I want his drill-head well into the tank."

"That's good," the Chief said after they had done what he said. "Now back off." He reached out and grabbed the valve's wheel and spun it. Sprocket twisted, but didn't react otherwise. I felt a sharp pain shoot through my own mouth in sympathy when the Chief gave it one final tug to cinch it down tight. Actually, it couldn't have hurt Sprocket at all, considering the abuse his tongue took downhole daily.

The Chief looked at me. "Sorry. I wish I didn't have to do this. I closed it enough to trap his drill-head on the other side of the valve. That ought to neutralize him for the time being."

He kept the gun against my head. "Okay. Next step is to put the rest of you somewhere safe."

We waited until everybody from the engine room and the wheelhouse had assembled on deck. The Chief counted heads until he was satisfied. When

Captain Johnson stepped to the front of the crowd and opened his mouth, the Chief shook his head and waggled the gun. "Don't waste your breath," he said.

He took me by the arm again. "I want all of you to follow us."

The entire crew marched behind as we headed toward the fantail, straight down the catwalk that ran the length of the ship. Finally, he stopped when we stood beside a sealed and locked hatch.

"Purser! Front and center!"

Eight large C-clamps secured the hatch. They were twisted down as far as possible. A hole in the tightening knob lined up with a hole punched in a heavy metal tab, that jutted out from the edge of the hatch. A lock had been passed through the holes on each clamp.

The purser came forward. "Unlock that hatch, please," the Chief said. Several rings of keys dangled from the purser's belt. Without a word he bent and began to open the locks.

When the purser was done, the Chief had me pull the hatch cover up and push it aside. I could see the floor of an empty hold ten feet below the deck. About then, I figured out what the Chief planned for us.

He nodded and smiled when I looked at him.

"That's right, Henry Lee. You're all going below for awhile."

"Chief, you can't run the ship all by yourself. Especially not with a hurricane blowing up."

"I don't plan to. I merely need you out of my hair," he patted his bald head and smiled again, "while I disable the radio, gather up my belongings, and escape. I'll pilot Mr. Pickett's speedboat to shore. I can get to Freeport or Bolivar in an hour. The ship will require five or six hours. I'll return for you in a few minutes. You help me cast off in the motor boat, then let everyone else out."

He turned to the waiting crowd. "All right, everyone into the hold."

A few minutes later, we stood in a clump in the hold, with the Chief outlined above us. "I won't be long, gentlemen. Try not to get too bored." He dragged the hatch shut until it sealed over the edge. It was quiet enough that you could hear him screwing down the clamps. He didn't bother to snap any of the locks in place.

Doc struck a phosphorus match, making a tiny, wavering circle of light in the hold. "Anybody got any ideas on how we can stop this lunatic?" he asked.

Nobody did.

While we waited, we explored the rest of the hold. It was completely empty. No handy dynamite or welding rigs or giant economy-size can openers. No doors leading out. We were locked tight inside a bare metal box.

After what seemed to be forever, we heard the Chief's footsteps overhead again. He rapped on the hatch cover. "I've been thinking, boys. Five hours isn't enough lead time. Better if everyone thinks I went down in the storm with the rest of you. Much easier for me to slip into my new life without the law after me. Sorry."

Shouts drowned out his leave-taking.

"The bastard's left us adrift," Captain Johnson said. "When the hurricane hits . . ."

We heard the Chief fire up T-Bone's speedboat. The sound diminished as he motored away, and the hold grew quiet and still enough for me to notice a whooshing, rolling sound around us. The more I listened, the louder it sounded in the dark.

"What's that noise, Captain?" I asked the Captain.

The hold grew silent, and we could all hear the gurgling and slapping.

"Oh my god," Captain Johnson whispered. "He's opened the sea cocks."

The hold got noisy again for a few minutes.

"I can't believe he's just left us here to die," I said when it got quiet for a second. "Maybe while we were all yelling before, he undid the clamps on the hatch."

"You climb up on my shoulders, Henry Lee," Doc said. "You're probably the strongest on the crew. How about a couple of you hands help me hold him up?"

The hatch was still clamped down. For ten minutes, I strained and grunted, but it wouldn't lift an inch. When the clamps were down, the cranes probably couldn't have pulled the hatch loose.

We were dead men, all of us.

"We should have jumped that bastard and taken our casualties when we had the chance," Razer said.

After a while, we all sat together and rocked back and forth. Listening to the water rush into the holds around us.

I thought about the Chief speeding away, leaving us behind to drown like rats. He could have let us live, but he didn't. He killed us. Not because we threatened him anymore. His original plan would have worked. He'd have gotten away. But he chose to kill thirty-three men—and Sprocket!—because it was more convenient for him that way. I never knew people like that existed. I was sorry I ever found out. I felt stupid that he'd followed me the way he did. I was just a big ol' dumb country hick. Couldn't tell the difference between a real friend and a mad dog killer. On top of everything else, he'd let me twist in the wind for weeks while everybody thought I was the one who killed Pegleg.

About the time I was feeling as sorry for myself as I could, new footsteps approached the hatch above us. Hundreds of them.

Sprocket's footsteps. He must have been playing his tongue out behind him to come to us.

I jumped up and started yelling. "Sprocket! Kick the clamps loose! Kick the clamps loose!" We pounded and shouted at Sprocket, but there was no way he could have understood us. All he understand was making a well and playing tricks on people. He probably couldn't have kicked the clamps loose anyway. They were made of heavy stainless steel and were practically flush with the deck when they were screwed down.

The ship settled lower in the water.

Then Sprocket screamed. I hope I never in my life hear another sound like it. It started low and ratcheted higher and louder until it keened so high we could barely hear it.

The scream cut off abruptly. A minute later Sprocket began shuffling about on deck again, grunting and moaning horribly. This went on for five or ten minutes. Then the hatch flexed twice and was wrenched into the air and out of sight. A second later, it clanged to the deck. Unbelievably, Sprocket had torn away the clamps.

I jumped up and grabbed the edge of the hole and levered myself outside. The clamps hadn't been torn loose. They had been unscrewed. They, and the deck for yards around, were covered with a viscous golden liquid that looked a lot like highly refined light crude.

Sprocket stood near the rail with his eyes closed. He might have been asleep, except that his whole body trembled.

I thought back to the Bali Room parking lot. Those clamp knobs resembled gas tank caps. He must have used his tongue to twist them loose. Then hooked it through the crane eye in the center of the hatch and lifted it off.

But his tongue had been trapped downhole!

Doc looked like he wanted to cry. He knew immediately what Sprocket did to himself to get loose.

"C'mon, Henry Lee. Razer. We've got to stop the bleeding."

Sprocket had used his eating mouth to bite his drill head off, then freed us with the ragged end. The golden liquid splattered all over the deck was his blood. Only the most complete desperation could have driven him to do what he did. Then a wave rolled over the rail and I realized how close to sinking *Miz Bellybutton* was. Sprocket must have realized it too. The next wave was higher.

I felt calm while we forced Sprocket to open his mouth and let us look at the smashed, gnawed ruin where his drill-head used to be. I guess I was in shock. I stroked his hide and held the tip in my hands while his blood soaked my jumpsuit. Razer entered through his mouth, slipping and sloshing through the golden pool inside it, then came back with the medical kit.

Captain Johnson and his crew had all rushed off to see about trying to keep *Miz Bellybutton* afloat and headed toward the coast. The Captain had looked

over the railing and shook his head when he saw how
low she rode in the chop.

While him and Doc worked on it, sewing, closing off
the flow of blood, then smearing anesthetic grease
and coagulants on it, all I could do was shake and
think about how much I wanted to catch up with the
Chief and make sure he never hurt anybody again in
this life.

I looked up from Sprocket's mangled tongue, and
stared out to the storm clouds gathering on the horizon, lost in a happy dream about how the Chief's
face would look after it had been punched hard for
maybe a half-hour. A speck bobbed up and down on
the waves a couple of hundred yards away.

I must have squeezed Sprocket's tongue, because
he winced and moaned. Doc shot me a stern look.

"Get yourself organized, Henry Lee."

I pointed at the speck casual-like. I still couldn't
believe what I saw.

"Take a gander over there, Doc. You suppose the
Chief was havin' second thoughts about leavin' us?"

The speck was the speedboat. The Chief stood in
the cockpit, watching us over the windshield.

Sprocket hissed and jerked his tongue from our
hands. He marched over until he butted up against
the rails. His eyes widened and started to spin.

"I suspect he's just waiting to see us sink," Doc
said.

Razer pulled at Sprocket's mouth crease to get him
to open up. "I wonder if that ol' deer rifle of mine
will take him out at this distance? Even if not, it'd be
fun to try."

"Good question," Doc said. He scratched his jaw.
"Way that boat's moving around, it'd be tough to
lead him right. Howsomever, it might not be a bad

idea to let that ol' boy know we ain't forgive him for what he done. How about getting my carbine while you're in there?"

"I got a twenty-two in my room, Razer," I said. "Box of long-rifles in the dresser."

None of us much felt like turning the other cheek. Sprocket least of all, as we found out in a second.

His mangled tongue shot over the bows and arched high in the air toward the speedboat. Everybody crowded against the rail to watch. The tongue-tip fell a couple of dozen feet short of the speedboat and the Chief spun the wheel. The speedboat turned sharply, throwing up spray in its wake. Sprocket's tongue played out of his mouth the way it had when the shark was running with it.

It sliced through the water in the speedboat's wake, gaining steadily. Then about twenty feet of it pulled out of the water like a giant sea serpent. It towered over the fleeing boat, then darted down and punched into the Chief's back. Knocked him away from the wheel. He fought with it as it wrapped around him. For a second he got loose and stumbled toward the wheel, but it wrapped around him again and jerked him clean out of the cockpit and over the gunwales into the water. The speedboat kept going, heading for the horizon.

Everybody on the deck cheered while he reeled the Chief in, twisting and yelling. The last fifty yards or so, the Chief didn't struggle so much. Sprocket wasn't doing a great job of keeping his head above water. Matter of fact, if I hadn't known what a gentle critter he was, I might have suspected he was semi-drowning the Chief on purpose.

The Chief spluttered weakly when Sprocket hauled him upside down into the air, then dropped him

headfirst the last couple of feet onto the deck. He
choked and spewed seawater real pitiful-like but from
the looks on the faces around him, nobody seemed to
be wasting a whole lot of sympathy in his direction.

Finally, he rolled over and looked at us. "Crap."
He spit out another couple of tablespoons of sea
water. "Ah, hell. Maybe it's best this way."

"Damn right," Razer said. "We said our prayers in
the hold, asshole. It's your turn now." He grabbed
the Chief by the shirt and yanked him to his feet. He
shoved him toward the rail. "You was so eager to get
ashore. Let's see how you make it without a boat."

"Razer, this ain't Amarillo," Doc said.

"Aw, Doc . . . he tried to *kill* us! And look at
what he done to Sprocket!"

I noticed Sprocket's stitches had opened up and he
was dripping golden onto the deck again. He didn't
seem to notice. Just watched Razer and the Chief.

"No sir," Doc said. "The man's gonna get a fair
trial. Then the State of Texas is gonna teach him how
to air-dance."

"You're just a goddam liberal, ain't you, Doc?"

"Come on, buddy. Act right."

"Shitfire!" Disgusted, Razer yanked the Chief back
from the railing.

A look of panic appeared on the Chief's face. If I'd
been him, I'd have got upset when Razer grabbed
me, not when Doc talked him out of giving me a
swimming lesson.

"Oh, my God!" the Chief said. "The engines! Did
you kill the engines?" He looked wildly toward the
fantail. "I drained the oil and throttled them up
to—"

The engines seized and tore loose from their mountings. Sounded like thunder. *Miz Bellybutton* shivered hard enough to throw everybody off their feet.

When I staggered upright again, the sailors had already run to unship the lifeboats.

"You rotten son of a bitch!" Captain Johnson said from on his knees. "You didn't want us to have any chance at all, did you?"

It went quick from there. Ten minutes later we watched from lifeboats as *Miz Bellybutton* started a whirlpool dive to the bottom.

I'd never seen Sprocket swim. For that matter, nobody on the crew ever had either. But he had calmly trotted to the break in the railing where his gangplank was laid when we were docked. He ran off the side of the ship and splashed into the water and floated quite comfortably at about his eye level. Couldn't steer worth a damn though. No rudder, and his stumpy legs were mostly useless as propellors. Razer and a couple of the guys brought their lifeboat alongside him and scrambled up his side. With their weight, he sank noticeably deeper in the water.

A couple seconds later, Razer came back out with some rope. We moored Sprocket and all the lifeboats together. Razer stayed on board Sprocket, half-poked out of a hole in his top. Nobody else was invited aboard, though. We was afraid of swamping Sprocket.

Not much to do after that. Nobody even bothered to suggest that we try to row ashore, fifty miles away. At least not with the rising swells. The hurricane was coming. We mostly just waited for it to hit and hoped it didn't drown us all.

Beside me in the lifeboat, Doc hefted a small leather bag in his left hand. We'd found it hanging from a strap around the Chief's neck when we searched him to make sure he didn't have any other weapons on him. The Chief had been real unhappy when we confiscated it. It contained dozens of emeralds. None of us knew anything about jewels, but I suspected the emeralds weren't junk stones.

Doc squeezed the bag and looked at the Chief. "This what everybody's been dyin' over, Chief?" The Chief stared at the bag dully. "I asked you a question, bud," Doc said. "We're all probably gonna drown out here. I'd just as soon know why. This is why you killed Pegleg, ain't it?"

The Chief shivered and his eyes focussed. "He came to the Goody Room that night after everything was battened down. He was half-drunk, as usual. He had a gun. When I got the chance, I tried to take it away from him. We rolled around and busted open a couple of cans. I guess the Muracon-E was one of them. I managed to knock him out. I thought he was dead. I decided to dump him over the railing, but when I carried him topside, it seemed like no matter where I turned somebody was in the way. It was dark enough that nobody spotted us. I carried him over my shoulder, but I kept having to dodge behind a pile of casing or stumble away from the side of the ship to keep from being seen. It was a nightmare. I just couldn't get rid of the damn body. Finally, I ended up near the wellhead. I could hear voices coming toward us from both sides. So I dropped him in the moon-pool."

"So it *was* all self-defense," I said. "You were just keeping him from shooting you with his gun. Same one you pulled on us?"

"Yes. I kept it."

"Then what on God's green earth made you act like you did with us?"

"They'd have found the emeralds on me if I surrendered to the Coast Guard. I figured that I couldn't hide them aboard *Miz Bellybutton*. Even if I beat the murder charges, I'd never be allowed back on her. And what if I was convicted? It didn't look good, me disposing of the body that way and then staying quiet about it for so long."

"And the emeralds were the reason he pulled the gun on you in the first place?" Doc asked.

"No!" Then he sighed. "Yes. He overheard me arguing with Axis Ortell in a waterfront bar. He told me about it. He was in a booth behind us, a booth that we thought was empty because he was slouched over, almost passed out. Too bad he wasn't too drunk to listen in."

"Who's Axis Ortell?" Doc asked.

"The captain of the *Belle Butange* before Johnson. I had to kill him. We had gotten the emeralds on our last voyage, after they were smuggled out of the Aguario mines in Venezuela. We were going to be rich. Then Ortell started demanding a bigger cut because he put up more money. That wasn't the deal. We were even partners. We'd never have gotten the emeralds at all without my contacts at Aguario."

"So Pegleg heard y'all arguing about the split."

The Chief nodded. "And he followed us out of the bar. He saw us fight in the alley. He saw me feed Ortell to the fish. The body never washed ashore. That was a break for me." He laughed bitterly. "About the only one in the whole mess."

"But Pegleg ruined it."

"Yes. He wanted the emeralds, or he'd tell. All of the emeralds. I couldn't do that. I didn't even have the emeralds then. When I went back to get them that night and head for Colorado, I found that Ortell had moved them from our original hiding place. I had searched his body and his duffel before I disposed of him, so I knew he hadn't been carrying them. I looked in a couple of likely places, but couldn't get into his cabin."

He laughed again and shook his head. "He'd locked it, and I hadn't thought to take his keys. He'd never locked his cabin before. The only other person with the keys was the purser. It would have looked too suspicious if I asked for them, but I was convinced that he'd hidden the emeralds there. The next day, Mr. Pickett had the ship put in dry-dock for the drill ship modifications. He wanted to keep the project secret for awhile, so he had us all moved to a hotel on the island while the dockyard did the work. After we had got the emeralds, Ortell had been hinting to the crew that he might be quitting, so it was easy enough for me to put out that he had just upped and left that night. By the time I got back on the ship, Johnson was aboard, and he routinely locked his cabin. I checked almost every day, and he finally left it unlocked. I found the emeralds taped inside one of the bunk's rails."

He shook his head. "It's been crazy. Everything I did turned out wrong. I never imagined it could go this far. Simple attempts to straighten things out would mutate into disasters. It's like I wasn't meant to get away with this."

"I ain't sure anybody is meant to get away with murder, bud," Doc said.

About then, the sky opened up and dropped its own ocean into the one we were floating on. It also brought lightning and thunder and a few minutes later, a big enough wind to take us to where Dorothy and Toto went.

We tried to row into the waves, but Momma Nature wasn't cooperating. When I was swept out of the lifeboat a half hour later, I managed to keep a hand on the oar that I'd been using. I heard a few choked yells, then I was washed away into the growing darkness.

I worked into a kind of rhythm. The waves weren't the cresting kind you see on the beach, they were watery mountains that moved like express trains. I'd be shoved up the side of one, then drop like I was in a runaway elevator. About three times a minute. I managed to keep my head above water at least a quarter of the time. I was proud of that, considering the conditions. I hung onto the oar, knowing if I lost it I'd probably drown in minutes.

I told myself that if I could only do this for about ten or twelve hours, the hurricane would blow through, and I'd merely be stranded at sea, fifty miles from land. People have been in worse spots and made it through, I told myself. Sure, lots of people. Half-a-dozen, maybe, in the entire history of the planet. I was young and strong, and a good swimmer, and Momma Nature was gonna have to make it a lot tougher before I even *thought* about giving up. Damn right.

Then something brushed my ankle. I'd forgotten about the sharks. Momma Nature was a heartless bitch.

I tried, the best I knew how, to climb on top of that oar. Didn't work out too well for more than a second at a time.

Don't thrash around, I said to myself. That'll just

attract them even more. Lay still. They'll get bored and go away eventually.

Then it grabbed me around the waist and dragged me screaming into the depths of the ocean. I hadn't yet learned how to breath water, so I passed out shortly.

I woke up lying on my stomach, retching seawater. Doc leaned over me and pounded on my back in a misguided attempt to help me. It broke my rhythm and I near choked to death.

Finally, I just lay on my side and gasped. I was inside Sprocket. A couple of torches were lit, revealing his central corridor to be crowded with bedraggled sailors and all the crew.

The curtain that led to the outer world flapped open abruptly and Sprocket's tongue glided inside, wrapped around another limp figure. Doc crawled over to him and pounded his back, too.

I sat up. A sharp *ping-ping-ping* reverberated through Sprocket's body. It seemed to come from everywhere, including inside my head.

Doc crawled away from the sailor he'd been pounding on. "He'll be okay, too." He noticed my head cocked listening to the *ping-ping-ping*. "Yeah. Damnedest thing, ain't it? I never knew he could make that sound, either. He does seismic testing in three-dimensions, though. Why not sonar location, too? We figure that's how he found the ones that washed away when the lifeboats capsized."

"He get everybody?"

"You and that sailor was the last, if we've counted correct."

"What now?"

"I guess we're all too stupid to give up and die.

Maybe we can ride out the hurricane in Sprocket. He blew all the drilling mud out of his bladders and filled them with air. That gives him enough buoyancy to float, but we go wherever the winds and the waves push us. The winds will shove us further out into the Gulf."

He leaned back against one of the gently moving walls of the corridor. "We got a little food on board. Sprocket oughta have some fresh water in a bladder, if I remember correctly. If he didn't fill it with air, too. Shipping will be disrupted for awhile after the hurricane. We'll be adrift in a large empty area." He grunted. "We ain't got much of a chance, but it's better than it was a couple hours ago, locked up in that hold."

I leaned against the wall next to him. The bobbing up and down and side to side might have made me sick at one time, but I was way beyond that right now.

Just when I was starting to relax, a wild hooting sound reverberated through Sprocket's body. It whooped on a rising note for half-a-minute, then cut off abruptly. Everybody stopped what they were doing. The only sound was the *ping-ping-ping* and the whoosh of Sprocket and thirty-three men breathing.

In front of me, Sprocket's tongue stirred, then fed out through his mouth. Doc and me stared at it, mystified.

"What's he doing that for?" Doc asked. "He's done got everybody aboard."

The musky breath that ebbed and flowed down the corridor stopped for a few seconds, then started up again with a faster rhythm.

Sprocket's body tilted to the right, then the front end dropped down. After a moment, the rocking that had been caused by the waves disappeared. Doc scrambled to his feet and staggered toward the flesh curtain that closed off his room.

"I got a bad feelin' about this," he said over his shoulder. He pulled the curtain apart and stared up at the ceiling of his room. Then he turned and shouted down the corridor. "Razer! Big Mac! You boys check a couple of rooms. See if Sprocket has closed down the sphincters of the holes on top."

A few seconds later, Razer and Big Mac confirmed that all the rooms they had checked had the sphincters shut tight. Sprocket refused to open them when asked to.

"He's sinking!" Doc shouted down the corridor. "The weight must have been too much for him. We got to lighten his load."

Razer shoved forward through the crowd. He was dragging the Chief along by the elbow with him. He yanked the Chief onto his toes. "I know who we can start with," he said.

Doc frowned at him. "Thought we'd already settled that, Razer. I was figuring we could begin by emptying out the iron room. Them chicksans and long joints would make a difference right quick. I think we got a couple of plug containers and disposal packers in there, too."

The iron room was just next door to Doc's room, so we quickly yanked out a couple of chicksans and carried them over to Sprocket's mouth. But when Doc tried to shove aside the curtain into the back of his mouth, Sprocket clenched it and wouldn't let him. Doc looked puzzled, then pounded on the wall beside Sprocket's mouth.

"What's the matter with you, son?" he shouted.

"We need to unload some of this here iron. 'Less you want us all to drown."

I was surprised, too. Sprocket's mouth was made so he could have opened up the back of it, then closed it down, then opened up the front and blew out the iron. Wouldn't have spilled a drop inside his central corridor.

But he was deliberately refusing to allow us to lighten his load.

"Maybe he's diving on purpose," I thought aloud. "Maybe he don't want to be lightened up."

Doc frowned again. "That don't make no sense. Ain't no reason for it."

I thought on it for a second. Actually, there were a couple of good reasons. "This way we get below the rolling and tossing of the waves. Probably won't get blown out to sea so much that way. Just float in one place below the surface. And maybe he was getting seasick again."

Doc looked thoughtful. "Huh. Might not be a bad idea at all. What if he springs a leak?"

I looked down the corridor. Sprocket had forty-six sphincters along the top of his body, plus the thirteen on each side which let into various bladders, which cross-connected into his tongue and mouth and various other places. He was a complex network of air and fluid lines, with internal and external sphincters acting as valves to control flow and mixing. If only one of them failed, his interior could be flooded with water within a few minutes.

"Let's hope he don't. Besides, he can surface immediately if he has problems."

Doc shook his head. "Can't you feel it? We're still diving. Sprocket's going deep."

He was right. We were still angled on a downward slant.

"He's sinkin' like a rock," Doc said. "Hey, Razer! Find Captain Johnson for me!" he shouted.

A couple of minutes later the Captain joined us. He had to brace against the wall, as we all did. The angle of Sprocket's dive had increased sharply.

"I remember it was about five hundred feet to the bottom of the ocean where we were drilling," Doc said. "But I heard one of your hands say it got deeper not much farther out.

The Captain looked as bedraggled as the rest of us. He rubbed his chin. "Right. We got a sonar reading of 529 feet where we had anchored. But we're near the edge of the continental shelf. It drops off fast, to depths of thousands of feet."

Doc disappeared into his room for a second and came out thumbing through the pages of the red book.

Doc came to the page he was looking for. "Here we go," he said. "American Petrogypsy Institute Hydrostatic Pressure and Fluid Weight Conversion Tables." I'd used that one many times to figure out bottom-hole pressures. A column of drilling fluid exerts increasing pressure in a way that is directly proportional to the depth of the hole.

He flipped back a couple of pages to the Weights and Measures listing. "Let's figure the water as dense as possible," he said. "Saturated salt water is 74.7 pounds per cubic foot." Doc continued. "Pressure gradient would be about .5190 psi per vertical foot. Let's say we go down six hundred feet. The pressure on Sprocket will be, ah . . ." He pulled out a pencil from a side pocket and scribbled in the margin of the page. "Three hundred and eleven point four pounds per square inch."

I couldn't keep from putting in my own two bits. "Plus fourteen point seven for the weight of the atmosphere."

"Smartass," Doc replied. He added my numbers to his figuring. "Three hundred twenty-six point five p.s.i. That don't sound too bad."

I didn't say what came into my mind. Maybe the pressure didn't sound like much, but it was twenty times what Sprocket's hide usually encountered. Sure, his mouth could handle pressures of thousands of psi when he used it for a blowout preventer, but the rest of his sphincters never encountered that kind of pressure. And a leak in the wrong place could kill us all. Doc already knew all that, anyway. He was trying to put the best face on it that he could.

And if we had the bad luck to have drifted off the edge of the continental shelf, we could run into pressures three and four times as high as those that he had calculated.

Right then Sprocket's nose bumped the ocean floor. He bucked and burped. We heard a whooshing, bubbly sound and his body settled more heavily to the bottom.

"I think he just blew the air out of a couple of his bladders," Doc said. "He's acting just like a submarine. Increasing his ballast."

"If he blows too much, we could run out of air to breathe down here real quick," Razer said.

"I don't believe so," Doc said. "I been thinking about why he run his tongue back outside. Smell the air he's pumping to us. If I got him figured right, he has his tongue at the surface. He's sucking fresh air through his drill-stem."

The *ping-ping-ping* quit for a second, then resumed. Sprocket started to march. "That son of a gun!" Doc exclaimed. "He can't swim worth a damn, so he decided to walk back to shore!"

After a minute, the whole corridor reverberated with whoops and laughter. Looked like we was gonna survive this adventure after all. All Sprocket had to do was take a stroll. We'd get surface air through his tongue, while he navigated around obstacles and such with his built-in sonar.

We found a couple of bottles of heart-starter scattered throughout the rooms in Sprocket. Didn't look like there was much else for us to do, so most of us proceeded to relax.

Not too much later I found myself feeling pretty good. We'd made it through the hurricane. We'd survived the Chief trying to murder us. Because I hadn't given up while floating alone and lost, I'd survived being stranded at sea, too. I looked forward to holding Star soon and telling her about the big adventure.

Of course, when I started feeling real good about everything is when it hit the fan again.

Me and Big Mac and Razer and Doc lounged in Doc's room passing a bottle between us. The bottle wasn't near dead yet, but it had been terribly injured. Just as I reached to take it from Big Mac for another dose, Sprocket's body rolled over completely.

The sphincter in the ceiling relaxed for a second and a jet of water drilled me in the side as I flew through the air.

Sprocket twisted and convulsed, flipping around like a leaf in a high wind. His illumination warts flared, then went dead, so we took more flying lessons in pitch darkness. The sphincter irised shut before water filled the room.

I finally managed to hook an arm around the railing of the bed that was bolted into Sprocket's wall. Next time another body crashed into me I grabbed it. It was Razer. Between us we got Doc and Big Mac anchored. After that, we couldn't do a thing except hang on for our lives until it stopped.

Sprocket quit pumping air.

He bucked and twisted for a good thirty minutes, with three or four quiet periods less than a minute in length each. I could hear the screams of everybody inside as it went on and on and on. Sounded like some folks hadn't got off easy as us. Doc had broke a finger, he thought, and Razer said it felt like his left leg was wrenched out of the socket. I was okay except for a couple of bruises that were gonna be classics if I lived long enough for them to purple up properly. And you couldn't hurt Big Mac with anything less than a five-pound sledgehammer.

"I know this sounds stupid," I said to Doc as he grimly hung on beside me. "But it feels like something has grabbed Sprocket and is yanking him around."

"There ain't nothing big enough to do that. Unless . . ." He almost lost his grip on the bed when Sprocket did another end-for-end flip. "You don't think a whale has attacked him, do you?"

Before we could speculate further, Sprocket surfaced. He bounced halfway out of the water, and all of his sphincters blew open simultaneously. For a second there, I thought we was all dead. The rain came down so hard, it almost seemed like he'd opened up while still underwater. But you could tell that we was on the surface from the screaming howl of the gale-force winds, and the sickening way we lurched up one side of a wave and down the other. I remembered that sensation too well from earlier in the day.

If something had been tossing Sprocket around, it had let him go for the time being. I sucked at the cold air that poured in with the rain.

I knew what I had to do. I didn't much like it. "Hold on a second here," I said. "Somebody needs to check out the situation topside."

I staggered and fell a couple of times, but I made it to the bottom rung of the ladder and climbed it until my head stuck through the hole in top of the room.

I couldn't see much. Between Sprocket careening around sickeningly, plus the heavy rain and water from the waves washing across me, combined with the dark caused by the clouds blotting out the sun, mostly all I could perceive was a strong impression that it wasn't a fit place for man nor beast.

I climbed to the top rung, trying to peer around me in the dimness.

Something rubbery wrapped itself around my shoulders, tore loose my grip on the ladder, and yanked me into the ocean chaos again. I didn't even have a chance to scream.

I hit the water and this time managed to hold my breath. Whatever had ahold of my pulled me away from Sprocket like I was on greased rails. Before I could blink twice, I was approaching a huge dark hulk that tossed in the storm. Whatever had wrapped around me was not Sprocket's tongue. It was too broad and flat.

A couple of other bands wrapped around me and pulled me closer to the dark hulk. Then I did scream.

I was completely tangled up in the bands, as they wiggled around insanely like gigantic snakes.

A small part of my mind that kept thinking told me that they were tentacles, and I'd been snatched out of Sprocket by some kind of enormous octopus.

Only, I was wrong. The tentacles drew me against the hulk and it split wide into a gaping, toothy mouth. I'd seen pictures of octopusses, and they had little beaks like birds. This was some other kind of sea monster entirely.

That mouth was big enough to swallow me whole. Whatever had me wouldn't even have to tear me up into bite-size chunks.

I gave up as the tentacles drew me to that cavern. I was about to be eaten by some kind of fearsome sea monster that was big enough to whip up on Sprocket, in the middle of a goddam hurricane, still fifty miles out to sea. There wasn't no way to live through that combination of good luck. I quit struggling and screaming.

The mouth opened wide, and I said good-bye.

Then I had second thoughts.

The Chief had betrayed me and damn near killed me, and the hurricane had damn near killed me, and the ocean had damn near killed me, and I'd lived through them all, and just when I thought it was safe, this goddam, meddling sea monster showed up out of nowhere and decided to fuck up my afternoon even worse than it already was. Well, to hell with him! He might figure Sprocket would make a tasty dinner, with me being the appetizer beforehand. He might be right. But he was going to have to work for his meals like the rest of us did.

I grabbed ahold of one of the tentacles that wrapped around me and tore it loose from my body. It felt all

rubbery and cold and wet, but I didn't flinch from it
anymore. I didn't struggle and try to escape. I
gripped it fiercely, doing my best to press my fingertips and thumbs into it. I was gonna strangle that
goddam tentacle to death.

I started to scream again. In a killing rage.

The rubber tore under my hands, and blood spurted
into my face. Suddenly, the tentacle became even
slicker than it had been before. I ripped chunks of
flesh loose and threw them at the body above me
and went back for more. The tentacles around my
chest tightened convulsively, almost squeezing the
breath out of me, then loosened.

I choked on water and monster blood and pulled
myself closer to the base of the tentacle that I'd
injured. The mouth gaped open right under my boots.
The monster sucked water in, trying to suck me in
too. I held on and gouged the base of the tentacle.
My fingers went in easier this time, and the blood
spurted quicker. I screamed louder. The blood tasted
good!

The major tentacle around me loosened some more,
but I began to slip inside his mouth. I kicked at him,
but the lips of the mouth closed around my waist and
started to draw me. I braced my feet rigidly against
his teeth to keep out of his mouth. If he ever got me
in between those choppers he'd tear me in half, like
he must have done that shark that him and Sprocket
fought over earlier.

I was completely insane by now, tearing and biting
at the base of the tentacle that I held onto.

Then another tentacle groped at me. I tried to bite
it, but this one was too tough. It lassoed me around
the shoulders and yanked at me. Tore me away from
the tentacle I'd been ripping into. I knew I'd had it

then. All the monster needed to do now was stuff me inside and chew a couple of times.

I still didn't stop fighting. If I had to, I'd fight my way out of the bastard from the inside. Henry Lee MacFarland wasn't nobody's appetizer.

I clawed and screamed and choked and tore at the tentacle wrapped around me, but it didn't loosen an inch.

Then it did a funny thing. It yanked me right out of the monster's mouth. Popped me loose like a cork out of one of them wine bottles back at the Bali Room. A couple of smaller tentacles were still wrapped around me, and it tore me loose from them too.

In a second, I was shooting through the water again. Only this time, I was moving *away* from the sea monster. For a long, terrifying moment, my mind flashed images of two giant sea monsters fighting over little old me.

Then I realized what had grabbed me out of the monster's mouth and I quit fighting it. I grabbed it and held onto it for my life. I ignored the tentacle from the orginal monster when it came from below and wrapped around my waist again.

Matter of fact, I held it to me. I had a plan for it.

A second later, I drew up to another huge dark hulk tossing in the water. And another huge mouth gaped open in front of me. And I didn't fight it the tiniest bit when it swallowed me right up.

I landed in the corridor, practically exploding into the midst of the crew when Sprocket's tongue reeled me inside.

The tip of the big tentacle from the sea monster still circled my waist. He wasn't nothing if not persistent.

Sprocket's mouth chomped down hard as it could,

and the tentacle convulsed loose from me. Sprocket's drilling mouth doesn't have any teeth, but lips that can hold in a ten thousand-pound kick can put some pressure on and hold it.

The anger hadn't left me yet. I was mightily relieved that Sprocket had come to the rescue again, but I was also hacked off at the entire world, with most of that feeling focussed on the sea monster that had grabbed me. I wasn't done teaching it who ate who on this particular planet.

The tentacle started to slide back outside and I fell on it. I wrapped my arms and legs around it and dug in. "Come on, people! Help me hold this thing down." Nobody but me knew what was going on, but everybody piled right on and pinned that tentacle to the floor.

Razer was one of the ones near me. I let got of the tentacle when it seemed to be trapped pretty well. "You hands just hold onto it for a minute. Razer, you still got that ugly ol' bowie knife in your room."

"Surely do, Henry Lee. You figure on relaxing with a little whittlin' after your invigoratin' swim?"

"Sort of. There's some kind of sea monster outside that tried to eat me, and I'm aggravated with the son of a bitch."

He went to get his bowie knife while I turned to the iron room and pushed its curtains aside. I rummaged around until I found what I wanted. I pulled out two ten-foot lengths of three-inch line pipe and hammered the wing nut down on the unions to make one twenty-foot length. Then I dug out a carton full of victaulic clamps.

Everybody watched me while they hung onto the whipsawing tentacle. Razer pushed out of his room and handed me the bowie knife, still in its scabbard.

I unsnapped the catch and shook the scabbard off. Ten inches of gleaming razor-sharp tungsten carbide steel glistened in the torchlight.

The four- and five-inch victaulics were too small, but the six-inch one fit just right when I slid it over the tip of the three-inch pipe, then slipped the bowie knife in between its gasket and the outer wall of the pipe. I pulled the clamp arm down and it snapped tight over the haft of the bowie knife. The blade protruded over the end of the iron pipe just right. I stood up and hefted it in both hands.

I was half-proud of myself. I'd made a pretty good harpoon out of things that were laying around the house.

I pulled aside the curtain into Doc's room and maneuvered the length of the harpoon until the tip pointed at the hole in the top, which was sphinctered closed.

"Sprocket!" I yelled. "I'm going outside!"

I turned to the people that were watching me. Behind them, the tentacle was still being held down by another group.

"I doubt the first one will do the job. If y'all could see about finding some more knives and making more harpoons, they might come in handy." I raised my voice. "Those of you holding down that tentacle—soon as I get situated topside, start pulling it in as much as you can. We need the monster as close up as can be managed."

A minute later I was poked halfway outside in the howling hurricane again. Sprocket pitched around, and slung sideways, and crashed half through waves on occasion, but it was practically peaceful compared to the banging around I'd gotten when the monster had me.

The harpoon felt light as a toothpick in my hands. It only weighed about a hundred pounds. Exactly the right length and weight for skewering uppity sea monsters.

I didn't see nothing for a few minutes. It took that long for the boys inside to haul in that tentacle. Then, slowly, thrashing and fighting, the sea monster was drawn closer. I still couldn't make out the details of it in the dark, but I could see enough to aim the harpoon.

I wanted to wait until it was slid right up next to Sprocket. Tentacles whipped through the air, slapping onto Sprocket's body and curling around him. For a second one of them was in reach of the harpoon. I jabbed at it. The bowie knife sliced into it, and the tentacle recoiled and disappeared into the darkness again.

Then the bulk spurted nearer. The monster wasn't trying to get away at all. It didn't mind getting in close and dirty. Flailing tentacles surrounded me. A couple of them wrapped around the harpoon and tried to tug it out of my hands, but I held on. Sprocket bucked and sunfished under me, then the monster got a good grip on him and dragged him underwater. Sprocket reflexively closed his sphincter around my waist. I held onto the harpoon while the water swirled around us. Then the monster flipped Sprocket completely upside down and I lost the harpoon.

I pounded on his hide to be let back inside, but I guess he was busy and didn't notice. I realized shortly that I couldn't hold my breath forever.

Fortunately, before I turned completely blue and exploded, Sprocket surged out to the water again, simultaneously relaxing his sphincter enough for me to slide back inside.

The room was dark. The warts had all gone out again. I felt my way toward the curtain leading to the corridor.

"Henry Lee?" asked the Chief, so close I jumped and gave out a yip. I reached out. He thrust a length of pipe into my hands.

"You put that last one into the monster?" the Chief asked.

I shook my head, then realized he couldn't see it. Sprocket lurched under us and I almost dropped the harpoon he'd given me. "No sir. But this one ain't gonna be wasted."

"Good. They got a little assembly line out in the corridor by the iron room. More knives and other pointy objects in Sprocket than I would have thought possible."

Sprocket seemed to settle for a moment, so I grabbed the bottom rung and pulled myself upright.

"Thanks, Chief."

"Sure. I'll be waiting with another one when you want it. Uh . . . Henry Lee?"

I was halfway up the ladder. "Yeah, Chief?"

"I really was your friend until everything got in the way. I'm sorrier than you'll ever know about how it's all turned out."

Sprocket's sphincter opened and I maneuvered the harpoon through the hole. "Me too, Chief." I don't know if he heard my words. The wind might have blown them away. I went back into the storm.

Matters hadn't changed much. Sprocket and the sea monster still wrestled.

I got a sighting on the monster. I waited until the pitching stopped for half-a-second, then drew the harpoon back over my left shoulder with both hands and twisted around halfways to pull my back and arm muscles as tight as possible. When they'd reached maximum tension, I held for an instant longer, then whipped the harpoon around as powerfully as I could. I didn't see it hit, but I heard the whistling shriek the monster let out when it drove deep into him.

I pounded on Sprocket and he loosened his sphincter again. I dropped into the room. The illumination warts glowed feebly now, enough to show the Chief's smile as he handed me another harpoon.

When I got outside again, I saw that I wasn't alone any more. Doc and Razer poked out of holes nearby.

"You didn't think we was gonna let you hog all the fun, did you, Henry Lee?" Razer shouted.

Then Big Mac started laughing behind me, poked out of his own hole.

"Hot damn!" he yelled. "This here beats the wrestling matches seven ways from Sunday! Sprocket and the Crew versus the Mystery Sea Monster in a winner-take-all title bout!"

Another long screech erupted from the sea monster when four more harpoons slammed into it.

When I came back up with another harpoon, Big Mac had one, too, but Doc and Razer had decided on a change of weapons. Doc cranked up this thirty-ought-six and pumped slug after slug into the sea monster, alternating with Razer blowing holes in it with his .40 caliber rifle.

Big Mac flung his harpoon. I drew back and was about to let fly, when Sprocket's tongue slapped me lightly on the chest. The length of it wound around me, sliding up my body until it reached the harpoon and curled around it.

I got the idea. I let go of the harpoon and Sprocket whipped off into the darkness with it.

"Go get him, boy!" I shouted hoarsely. "Now you got something to do it with!"

It was downhill from there for the sea monster. Between us all, we'd messed it up good. Sprocket put the finishing touches to it. He drilled it to death.

Shortly after the sea-monster-attack part of the day ended, we got back to the submarine-adventure part again. We were still far from shore in the middle of a hurricane.

Sprocket blew the air out of his bladders and dove for the bottom. Doc found under his bed, miraculously unbroken, the bottle that we'd been passing around. The same bunch of us congregated again in Doc's room and passed it around while Sprocket headed for bottom.

After a few sips, I started to relax. The hard part was behind, I figured. Then the sphincter in the ceiling blew loose.

I went from leaning comfortably against a wall to drowning in the darkness within two breaths. Doc and Razer gagged and choked somewhere nearby. The flood swirled me against the ladder and I managed to grab one of the rungs as it went by. The ladder was directly underneath the high-pressure jet of water blasting in through the sphincter. For a second, it dwindled to a trickle, as Sprocket tried to tighten down again, then spurted out again to a three-inch wide gout.

Sprocket had been weakened by the fight with the sea monster, and he couldn't keep that sphincter ring muscle tightened down completely against the outside water pressure.

Without even thinking about it, I lunged up another couple of rungs and plunged my fist through the sphincter. I forced it through the ring muscle until I was up past my elbow. Sprocket's muscle tightened down around my biceps. With something other than itself to clamp down on, the sphincter was strong enough to shut out the water.

I hung there while the room slowly drained. We later figured out Sprocket sucked it in through the tip of his tongue, then pumped it into a bladder through his internal valve system.

Within a couple minutes, Doc found a five-inch bull plug in the iron room. After I pulled my arm loose, we forced it, rounded end first, against the incoming water until it fit snugly in place of my arm. The sphincter clenched around it just fine.

I sat down on Doc's bed, trying to flex some life back into my paralyzed arm. Sprocket had clamped down on it pretty hard. We all watched the bull plug for signs of another leak.

"Might look through the iron room some more," Doc suggested to Razer. "We better be ready if another one gives way."

A couple did, mostly up front. Sprocket had gotten so wrenched around by the sea monster, not to mention the other fun during the past few hours, that some of those muscles must have got just plain exhausted. We plugged them off and they held. But we stayed paranoid the next couple of hours.

I was dreaming of being dry. "Henry Lee, wake up. Something's wrong."

I snapped to attention and rolled out of my bed before I was awake. The words whispered to me had ruined my sleep dozens of times before. They could mean anything from stuck pipe to a flaming, explosive blowout. I relaxed when I realized where I was and that the Chief had been the one shaking my shoulder. "What's that matter? Sprung another leak?"

"No. I think we're on shore."

We stepped out of my room into the corridor. It was littered with sleeping bodies. Beyond a certain point, we had all been forced to quit worrying and catch up on our sleep.

"What makes you believe that?"

He led me to the front of the corridor, just behind Sprocket's mouth.

"Listen," he said. "What do you hear?"

I leaned forward and cocked an ear. "A high whistling sound. Real faint."

"Right. Like the hurricane blowing. But if we were on the ocean floor, we wouldn't hear that. And if we were floating, where we *could* hear it, Sprocket would be rolling in the chop. He's steady as a rock."

"You know, you may be right, Chief." I grinned and rubbed my hands together. "We made it! Goddam, we made it!"

He shook his head. "I don't know. There's a problem. He won't open up."

"What do you mean?"

He pulled at the thick curtain of flesh that was the back of Sprocket's mouth. "I mean this is clamped shut. He won't let us out."

I looked at him pityingly. "You mean he won't let *you* out, Chief."

He turned red. "Maybe that's it."

I rapped on the corridor wall to get Sprocket's attention if he wasn't already listening. "How about letting us out now, buddy?"

When I tried to pry the curtain open, Sprocket refused to relax it for me, either.

"Huh. Maybe he's still protecting us from the hurricane. I imagine it's pretty rough out there if we can hear it from here. Probably all kinds of debris flying through the air." I raised my voice. "I just want to take a quick look, Sprocket. Won't even step out of your mouth." He still wouldn't cooperate.

"What the hell," I said to the Chief. "Might as well take it easy till the hurricane blows over. I trust Sprocket to let us out when it's safe, and not a minute sooner."

"It's hard to wait, after all we've been through."

"How come you're in such a big hurry to get out there, Chief? You got some music to face, you know."

He shook his head. "Not if I can help it. That's why I want to leave now." I looked down when I felt the point of the knife in his hand press into my stomach.

"Aw, Chief."

"I tucked it away when we were making harpoons, Henry Lee. Tell Sprocket to let me out."

"Or you'll cut me?"

"I don't have any choice."

"You never seem to have any choice but to hurt people, do you? When are you gonna learn? Every time you pull this crap, you just get in further over your head. Go ahead. Cut me. I ain't cooperating any more."

I held my breath while he nudged me with the point again. I guess I was still being a dumb ol' country boy. I couldn't make myself believe he'd actually stick it in me.

After a second he sighed and pulled the knife back. "I can't do it."

"Good. Now, let's go back, and—"

"But I can slash my way out of Sprocket if I have to," he interrupted. The edge of the knife moved to press against the curtain. "Tell him to open up or I swear I'll make my own opening."

"Chief, for the love of—"

He jabbed the knife into the curtain. Then again. Sprocket moaned. "Open the goddam curtain!" he screamed. He stabbed a third time.

The curtain relaxed and the Chief pulled it open with his free hand. I watched Sprocket's blood drip onto the hallway floor.

"You won't get far, Chief. It's all been a big waste. Everything you've done." Behind us, half-a-dozen hands woke up and watched us. The Chief ignored them.

"It wasn't as easy as it should have been, that's for sure." He undid two of the buttons on his shirt. The leather bag containing the emeralds hung around his neck once more. "But a half-a-million dollars should make it worth the effort."

He nudged me into Sprocket's mouth. The curtain closed behind us. I started to make a move in the darkness, but the knife pressed deeper into my side.

"Open wide, Sprocket," the Chief said. He poked with the knife again. "Time for me to check out. Open up Sprocket! Don't make me use the knife again." Sprocket's mouth opened.

Sprocket stood right inside the seawall, not a hundred yards north of the Bali Room. I'd been right about the serious major hurricane weather. The wind screamed into Sprocket's mouth, driving with it rain as cold and hard as frozen buckshot.

Suddenly my ears felt as if ice picks had stabbed into them. I yawned enormously and they popped.

The Chief did the same, keeping the knife firm against my side.

"You won't get twenty feet in that," I shouted to the Chief.

"Not your problem, Henry Lee. So long." He stepped off Sprocket's lip and staggered as the full force of the wind hit him. It shoved him ten feet, then knocked him down.

Sprocket's mouth snapped shut before I could see whether he made it back up.

I thought about trying to convince Sprocket to let me go after him. Then I thought about where the Chief must have gotten the emeralds from and forgot about everything else.

Doc was lying with his head in a pool of blood when I tore into his room. He was still alive, though.

The Chief had bashed him pretty hard. We begged with Sprocket to let us get medical help, but he wouldn't open up, even when we got abusive. He plain refused to let anybody out.

I'm ashamed of the memory, but I was thinking about poking the curtain with a knife a couple of times to change his mind, until Doc came to on his own.

He said we should wait. He didn't know either why Sprocket was being such a pain in the rear about it, but we were all alive so far because of him. Best to trust him a while longer. We waited over nine hours. Doc seemed to have nothing worse than a terrible headache and a superficial gash. The first aid book listed all the symptoms of concussion and internal hemorrhaging and he didn't appear to be possessed of any of them.

When Sprocket's mouth finally opened and I

stepped out, the hurricane had moved on and a crowd stood around Sprocket. Star and Sabrina and the other girls from Lady Jane's crew were right at the front of the crowd.

Star tasted as good as I remembered.

We told the DPS troopers about the Chief being on the loose, armed and dangerous. They identified him an hour later as the mystery patient in the intensive care unit at UTMB Hospital. Just one floor below the ward Doc and half-a-dozen other hands from Sprocket and the ship had been checked into for observation.

Star and me went down to see the Chief. He'd been found unconscious in the street by a Texas Ranger on the lookout for looters. The hurricane had finished tearing up the island only thirty minutes after we came ashore.

The Chief had made it almost two blocks before he dropped.

Me and Star held hands and looked at him through the thick glass window. They had him isolated in a huge pressurized vessel, with one husky male nurse sitting beside his bed reading a book.

The intern standing beside us made a mark in the folder he held. "Interesting case." He looked over at me. "Oh, not that unusual, clinically speaking. But the circumstances . . . are you friends of his?"

Star squeezed my hand.

"We know him," I said.

The intern pushed his glasses up closer to his eyes and looked as knowledgeable as he could. "Lucky we got him into the re-compression chamber as quickly as we did."

"Re-compression chamber?"

"You people were with him, weren't you? I heard part of the story. About how your Driller walked ashore. Hasn't anybody told you anything?"

"We been busy with another injured friend."

"Is it true that your Driller decompressed you himself?"

I must have looked totally confused. He proceeded to explain about their theory of what had happened. The Chief had a severe case of decompression sickness. Otherwise known as the bends. When undersea divers go down past certain depths and stay too long, the gases in their bloodstreams are compressed and concentrated because of their increased partial pressures. When the divers surface, unless they do it in stages, the gases expand inside their bodies and cause the bends. Air embolisms in the wrong body organs can kill. The lengthy pauses on the way up give the body enough time to throw off the excess gas safely.

Sprocket had apparently been forced to increase his internal atmospheric pressure after the fight with the sea monster, in order to somewhat offset the water pressure trying to broach his hull. The Chief forced his way out right after we got to shore and suffered a bad case of the bends. We stayed inside, trusting Sprocket, and he decompressed us safely.

The medic pushed his glasses back up on his nose again and peered at me. "The amazing thing is that your Driller knew to do what he did. I'm told there were some sailors with you. Did they instruct him about the proper procedures and timing?"

I shrugged. "Nope. They mostly slept through the whole thing. Sprocket just knows how to deal with pressure. Downhole or underwater; I guess it don't make no difference to him." I didn't say it, but what

I figured was that whoever had made his kind had thrown in some features we hadn't known about before.

"Too bad your friend didn't stay with the rest of you. We don't know yet how serious the spinal cord and brain damage will be, but it doesn't look good for him right now."

"It hasn't looked good for him for some time now," I said.

The Chief began to convulse. He died a few hours later.

In-Between

I almost broke my face when I stuck my foot in the hole and tripped. Doc and Razer and Sabrina laughed at me while Star helped me get up. My fault. I knew better than to walk around the pasture without keeping an eye on the ground.

After a second, one of the culprits ambled up and demanded to be petted and stroked by us all. Munchkin had dominoed right in the middle of the hurricane. According to Star, her crew got nearly as tensed up as Sprocket's crew was at the time. Must have been some hairy maternity adventures there.

She'd birthed four healthy Drillers, two males and two females. A big litter.

Her and Sprocket made a handsome pair, nuzzling together in the pasture, watching the kids frolic. They were all little whirlwinds, squealing with baby enthusiasm as they charged around the pasture. Each was about the size of a grizzly bear, but as friendly and cute as a collie pup.

Trouble is, they wasn't housebroke yet. The whole

pasture was a mine field of holes. They all drilled. Not to find oil yet, or even water, since they couldn't get much depth. Just for the sheer pleasure of drilling.

One of them, who'd already acquired the name of Spivey, wandered over and cuddled up against Razer. Razer climbed on top of him and they wandered off.

Sprocket's eyelid opened lazily when I rubbed it. He hummed in greeting. "You gotta control those little monsters," I said. "I damn near wrecked myself getting here. Have 'em do it over in one corner or something."

Sprocket watched Spivey and Razer rolling around in the grass. His lips flapped derisively at me. He wasn't gonna rein in his kids. Birds got to fly, Drillers got to drill. We both knew that.

Doc squatted and poured himself and Sabrina a couple of cups of coffee from the pot hanging over the fire. "Looks like Spivey and Razer might make a good team," he said to Sabrina. "Razer's gonna have to settle down a bit, but I believe he's got the stuff in him to work out. I'm gonna miss him when he's gone."

Sabrina nodded. "Uh-huh." She looked at me. "You figured out who your new *segundo* is gonna be, Doc?"

"Uh-huh. I figured I'd make the official announcement this evenin'."

"Wait a minute," I said. "What's this about Razer goin' somewhere?"

Doc took a sip and squinted up at me. "Well, hell, Henry Lee. Somebody's gotta head up the crew on Spivey when he gets his growth on him. Him and Razer get along fine."

"But—"

"Oh, it'll be a year or so before Spivey's big enough. They'll do the basic training for him and his sibs up at Aggie Station. While Sprocket's drill-head regenerates, I figure we might as well go to school up there, too. They got a big music competition sponsored every year by the API that I want to put my latest piece in. Besides, everybody on the crew could use some more training. A couple semesters of cracking the books and Razer'll have his Bachelor's degree in petroleum engineering. He's been putting off finishing it for too long."

"Razer? A college degree?" My mind boggled. I knew some gypsies went to Aggie State for schooling on occasion, but nobody on Sprocket's crew had talked much about it. It had sounded more like vocational education than anything else.

"In a year, Sprocket oughta be ready to get back to work," he continued. "You should have enough schooling to handle your new job by then. With me and Sprocket keeping a close watch and polishing you up in the field, you'll make a half-assed decent *segundo*."

My mind re-boggled.

"Who, me?" I finally squeaked.

"It's a ugly job, but somebody's gotta do it."

I leaned against Sprocket. A gentle hum from inside of him vibrated against my back.

"But—but—what about the other hands? Everybody on the crew's got seniority over me."

Doc looked disgusted. "We don't go by seniority, son, just ability. I ain't gonna sit here and slobber all over myself about how wonderful you are, but we figure we got the best man for the job. Ain't nobody on the crew gonna be jealous or give you a hard time. Except when you earn it. Most of us halfways like you, boy."

I was overwhelmed. "I'm overwhelmed," I said.

"Don't let it go to your head. Mostly, it's a pain in the ass."

I gulped. "I won't never let Sprocket down, Doc."

Sprocket chirped to his three kids that had quietly drifted into place behind us. Three blasts of drilling mud hit me in the rear end and knocked me on my face. I twisted around and grabbed ahold of one of the tongues before it could creep up my sleeve and fill my coveralls with mud. The kids continued to spew mud out, over all four of us and each other until we were completely covered.

We wrestled with the tongues and each other for a while, with it somehow working out that me and Star mostly rolled around together, and Doc and Sabrina mostly rolled around together, and the kids mostly sprayed us all impartially.

Doc finally sat up and wiped mud out of his eyes. "I guess that's their subtle way of congratulatin' you on your promotion." He eyed Sprocket. "Their daddy is already teaching 'em his bad habits."

He pulled a broken conductor's baton out of the pocket running the length of his leg. "The problem ain't letting Sprocket down, Henry Lee." He sighed. "The problem is puttin' up with him."

Sprocket Goes to School

It was the loudest, most bizarrest conglomeration of machinery I'd ever seen or heard.

The crowd surrounding it seemed to feel they were getting their entertainment dollar's worth. Every half-a-minute or so they'd erupt into cheers and whistles. The whole thing was set up about fifty yards in from the street, over by a clump of trees. Next to it somebody had assembled a refreshment stand and a small set of portable bleachers for the faint of leg and back.

We had a good viewpoint, being on top of Sprocket as he churned down University Drive. Since Aggie Station is a college town, and the college is Texas Petrological and Agricultural, the streets had been built to size, wide enough for use by Drillers and Cementers and Mud Mixers and Casing Critters and all the others. Not like a lot of them narrow, twisty country roads out in the ass end of god-knows-where that we have to make do with most of the time.

The day was bright but unusually coolish for late

August, with a wind coming down from the hill country to the northwest. This was good news for the dozen fellas scrambling all over the strange machines. Looked like they'd have dropped on a normal summer day, with all the exertions they were making.

Doc and Sabrina and me and Star lounged back in our folding chairs on top of Sprocket's back, under a huge grass-green sun umbrella we'd bolted down. Five other umbrellas dotted Sprocket's length, with most of Sprocket's and Lady Jane's crews up top socializing.

Doc picked up the jug of iced lemonade on the table between us and topped off our Mason jars.

"What on Earth is that ridiculous-looking contraption?" I asked Star.

Doc grinned. "Hey Sprocket!" he sang out. He stood up, folded his chair, and whacked Sprocket over the left eye with it. "Over thataway! Let's us watch the show some." Sprocket growled to himself, but he slowed and gingerly climbed over the curb, taking care not to spill anybody's drinks. He could be thoughtful that way when he chose. It wasn't all that often that he chose, mind you.

Lady Jane politely followed behind. She'd stayed with us when the rest of our convoy split off to head for the camp east of town.

Two derricks stood side by side. Under one of them a Driller was doing his business, making hole with a high musical whine while a gypsy band played for him. He was hooked up to a Mud Mixer and a Gas Tanker, both of them apparently asleep despite the noise of the crowd. That part was all as usual.

However, machines, and lines, and platforms, and all kinds of unrecognizable equipment had sprouted all over the other derrick, especially down around the drilling floor. A thick braided steel cable hung from an oversized hay pulley. A hellaciously noisy diesel engine rolled one end of the cable onto a drum that was bolted to the drilling floor. The cable went straight down to where the wellhead would have been if a Driller was drilling there. The cable and drum looked kind of like a wireline setup, but I had no idea what all the other machinery could be.

"Them Aggies never give up, do they, Sabrina?" Star said.

"I guess not, honey." Sabrina clicked her knitting needles together. She was just starting some red wool long johns for Doc. He was only slightly embarrassed that she was doing it in public. "I was here for the first contest. When was it, Doc? Nine years ago? Ten?"

"Ten," Doc said. "We met that year, I believe."

"Why, so we did. I remember." She pretended to prick him with the tip of a needle. "You were such a big stud back before you got old. Cut through the co-eds like a red-hot poker through a basket of kittens."

I winced at the image that created. Doc muttered something none of us caught.

"Eh, dear? What was that?" Sabrina asked him.

Doc leaned over and kissed her on the ear. "I said, I ain't so damn old. How do you know I ain't immoral like that no more, darlin'? Henry Lee and me both could probably leave a pretty broad wake behind us here if we decided to."

"Yeah!" I said loyally. Star dug an elbow in my ribs. "Uh—I mean—you leave me out of this! I'm an innocent bysitter, and besides, what the hell is all that machinery doin' over there anyways?"

"You better just keep on bysittin', bud." Star said. "And that is a drilling rig over there."

"I *know* that, smarty. I'd recognize a Driller from the smell alone. But what's all that stuff next to it, on that other derrick?"

"Star just told you," Sabrina said. "It's a drilling rig, Henry Lee. A *mechanical* drilling rig."

I stared at it for a long eight count. Then I busted out laughing. "Well, if that don't beat all!"

"Uh-huh," Doc said. "About half-a-dozen schools at the university here cooperate in designing and building machines to imitate the real thing. They've spent some serious research money on it, and they've come up with some purty ingenious stuff. See that cable going in the hole?"

I nodded. The drum reversed, pulling the cable out of the hole. A couple of fellas sweated over a control panel beside it.

Doc continued, "They got a pointy tool attached to the end of that cable, with some heavy-weight collars screwed on above it. They pull it up a-ways and then drop it free-fall to the bottom of the hole. The tool fractures the rock and they circulate the particulates out while they're pulling the tool back up the hole. Works damn well, all things considered. On a good day, I've seen 'em make three, four hundred foot of hole. Then something breaks down and they spend the next three days fixing it."

"What's that Driller doin' next to 'em, then?"

"Drilling," Star said. "Every year they have a big contest, and the Aggies trot out their new, improved version of a mechanical drilling rig and stage a contest to see who can make hole the fastest and the bestest, down to ten thousand foot. The losers spring for a big party the weekend before school starts."

I marvelled at the ingenuity of the Aggies. The cable tool abruptly released and the cable whined into the hole. The crowd cheered again. Then I had a alarming thought. "Wait a minute! What if them fellas make a machine so good that nobody needs Drillers no more? Just put it on automatic and come back when you're ready to go into production. We'd be in a fix!"

They all laughed. "Ain't too likely," Doc said. "Sometimes we forget just how complicated it is to make a well. They ain't won a single drilling contest yet. Nobody can't make machines good enough to compete with living critters made for the purpose. The technology just ain't in place, maybe never will be. It costs too much, it breaks down too often, and it just don't make hole fast as a Driller."

The cable started winching out of the hole again. Next door to it, the Driller quietly, steadily hummed to itself as its tongue ripped a hole into the earth. Not all noisy and dramatic like the machines. Merely taking care of business and getting the job done.

"I guess," I said doubtfully.

"Hey, Sprocket!" Doc called out. He went through the folding and whacking procedure again. He was just too lazy today to go to his room and get the crowbar that he usually drove with. "We need to get on over to the vet building. Gonna miss your appointment if we don't get it in gear. Vet building, boy!" Sprocket groaned; once he got stopped he didn't much like to fire up again. "We'll come on back here later, Henry Lee."

"Yeah, I'd like that, Doc."

The drilling contest receded behind us. I turned and watched it until a building got in the way.

I don't know why; I started to hum a little tune to myself. I don't remember all the words to it. Something about John Henry, he was a steel-driving man.

*   *   *

P&A was tucked away in the hill country in the middle of the state. I'd imagined it would be crude and primitive, not much more than a bunch of shacks and ugly brick buildings, since Aggie Station had a reputation for not being a completely civilized place. Instead, the campus looked modern and well manicured. It was also five times as large as I had thought it would be. It looked like a small city, with its own miniature skyscrapers. I liked it. The buildings tended to be crowded together and the streets were mazes, but Sprocket knew where he was going, as he had visited the vet more than once. I had found out that oilfield critters, whenever possible, spent their first year or two at Aggie Station for pediatric care and basic training.

Eventually, we drew up on a building six or seven stories high. Sprocket chugged around to the back. A down ramp led to an open bay wide enough for three Drillers to march in side-by-side.

The entire bottom three floors of the building was actually one huge room, broken up into cubicles around the edges by little head-height dividers. All sorts of equipment was scattered over the floor. Five separate areas, like oversized repair bays in a garage, were boxed by blue lines on the concrete floor. A Mud Mixer was in one of them, with a dozen people in white coats crawling all over it. A Cementer faced the wall in the bay farthest from us, apparently unattended and asleep. Sprocket proceeded to park in one of the open bays. He acted strangely eager to get to his place.

I figured it was just because he had been on the road for a week and was ready for a rest.

A big shiny piece of square gray glass, at least three yards across, hung on the wall twenty feet in front of his eyes. A long cable with a box covered with buttons the size of dinner plates on the end, hung on a clip next to the glass. As soon as Sprocket stopped moving, his tongue shot out and grabbed the cable and pulled the box toward him.

He dropped the box to the floor in front of him and his tongue-tip started pushing buttons. The bandages didn't seem to slow it any. The square of glass lit up with moving colors and noise blared from a grill beneath it.

"Turn that goddam thing down!" Doc yelled.

The noise dropped in volume. The pictures on the screen flicked from one scene to another as Sprocket checked through the selections available.

"He loves that moron thing," Doc said at a more conversational level. "Ever time we been here he stands in front of it like a idiot for hours and hours on end. Doesn't even notice people working on him. They're all like that; Drillers, Cementers, you name it. It's like it sucks their brains right out of their heads. If we had these things set up on location, we'd never get nothing done. They'd all just stand around dribbling on themselves watching the goddam tee-vee." I knew about tee-vee, of course. I'd seen 'em in bars all over the state. But this screen was about ten times bigger than any other I'd seen. Obviously custom-made for oilpatch critters.

Sprocket settled on a beach scene with lots of girls bouncing around in teeny-weeny bikinis. Strange choice for a Driller, I thought. But Sprocket still surprised me with himself about once a day, so I didn't dwell on it much. I also tried not to dwell on the girls in bikinis as we folded up the umbrella and chairs, but I caught Star smiling at me tolerantly anyhow.

"Hey, Doc! Long time no see!" A girl appeared in the doorway of one of the little offices along the wall and took long strides toward us.

She had her hair cut short as a boy's, which was a horrible mistake, since she was otherwise definitely a female.

"Hey, Hillary! How you doin', sweetheart?" Doc slid down Sprocket's side and hugged her with great sincerity when she got close enough. I kept an eye on Sabrina. She didn't seem to be getting no emotional problems about Hillary and Doc. Not that she was the jealous type, mind you.

She finished stowing a couple of chairs and slid down Sprocket's side and hugged Hillary herself.

"Hillary was on Sabrina's crew for a couple years before she decided she liked vet work full time," Star said beside me. "Casing gypsy, born and bred."

"Oh," I said. "I wasn't sure for a second whether she was one of the kittens in Doc's basket."

Star shrugged. "Doc had a lot of kittens, and more'n one basket. Maybe still does. You'd know better than me about that."

In the last year or so, I had learned some good times to keep my trap shut. This was one of them.

"Anyway," Star went on, "I don't think Sabrina figures she has exclusive ownership rights."

"They sure been acting otherwise for the last six months."

"Yeah. It ain't like either of them."

"Getting old, I guess."

"Must be." She finished with her umbrella. "Henry Lee, we ain't talked about it much, but I don't figure

I got exclusive ownership rights on you either, you know."

"I know that."

"And vice-versa. I grew up a casing gypsy. Moving from camp to camp, location to location. I learned early on that nobody ever owns anybody."

"I understand that, Star. I never tried to hold you down, did I?"

"No, you never did."

Doc called us to come down and be introduced to Hillary. Star had been moody for the last two weeks and I had the feeling somehow that we had just finished an important conversation, but I didn't know whether I'd screwed up my end of it or not.

Hillary and an assistant in a white coat dragged the tongue-tip over to a bench and clamped it gently in a large cushioned vise. Sprocket didn't seem to mind; his eyes never left the tee-vee screen.

"Now, let's see what we've got here," she said as she unwrapped the bandages. The tongue twitched a little when she came to the last layer, but Sprocket still kept on watching the tee-vee.

"Oh, my," Hillary said. She lifted his tongue-tip, turning it over and looking at it from all sides. "No sign of infection. The wound is uncharacteristically ragged. Usually the cut's much cleaner."

"You mean this kind of thing happens all the time?" I asked.

"Oh, no. Not at all. It's fairly rare. I've seen it maybe a dozen times. About the only instance that will cause a Driller to lose a length of tongue is when he's involved in a hole collapse or casing implosion. He gets trapped in the hole, and the crew has to run a tool downhole on wireline as far as possible and shear him loose. But that's not what happened here, is it? Looks like the collapse itself severed it. Very messily."

"Wasn't a hole collapse," Doc said grimly. "He chewed off his tongue, about fifty feet behind the drill-head." He saw the question on Hillary's face. "Oh, he didn't go psychotic on us, Hillary. He saved our lives by what he done. It's a long story. Tell you the details tonight."

"Hmph. Okay." She examined the tip some more. "Good thing he only lost about fifty feet of length."

"Why's that?" I asked. "Take longer to regenerate otherwise?"

"No. The drill-head will regenerate approximately two yards forward of the edge of the wound. What's gone in length is gone for good, though. I had one last year that lost almost ten thousand feet. Ruined him for deep wells. Sprocket got off easy in that respect. He looks healed up enough that we should leave him unwrapped from here on. Air and sunlight and exercise of the tip will be beneficial." She unclamped the vise and allowed Sprocket's tongue to slither back in his mouth.

"Well, Henry Lee, we gotta go over to the camp and find some medicine for this terrible dry throat I have acquired," Doc said casually. "You mosey on over when you finish up here."

"What! I gotta stay here while y'all party?"

"Just till Hillary and her bunch finish up on the preliminary exam. Shouldn't be more than a couple hours, right, Hillary?"

Hillary looked up from a clipboard she was examining. "Hmmm? Oh, I imagine, about that. We'll shut down around 'fivish' or 'sixish' regardless. Meet y'all at the camp?"

"Oh, sure. Henry Lee and Sprocket'll give you a ride."

"We will, huh?"

"Now, now. I told you that being *segundo* on a crew is mostly a pain in the butt. You might as well practice bein' left behind, starting right now. It won't be the last time. Matter of fact, long as you're here, you might get the red folder off my desk and make a head start on that inventory of all Sprocket's equipment that we were talking about."

"You gonna stay with me, Star?"

"Sorry, Henry Lee," Sabrina said. "I need her to help get us and Lady Jane settled in at the camp."

"You're a big boy now," Star said sweetly as she kissed me on the cheek. "You can handle it. Watch tee-vee with Sprocket."

Wasn't much I could do but stand there and wave bye-bye, like a big boy, while they all piled into Lady Jane and trundled on out of sight.

I begun to suspect that maybe Doc wasn't merely trying to keep me from getting a swelled head when he told me that people didn't fight and die to be the *segundo* on a crew.

Hillary made it clear that her and her bunch considered me to be unnecessary to their exam, and Sprocket wasn't the least bit sociable, hypnotized by the tee-vee as he was. He changed channels to some kind of nauseating nature film thing about snakes and frogs and insects slurping mucus and eating each other. So I spent about thirty minutes inventorying tees and crossovers and swages and such before getting terminally bored.

Hillary said she didn't mind, when I asked her if I could wander around the place a bit, as long as I kept my hands in my pockets. Wasn't that she didn't trust me, she just didn't want me bulling around messing with her expensive scientific equipment. By then the other two critters had cleared out, and the examiners that had been working on them had disappeared, so we had the hangar to ourselves.

All the bays were practically identical, so I finished checking them out shortly. I didn't have the leastest idea what most of the equipment was for, anyway. After awhile I found myself at the foot of one of the stairs that climbed to the catwalks on the second and third floor levels. Situated at several places around the perimeter were controls for various cranes and hoists that hung over the whole area.

Hillary glanced at me when I got to the second floor level right over Sprocket's bay, so I leaned over the rail and called out, "Hey! What's these cranes and stuff for?"

She took her pen out of her mouth and strolled over to the foot of the stairs.

"Sometimes we have to lift our patients completely off the ground. Late last year, for instance, a Tanker and a Driller were caught in a blowout that ignited, over by Hempstead. They were brought in, unconscious and severely burnt, by a couple of Army Corps of Engineers' heavy-haulers. We used the cranes to transfer them into and out of liquid bath tanks while they healed. We'd debride the dead flesh and then keep them bathed, antiseptic, and gravity-neutral."

"They make it okay?"

She shrugged. "The tanker was physically all right in a couple of months, but she's phobic. Won't go near the wellhead anymore. We're still doing therapy on her, trying to desensitize her to her fear."

"How about the Driller?"

"He's fine," she said. She frowned and went on more slowly. "About the only thing that can make a Driller phobic is for it to lose a piece of itself downhole."

"Like Sprocket did."

"Like Sprocket did, yes. Have y'all tried to get him to run into the hole since the accident?"

"No, ma'am. No reason to. How do we find out if there's going to be a problem?"

"If he won't go in the hole anymore, there's a problem. We'll check it in a week or two, after his tongue has healed more."

"What if . . ."

Hillary shrugged. "Some get over it. Some don't. I'm sure he'll be all right. Sprocket's a young Driller, and they're resilient."

I wandered up to the third floor and took the seat behind one of the crane control boards for awhile, looking over the hangar below. Just as I was getting comfortable, I heard a scratching sound behind me and turned around.

Standing on the ledge outside the window, not five feet from me, was a creature I'd never dreamed in my worst nightmares. It stood tall as a man, all black leather and bat wings and long, sharp beak. The monster spread its wings and I saw that deformed hands with long claws twitched at the wings' midpoints. Its head cocked sideways. It glared at me with beady red eyes and clacked its beak metallically. I knew exactly what it was thinking.

My, that certainly does look tasty. I think I'll crash through this window and eat it right up.

It clacked its beak again and took a step closer to the window. I let out a yowl and scrambled out of the control seat. I made it to the floor of the hangar almost as fast as if I'd simply dived over the rail.

I was leaning against Sprocket's flank and trembling when Hillary stepped out of his mouth. "Something the matter, Henry Lee?" A couple of her crew popped out of holes along Sprocket's top and stared at me like I'd lost my brains. Sprocket glanced at me, saw I was all right, and went back to watching the tee-vee.

"I . . . he . . . it . . . Uh, wings, claws! Big, black monster! Acckkk!"

They all looked puzzled, then Hillary started to snicker. "He must have seen Maureen or Sonny," she said to her crew. They laughed, too. I didn't appreciate it one little bit.

She hugged me, which actually provided a nice distraction from the mortal terror I was experiencing. "There, there. Maureen and Sonny look like something from the backside of hell, but they're harmless."

"Didn't look harmless," I mumbled, hugging her in return. She smelled real good. "Looked hungry."

"No, no. Maureen and Sonny don't eat anything bigger than sheep. You probably scared the poor dear half to death." She let go of me and stepped back.

"What the hell are Maureen and Sonny anyways?" I asked.

"Dactyls." She looked at her watch. "Tell you what. We'll be messing with Sprocket for another forty-five minutes or an hour. Why don't you go up to the top floor and get another look."

"I don't think . . ."

"They're interesting critters. You may never get a better excuse."

"Yeah . . ."

"And you need to make sure Sonny or Maureen is all right after the scare you gave it." She turned me around and swatted me on the rear. "C'mon. You'll enjoy it. Elevator's down that hall and on your left. Seventh floor. Find Stevie Goolsby. He's their keeper. He'll be happy to introduce you to them."

"Uh . . . how about another hug to reassure me some more?"

Actually, once she told me they didn't eat Henry Lees for dinner, I was kind of interested in getting a more formal introduction. So I took the grungy elevator to the eighth floor. When the doors opened, there was a long hallway in front of me. None of the nameplates on any of the doors had Stevie Goolsby's name on them. I tried a couple of doors and they were all locked, so I wandered down the hallway to where it tee'd, looking for signs of life. I took the right-hand branch and tried a couple more doors, with no luck.

I heard a door clack open back around the corner from where I had come. I started back, to get directions or see if it was Stevie Goolsby. I could hear two of them talking. The woman had a accent that dripped honeysuckle onto the floor. Just before I turned the corner, I realized she was in the process of chewing his ass off, so I held back.

"Actually, Steven, Ah b'leeve the depahtment has just about come to the end of the road with yoah sloppiness."

"But I'm just on the verge of—" His voice was high and uncertain.

"You've been just on the vudge, suh, evah since the depahtment brought y'all heah. Frankly, ah haven't seen any real puhformance out of you in the last foah yeahs. Just promises and a specialization in a bizarre, unprofitable lahn of research that drains much-needed funds from awuh school."

"The dactyls are not bizarre and unprofitable, René!"

"The budget committee is beginnin' to thank otherwise. The dactyls have not fulfilled awuh expectations, have they? Money is tight. We ah goin' to have to make some cuts this yeah. If we don't see some tangible results by the next fundin' cycle . . ."

"Aw, come on, René! You can't do basic research by the clock."

"Puhhaps, but I'm afraid yoah clock is tickin', Steven. Good day, suh."

I hung back out of sight, not wanting to eavesdrop, but not wanting to walk in on the middle of their happy discussion, either.

I heard her heels clicking away from him down the hallway. The elevator doors whooshed open and shut.

I waited a minute, so he could go back in his office and I could come in without him knowing I overheard their conversation.

When I peeked around the corner, he was standing in front of his office, staring absently at the wall beside my head.

His eyes focussed, and he stared at me instead, for a few seconds.

I stared back. He was a short, wiry guy; made me think of an elf with bad eyes. His glasses were so thick they looked like Coke bottle bottoms strapped on his face with chicken wire. He was wearing a dirty green dress that I later learned was a lab smock. The screaming red hair on his head tried to escape in all directions, but his scraggly beard looked too sick to do more than drip limply off his face. A thick gold ring piercing his left ear looked completely out of place.

I cleared my throat.

"I didn't know we had an audience," he said.

"Sorry. Uh—I didn't mean to be an audience. Uh—Hillary told me to find you, and I was looking around up here, and . . ."

He shrugged. "What the hell. The Stone Magnolia probably would have kept eating on me if you'd been standing beside us doing a tap dance and singing 'Camptown Races.'"

I shrugged uncomfortably. "Sorry."

"Not your problem," he said. "What does Hillary need?"

"Well . . . she thinks maybe I scared Sonny or Maureen when one of them terrorized me, and she wanted me to check with you. She said you'd introduce me to them."

His whole look changed. His eyes swole up happily behind his glasses. "Yeah, I'll introduce you to my babies."

He took me through the door he and the Stone Magnolia had come out of. The large room inside was a laboratory, with mysterious equipment scattered around on big marble-topped tables. I always thought doing science would be clean and tidy, with smart-looking guys talking fast while they drew diagrams on blackboards and cooked stuff in funny-shaped glassware, but this room was a ungodly mess. It did have a lot of funny-shaped glassware on the tables, though. Most of it was dirty. I didn't get much chance to look around, because he grabbed a ring of keys out of the drawer of a desk against the far wall and took us back out in the hallway.

He led me to the door next to the elevator. We

went into the stairwell and climbed up a short flight of stairs. "Gotta keep the tourists off the roof," he explained as he used one of the keys on the ring to open a door at the top of the stairs.

The dactyls must have heard us coming.

When Stevie opened the door they jumped us, screeching and flapping and cackling. They both looked ugly, and mean, and hungry, and unprincipled, but Stevie held his ground, so I did, too. Then I noticed they both had still-damp blood staining their beaks.

Stevie started making little burping noises and grabbed a beak with each hand. He shook their heads back and forth vigorously while they tried to crowd us back into the stairwell so they could kill us out of sight from the public. After a minute of this foofaraw I figured Steve and them were merely demonstrating how happy they were to see each other. He started scratching their heads where their ears would have been if they had any ears, then shoved them back out on the gravel-covered roof.

In the late afternoon sunlight I got my first clear look at the dactyls. They both spread their wings and made funny wooka-wooka sounds, their beaks jabbing at the sky while the claws at the leading edges of their wings flexed and clasped. Their wingspans exceeded twenty feet. They differed from each other in a couple of ways. The one that Stevie called Maureen stood almost a foot taller than Sonny. And growths of feathers, scraggly as Stevie's beard, blue and green and yellow and red, sprouted on different parts of their bodies.

Steve took up a rag hanging on a peg beside the big chicken wire cage that I figured they lived in. He dunked the cloth in a trough of water, then wrung it out.

"Come here, Sonny. Let Papa clean you." He made the burping and clicking sounds again, and Sonny echoed them. He furled his wings and waddled up to Steve. Steve took the cloth and began to wipe the blood off his beak.

"They went out for dinner this afternoon," he explained. "Usually they get by on what I bring them, but twice a week I turn them loose. The school has an arrangement with a sheep rancher a couple of miles north of town. They take one of his flock and we reimburse him at about twice the going rate."

I shivered. "Hoo, I bet that terrorizes the flock as much as it did me."

"Surprisingly, no. They drop out of the sky from a thousand feet up, grab one at the edge of the flock, and are gone in a half-a-second. Sheep are amazingly stupid. They don't even react. There's a cliff up near Mumford, north of town. They drop the sheep on top of it and have dinner."

He dunked the cloth in the trough again. Brown stained the water in it. "The cliff's necessary because they're what we call stooping birds." He squeezed the cloth and applied it to Sonny's beak again. "That means they can't take off from level ground. They have to drop off the edge of something and fall awhile until they gain enough velocity to fly. That's one of the reasons we keep them on top of the Vet Building. Once or twice they've gotten stranded on the ground and we had to bring them back up here in the elevator."

I nodded. "Uh-huh. I've never seen any birds that look anything at all like these." Maureen waddled over and cocked her head from side to side, inspecting me with first one eye, then the other. I held my ground. Then a long purple tongue snaked out the side of her mouth toward me and I jumped back.

Stevie laughed. "She just wants a taste. Like a dog licking you so she'll be able to recognize you better. They're not modern birds, Henry Lee. Their kind haven't existed on this Earth for millions of years."

Her tongue tickled as she ran it down the side of my face. She clucked and cooed. I reached out and scratched the side of her head like Stevie had. She hiccuped happily.

"Something interesting happened about ten years ago," Stevie continued. "A volcano blew up in Antarctica. You might have read about it."

I shook my head. "Nope, I'm just a country boy. Grew up reading the Bible and the Farmer's Almanac."

He rolled his eyes. "Ridiculous superstitious trash. Anyway, a team of geologists stationed at McMurdo Sound down there went to monitor it. It had cracked a glacier wide open. Purely by chance, one of the team spotted an ice boulder that encased a nest and a clutch of twenty-three pterodactyl eggs. In perfect condition." He finished up with Sonny. "Here, Maureen. Cleanup time, sweetheart. Amazingly, eighteen of the eggs contained viable genetic material."

Sonny went through the open door of the chicken wire cage and used his claws to walk up the wall until he got to a rubber-covered steel bar suspended on thick ropes below the tin roof. He climbed onto the bar and began to rock happily back and forth like a huge, repulsive parakeet.

"The eggs were transported to MIT, where I was a grad student at the time. To make a long story short, we studied and planned for five years. The pterodactyl genetic material was damaged in places, so we introduced material from modern-day birds into the

DNA chains after intensive computer-modelling and a lot of sweaty guesswork. Then we enucleated a couple of dozen ostrich eggs and took our best shot at it. We got ten live birds." I hadn't understood half the words he was using, but I got the general drift, so I just nodded and tried to look intelligent.

He finished up with Maureen and slapped her on the flank. She hiccupped and went to join Sonny. We hooked our fingers in the chicken wire and watched them.

"The project couldn't have succeeded without a lot of inter-university cooperation. Half-a-dozen schools contributed money, personnel, computer time, equipment. As part of the deal, P&A got a breeding pair when they'd matured enough to travel. Sonny and Maureen. And they got me." He sighed. "It hasn't worked out too well for any of us."

"How come? Sounds like everybody ought to be thrilled. Y'all got some live dactyls, didn't you?"

"Almost. Like I said, we injected foreign genetic material. Sonny and Maureen are part cockatoo. They're cockadactyls, not pterodactyls. We tagged the cockatoo sequences. The plan was to breed back to a pure form, gradually eliminating the tagged sequences. We estimated it'd take about a dozen, maybe two dozen generations." He sighed again. "But none of the dactyls have bred yet. They reached sexual maturity two years ago, and they don't even try. We're wondering if we screwed up their reproductive systems when we put in the cockatoo genes."

He turned away from the cage and stared out over the roof. "Some of the schools are getting impatient. Me and the Stone Magnolia got along fine until a year or so ago. I thought she was a pretty nice lady. Then she started to change. I don't know . . . maybe she just ran out of patience." He shrugged. "Now she foams at the mouth when the subject of cockadactyls comes up."

"Can she do anything about it?"

He gave me a lopsided smile. "She's my department chair, and, as you oil gypsies say, she has suction. Lots of suction, with P&A's board of regents. She can do damn near whatever she wants to. So far, she hasn't thought of anything."

He took off his glasses and squeezed the bridge of his nose. "But she will," he said. "She will."

Hillary had us stop off at her apartment complex on the way to the camp so she could pick up some clothes and other stuff. She planned on going out with us for the evening, and had decided to get ready aboard Lady Jane after supper. Her place was on the edge of town, in almost the same direction we would have had to go anyway.

While we waited for her, me and Sprocket meandered among a small field of pump jacks across the street. Jacks in various sizes were spotted all across the state, some places more than others. They pumped oil out of wells that didn't have enough pressure downhole to get to the surface otherwise. A jack looked like a large, black, horse-like animal with its nose dipping up and down tirelessly and the half-wheels on the rear kicking around like a donkey's. They pumped the oil into nearby storage tanks which would be emptied by vacuum trucks every week or so, depending on how much the wells produced.

Half the jacks were motionless, since the Railroad Commission strictly limited how quickly a reservoir could be depleted of its hydrocarbons.

We passed one that was partly dismantled for repairs and I got a bad idea. I took a hammer and a thirty-six from the iron room and opened the hole under the pump jack.

"Hey, Sprocket. Oil. Look, oil."

He didn't respond, so I got him to open his mouth and pulled his tongue-tip over to the hole.

"C'mon, boy. Run on in there. Get you a little snack."

He just stared at me. I pulled his tongue closer and tried to insert it into the hole. I had it in less than a foot when he jerked it loose and galloped out of the field.

I ran after him, shouting. I caught up with him in the street. He stood there trembling, with his eyes tightly closed.

Hillary came up behind me with a small suitcase and a large purse as I was rubbing the area over his right eye, trying to calm him down.

"I saw from my window," she said.

"Did I mess him up worse by pushing on him? I feel like such a idiot."

She set down her suitcase and started to rubbing him, too. "We'll see," she said. "I'm sure he'll be fine." She sounded like she was trying to convince all three of us.

It was the largest camp I'd been in, with maybe ninety critters on hand, which meant fifteen to eighteen hundred people. A lot of them worked the Austin Chalk and other fields around Aggie Station, but others were there strictly for educational purposes.

Hillary said the camp should grow past a hundred critters and two thousand people by the time the semester started in two weeks. Our convoy had grouped together near the center of the camp. Hil-

lary and me might have had a hard time finding our
bunch in the twilight, but I asked some kids playing
with a baby Cementer and they gave us directions.

I noticed that, aside from its size alone, this camp
was different from the others I'd been in. For one
thing, half a dozen permanent buildings were scattered around inside the fence. And there was an
awful lot of kids and young oilfield critters running
around. The ones you couldn't see, you could hear,
having a grand old time with each other.

They'd saved a slot between Lady Jane and Munchkin
for us. When Sprocket slipped in, dinner was ready,
which was fine by me. A growing young fella needs
lots of nourishment from what Razer called your four
basic carbohydrate groups—boudain, chicken-fried
steak, spaghetti, and chocolate pie. The smell rising
over the whole camp was making my tummy talk to
me.

After dinner I got introduced to another gypsy
custom that I could have done without. No other
camp that we'd stayed in had this particular way of
helping you to introduce yourself, but they did things
different, and stupider, at Aggie Station.

Me and Star was talking quietly, leaning up against
Lady Jane, when Doc called me over and motioned
for me to stand beside him. The crews for Sprocket,
Lady Jane, Munchkin, and Big Red all came to their
feet and stood behind us. The head of the camp,
Wiley the Wildman Throckmorton, solemnly pulled
forward a four-wheeled red wagon heaped neck-high
with white towels. Most of the rest of the camp
gathered behind him in a semicircle.

The Wildman bowed to us all formal-like. Doc
bowed back, then looked at me. I hastily bowed, too.

"Welcome to the camp, folks," the Wildman said loudly. "Always good to see our brothers and sisters come to school up here." He took a deep breath. I started to relax, figuring we was going to get a long-winded, boring speech.

"Y'all have fun. Make the stacks neat." He handed me the end of the rope that he'd tugged the wagon forward with. "We figure y'all oughta be done about midnight." He smirked and started moving away.

The crowd behind him cheered and whistled enthusiastically.

"What the hell was that all about?" I whispered to Doc.

"They expect us to dry and stack about forty million pieces of dinnerware," he whispered back. I looked at the towels packed on the wagon. There was a lot of towels, enough to wash and dry thousands of dishes. Then I looked at the long, long table that circled a huge trough in the center of the camp, about twenty feet away. It was piled high with dishes and glasses and cups and spoons and forks and knives. Gypsies had been putting them on the table all while we were eating, but there had already been a mountain before dinner. I hadn't taken much notice of it, since I was busy defending myself against starvation.

I looked at the wagon again. I began to wonder if we had enough towels. Doc took the rope from my hands.

"Appreciate the honor," he called out. He held the end of the rope up high, then dropped it. "But I don't believe we'll be needing these towels here."

The camp went deathly quiet.

"You mean you ain't gonna wash the dishes?" the Wildman finally choked, in a high, outraged voice.

The crowd started to mutter ugly mutters. I got

ready for a fight, which might be better than washing all the dishes they'd lined out for us.

"Not personally, we ain't." Doc let the muttering get louder for a minute, waited for the crowd to begin to edge toward us. Then he smiled. "But that don't mean they won't get cleaned." He turned to Sprocket and the crew. "Let's get it on, boys."

While the entire camp watched suspiciously, we followed Doc's directions and ran a couple of lines from the industrial-size faucets among the troughs. We half-filled one of Sprocket's bladders with nearly boiling water, then poured in a half-dozen sacks of 20-40 sand for scouring, then a barrel of well-cleaner, which ain't nothing but highly concentrated soap. Then, while Sprocket held the bladder's outside orifice wide open, we dumped into him all the pots and pans and dishes and spoons and forks and cups and bowls. All the dinnerware was metal, mostly aluminum and tin, since glass and dainty china don't travel all that well into the places our kind of folks end up going to.

Frankly, it looked to me like some of the pieces had been saved up for a couple of days, or maybe even weeks. I overheard a couple of comments in the crowd that didn't persuade me otherwise. All of the pieces had identifying marks scratched some place on them, so there wasn't any chance of them getting mixed up.

We played a little casual free-form jazz in C Dorian mode while Sprocket foamed up the water in the bladder, then turbulated it by marching in place and pressure-squirting water from bladder to bladder. You couldn't hardly hear the clanging collisions of all the stuff in his bladders over the music, which was maybe the idea.

After a half-hour, Doc called a stop to the playing. I hooked up a hose to the orifice that led off to a big disposal pit on the edge of the camp. Sprocket emptied the dirty, soapy, sandy water through it, then switched back to another hose with clean water and rinsed the dishes.

He stuck his tongue out and sputtered wetly at the crowd, then winced. Maybe not so good an idea until his drill-head grew back. He started to hum, quietly at first, then louder and louder. Four of his orifices gaped open and began to whistle as they sucked air in. He swole up like he had just before he blew out on my daddy's farm.

A geyser of steam jetted from the top of his head through his blowout relief sphincter.

Doc leaned over and whispered to me, "Razer and me figured this out last time these turkeys laid a month's worth of dirty dishes on the crew. We swore we wouldn't get suckered again."

After about five minutes, the geyser trailed away into nothing. A minute later the whistling died and the four intake orifices clenched shut. The orifice that led to the dishwashing bladder gaped open.

"High-pressure pneumatic drying," Doc said. He stepped forward, and gestured for the rest of the crew to follow him.

"Okay, folks, let's stack 'em. Neat, like the Wildman asked."

We stacked the last of the dishes around eight o'clock.

Doc yelled down Sprocket's hall while I was fumbling with my cuff links. "Anybody got any preferences where we start out tonight?" A chorus of contradictory suggestions came from all of the rooms.

"How's about we make it to Jon-Tim's Juke Joint?"
Doc asked. "Hillary says they got a band in tonight
that plays them dirty ol' low-down blues that Henry
Lee likes so much."

Everybody booed and howled.

"No, no! We hate that garbage!"

"Uh-uh! Anything but the blues!"

"I'd rather listen to cats fightin' under the front
porch!"

"Country and Western forever!"

"Bob Wills is still the king!"

"Well, it's settled, then," Doc said. "We'll go to
Jon-Tim's and take in some blues."

Jon-Tim's Juke Joint had been designed with oilfield
critters in mind. The place was actually a huge
wooden-panelled, rectangular pit, a couple of hundred feet on a side and eighteen feet deep in the
ground. An asphalt parking lot surrounded it. A pavilion roof, festooned on top and bottom with various-
colored lights, protected it from the weather. The
pavilion roof was a good fifteen feet above the ground.

Half-a-dozen stairways led from the surface down
to the sawdust-covered floor of the pit, which was
arranged like the standard inside of a good road
joint, with a bar running the length of one wall, the
bandstand against the opposite wall, a cleared dance
area in front of the bandstand, and a bunch of tables
and chairs densely packing the rest of the available
space.

Critters crowded most of the way around the edge
of the joint, their faces poked over partways into the
pit, but Sprocket and Lady Jane found a couple of
parking slots next to each other and glided into them.
Munchkin had stayed in camp to watch over her

young'uns, and Big Red and his crew had gone off to raise hell and shoot pool at a place called Fajita Rita's, where we were supposed to meet them later. After the crew climbed out through Sprocket's mouth he nosed up until a yard of his front end dropped over the edge of the pit. Lady Jane did the same as soon as she was emptied. I'd felt guilty before on occasion about leaving them outside while we went in and partied, but Jon-Tim's had solved that problem. They built so that the critters could attend the party, too.

As we was settling into a couple of tables, the band came on and began to fiddle with their instruments. A high-cheeked black man that had a red electric guitar strapped to him leaned into the microphone. He was dressed all in black leather. Had a big nose, a small moustache, and eyes that seemed to glow from inside with a smoky light.

"Well, folks, the band's passing through Aggietown on our way to someplace else again. Figured we'd stop off and play y'all some Chicago blues this week. Always real happy to make a showing for Jon-Tim and Cathy. We gonna start this set off with 'So Glad I'm Living.' "

He hit a chord, the rest of the band kicked in with a long piano, guitar, and screaming harmonica introduction, and they proceeded with the howlingest blues I ever heard.

He sang with a voice like whiskey that had rattlesnake heads soaking in it.

My baby's long and tall . . .
Shaped like a cannon ball . . .
And every time she love me . . .
Oh, you can hear me squall . . .

I cry Ummmm . . .
I believe I change my mind.
She said—I'm so glad I'm living.
I cry, ummmm, baby—I'm so glad you're mine.

About halfway through the song, he stepped back and surveyed the crowded room while the piano player burned down the place.

His froggy, glowing eyes widened and he smiled in our direction. I looked over and saw Doc smiling back at him and nodding while he rocked in his chair and tapped time with his foot.

When the song finished, we clapped for a goodly while. They were damn good musicians, every one of them. The song almost sounded like something I had heard in the Chief's collection, but I couldn't quite place it. The blues was maybe the only good thing I had brought away from the Chief.

"Well, well, well, yes sir," the fella with the guitar said. "I just seen one of my bad ol' friends slouchin' in the dark there, trying to hide in the crowd. He plays the piano all right for oifield trash. Come on up here, Doc. You ain't gonna get off tonight without workin' some. People, give the man a hand—Doc Miller!"

I looked at Doc in amazement. He showed me his teeth and stood up. His hand rested on my shoulder.

He nodded to the crowd, which was clapping and whistling.

When they quieted down, he shouted up to the band leader, "Hey, Muddy, I got a boy here wants to learn the blues. Think you and Willie can teach him some?"

Muddy laughed. "Hell, Doc, if we can teach you

the blues, we can teach 'em to anybody. Get him on up here."

"Come on, Henry Lee." He started to pull me out of my seat.

"What? Me? Are you out of your mind?"

"You been runnin' off at the mouth about how much you love the blues. You ain't never gonna find anybody better to play with than Muddy and Willie." He nodded at the squat man holding onto an upright bass. Willie grinned back. I got the feeling he was lookin' forward to the execution.

"Come on, Henry Lee. Time to fish or cut bait, son." The fellas at the table started shouting, "Henry Lee! Henry Lee!" and pretty soon the rest of the club took it up. I looked at Star; she just rolled her eyes and laughed at me. There wasn't no graceful way out of it.

Once I got to the bandstand, Muddy handed me his backup ax. It was identical to the one he was using, except for the gleaming black paint job. While I was strapping it on and hooking into the sound system and digging my best tortoiseshell pick out of my pocket, I watched Doc replace Otis, the fella at the piano, and run his fingers over the keys. I turned down the volume on the guitar and joined him in a couple of scale exercises for a minute. If looks could have killed, his hands would have got very sick. Instead, he just grinned and casually rolled a couple of rapid bass and treble walking riffs past me.

It helped that the guitar's fretboard was the fastest one I'd ever touched. It practically begged me to play thirty-secondth and sixty-fourth notes on it. I examined the guitar more closely. It was light, but solid, and felt alive in my hands. On the headstock was the word "Fender" in script, and in smaller block letters underneath, "Stratocaster." I'd played through a Fender Twin Reverb amp a couple times in a camp near Manvel, but the guitar was news to me. I already wanted one. It made my Epiphone feel like a boat oar with strings on it.

"You boys warmed up?" Muddy asked, after much too short a time.

"I am," Doc said. "You think you can handle the pressure, Henry Lee?"

"I'll fix your wagon for this one day, Doc. Fix it good!"

"We got a song that Willie wrote for me," Muddy said. "I believe you know it, Doc. It ain't too hard. We play it in 'G' this month. Called 'I'm Your Hootchie Cootchie Man.' " The crowd started to whooping and clapping again. I realized exactly who Muddy and Willie were, and I got even more petrified than I already had been.

"You ever heard the song, Henry Lee?" Muddy asked.

"Yes, sir, I sure have!" Muddy and Willie and Doc all grinned evil-like at me.

I wasn't going to give them the satisfaction of watching me fall apart. I'd never played the song with anybody, since I couldn't find anybody on the crew—lying bastards that they all were—that would admit to knowing about the blues, but I'd heard it on the Chief's phonograph enough to fake it. I hoped.

I looked up to the rim of the club and saw Sprocket. He winked at me.

That night I played the best I had ever played in my life. It was sheer desperation. I started out just trying to keep in tempo with the band, doing the simple five-note response that was required when Muddy finished his call, at the end of each measure.

They took it easy on me for awhile, I think. And the basic song itself ain't all that technically difficult.

Then they took off. Not that it got faster. Merely a whole lot *nastier*. Them fellas knew how to do it. And some of it vibrated its way into me somehow. I started bending and sliding my notes meaner, sneaking in a triplet run here and there, slurring my lead line against the dirty shuffle beat Doc and Willie and the drummer laid down, moving up to work the high part of the neck around the fifteenth fret, making that Fender music-monster scream and sing, slash and sting.

Long about the fifth verse, Doc started howling like a deranged wolf while he pounded out on the ivories a long, involved riff that I somehow managed to echo a fourth higher on my ax. Muddy whipped out a harmonica and jumped aboard. We got going, the three of us, challenging each other, twining and swirling blue, blue notes around and into the smoky air, while the rest of the band laid down the groove we careened through.

I got high enough to see the tops of the clouds in the sky above Aggie Station.

Forever later, when the last ringing note of the last song of the set died away, we stood for a minute and let the clapping and whistling wash over us. Muddy came over and hugged Doc and shook my hand. "Whoo, man, you two ain't bad for a couple of white boys," he said. "Not bad at all."

I gave him back his ax and floated down the steps of the stage. I waved to the folks at our table, and without breaking stride, headed straight to the stairway next to Sprocket. Suddenly, I felt like I was gonna explode, probably because that had been a couple of real bowel-clenched minutes up there until I had got into the groove. Not to mention the three pitchers of beer that a waitress had handed up during the set.

The restrooms were located on the surface in a small concrete building set a few yards behind and to the left of Sprocket's rear end. I made room for another pitcher while I read the wall literature. You can always tell whether a joint is any good by the quality of the writing. Jon-Tim's was a great joint.

When I came back out, about halfway back to my table, I almost stumbled over a leg that shot out in the aisle in front of me. A smiling Stevie Goolsby, seated alone at a table against the wall, was attached to the other end of the leg.

"Hey, Henry Lee. You were pretty hot on that guitar."

"Yeah, I was, wasn't I?" I said modestly. I sat down and blew out a big breath. "I was also on the edge of complete mental destruction for awhile, too."

He laughed and motioned a waitress over and ordered us a couple of beers. We talked for a minute about how great I had been, and were the dactyls all right. When the beers arrived, I picked mine up and invited him to sit in over at our table.

My chair was taken by a disgustingly handsome Joe College type guy who was talking real friendly at Star. She was smiling at whatever he was saying.

Beside me, Stevie muttered, "Uh-oh. I knew I was having too much fun for it to last."

"Beg pardon?" I said, looking around for an empty chair, not finding one right offhand.

"That guy, talking to the cutie with the long hair."

"Yeah?"

"He's the captain of the varsity football team.

Unbelievable pussy-hound. Obsessed. Gets more than any other four guys on campus. Fucks 'em and forgets 'em. A real nickel-plated asshole. Also the Stone Magnolia's favorite nephew."

The fella leaned forward and casually put his hand on Star's knee while he made some particularly important point. They both broke out laughing.

"Great. What's his name?"

"Billy Bob Dartmouth."

A couple of guys vacated the table next to us and I scooped up their chairs and wedged them in between Star and Billy Bob.

"Howdy, folks." I said. "Sorry about being gone so long, Star."

"That's all right, Henry Lee. I was just talking with—"

I stuck out my hand and he reflexively shook it. "Yes. You're Billy Bob Dartmouth. Captain of the football team. Heard *all* about you. My friend here, Professor Stevie Goolsby. I believe y'all know each other, Billy Bob. Stevie, this is Star—Star, this is Stevie." I grinned at him with every single tooth in my mouth, and squeezed on his hand a little less than I figured would take to crunch a couple of bones. He just smiled back. And squeezed back.

"Delighted to meet you, Henry Lee," he said. We both smiled and squeezed some more. "I was admiring your guitar playing earlier." He glanced down between us. "Must make for strong hands, staying in practice on that thing."

"Why, thank you, Billy Bob. You got a firm grip yourself."

"Appreciate you sayin' so, Henry Lee. I'm a quarterback. Lots of quarterbacks got delicate hands, but I never had that problem. Not even a little bit."

We both bore down a bit harder, our hands still pumping up and down a couple of inches.

"So. You been hanging out with the Herring, huh?" Billy Bob said.

"The Herring?"

He nodded at Stevie, who blushed furiously. "My biology lab professor there. Known as the Red Herring of Romance around the campus." He smiled maliciously. "Way he got the name is—"

Stevie was squirming in his chair, looking miserable. So I quit taking it easy on Billy Bob and gave his hand a medium strangulation.

Sweat broke out on his forehead and he went pale.

Star's hand overlaid both ours and stopped the up and down motion. "Looks like you boys ought to have introduced yourselves enough by now." I gave Billy Bob one last squeeze, along with my best lazy smile, then let go.

"Well, Star, it sure was a pleasure chatting with you," he said. He scraped back his chair and stood up. "I need to get back to the dorm. The team's workout starts at six in the morning. We got the big exhibition game against UT next weekend, and Coach is taking it serious."

"Maybe I'll see you on campus sometime soon."

"I'd like that a lot. 'Bye."

We watched him pick up a couple of friends from a table near the southside stairway and leave with them.

Star quit smiling and turned on me, furious. "Goddammit, Henry Lee, don't you ever—"

"Aww, Star. I was only—"

"I know what you was only! You ain't *about* to start choosing for me who I talk with. Or do anything else with, for that matter!"

"Okay! I'm sorry."

"Fine." She stood up. "I got a headache. I believe I'll go lay down in my room. See you tomorrow."

"Tomorrow!"

"Pleasure meeting you, Professor Goolsby." Some kind of invisible signal passed between her and Sabrina, snuggled up against Doc on the other side of the table. Sabrina unhooked herself from Doc, gave him a peck on the cheek, and followed Star away.

Doc saluted me with his beer bottle. "Way to go, slick. You have definitely got the magic touch." He took a sip and burped contentedly.

I woke up alone in my room the next morning to the smell of bacon and eggs frying on an open fire.

About the time I finished buttering my biscuit, Star came out of Lady Jane's mouth, marched over, and plomped down on the bench beside me. Doc and Sabrina and Razer made a big obnoxious deal out of quietly getting up and moving away so's to give us a little privacy, twitching their eyebrows and nudging and whispering at each other and making comments that I couldn't quite hear.

Star got her own breakfast, without saying a word, stealing a piece of bacon off my plate in the process. That encouraged me. Finally, I got up the nerve, just as I was using my last piece of biscuit to finish sopping up the egg yellow left on the plate.

"I'm just sorry as hell, Star," I said. I had figured that the smartest thing was unconditional surrender. "I was completely wrong. I won't never do it again. Even if I see you talkin' with Jack the Ripper, I'm gonna stay outta your business."

"Actually, it was kind of sweet of you, Henry Lee." She leaned over and kissed me on the cheek.

It seemed like a natural thing for me to turn over my plate then and start banging it against my forehead. Star didn't seem to mind. She patted my knee and kept on eating.

We rode Sprocket over to the Vet Building and parked him for more tests by Hillary and her assistants. Lady Jane followed into the slot next to him to get a general checkup. Both crews bailed out and headed a couple of blocks over to the administration building to register for the fall semester at P&A.

Doc had had me send off for a copy of my school transcript from Hemphill, but it hadn't arrived yet at P&A administration.

Star sat next to me and helped me fill out the application forms, of which there seemed to be a plenitude. Her own paperwork, and that of most of Sprocket's and Lady Jane's crews, consisted of one form, since they already had a record there. They merely needed to officially apply to continue their schooling, rather than having to start up completely new like me.

The forms generally made me feel stupid, since I couldn't answer half the questions. What was a SAT, anyway? And I didn't have a SS number that I knew of. I didn't even know what address I lived at.

We got to the section about educational background and began to fill in what I could remember without the transcript. I was embarrassed to let her see that I had only finished tenth grade, although I had thought it was pretty damn good at the time. When you work a farm, you take school when you can, and don't when you can't.

"Don't you worry about that, Henry Lee," Star said. "We're gonna enroll you in GED classes in the evening. You'll have your high school diploma in a couple of months."

"Hold it. How can I go to college before I got a high school degree?"

"Trust me."

"I don't want no special favors."

"Don't worry about it. This is all part of a deal P&A cut with the API. They ain't doin' you no favors. They just recognize that gypsies ain't exactly the normal type of college student. Half of us have bounced around the country all our lives." She looked at the clock on the wall and began to gather up the papers. "Let's finish this later. We can't really complete it until we get your transcript from the school in Hemphill. We need to get next door for our exams." Part of the application process included getting a clean bill of health from the school's clinic.

"What's your degree gonna be in, anyway?" I said when we were back out on the sidewalk. "You never have told me." I never even knew until a couple of days before that a *segundo* needed a degree. I figured it was all vocational training, and it turned out I was right for regular hands on the crew. But Doc had explained to me that I was going to have to learn everything from accounting to reservoir engineering to moderately advanced physics if I planned to keep my new job. I was beginning to wonder if I could hack it. I hadn't mentioned to anybody that the reason I never got past the tenth grade was I failed the eleventh. Papa said it looked like I had about reached as far as I should try. I was just as glad that the transcript hadn't arrived yet. I wouldn't have wanted Star to see about me failing.

"I was going for Chemical Engineering, like Sabrina's degree. It's a good one for somebody on a Casing Critter. But I'm thinking of switching to being a music major. She's been pushing me to pursue the violin more seriously. Wouldn't mind getting a Composition degree like Doc."

"Composition degree?"

"Sure. Didn't you know?"

"I'm beginning to believe that nobody ever tells me anything. I just seem to find out stuff accidentally."

"Well, he has a Doctorate in Classical Composition. Sabrina says he'll be on visiting faculty while we're here this year; teach a couple of small group seminars and participate as a student in a couple of others."

I felt my IQ drop a couple of more points.

At the front desk of the clinic, we handed over the papers that the admissions clerk had given us to authorize the physicals, and were asked to seat ourselves in the medium-crowded waiting room down the hall, which we did.

A few minutes after Star's name got called and she went off with a nurse through a swinging door, Stevie Goolsby stuck his head in through the entrance to the waiting room and looked around like he was trying to find somebody.

He spotted me, and waved and looked around some more before he wandered over in my direction.

He sat down next to me on the couch. "Going to get a going-over by the vets, huh?"

"Vets? You mean veterinarians, like Hillary?" He nodded. "They don't use vets in medical clinics. I ain't falling for that one."

"Students, actually. If you're in for a physical, you got a fifty-fifty chance of drawing a vet student."

"Naw! You're just messing with me."

"Uh-uh. People are just monkeys that got too proud to walk on their knuckles. The school trains vets to take care of humans in case of emergencies like floods and earthquakes and the occasional nuclear war. Interning in the clinic for a couple of months is part of the training. You'll know it's a vet student if he tries to strap you down and take your temperature rectally. Some of their habits die hard."

I must have looked alarmed. He smiled. "Just kidding, Henry Lee."

"I ain't a complete moron, actually," I said, though I wasn't sure anymore that was true. "It's just—I been running into so much new stuff at P&A that I don't know what to take serious yet."

"I've been here three years and I haven't gotten that entirely straight myself. I'll try not to kid you too much until you get your feet on the ground." He patted me on the head.

"Thanks a whole bunch," I said. I stuck out my hand. "Shake on it, buddy?"

He looked at my hand, then my face. Then back at my hand. "Uh—no thanks." We both grinned.

"So—how come you're hanging out in the clinic?" I asked.

"I'm a scientist. I'm looking for people to experiment on."

"Beg pardon?"

"No, not really experiment on. I'm participating in a government research project where I need to obtain a broad range of biological samples. Blood, hair, urine, feces, perspiration, that sort of thing. I pay twenty-five bucks per subject."

I sat up straighter in my chair. "Oh, really? What sort of subjects?" Being in a scientific experiment kind of appealed to me. Not to mention the twenty-five bucks that could go toward the purchase of a Stratocaster.

He shrugged. "I have a fair amount of latitude. The project is funded and controlled by the National Institutes of Health. They want samples from varied somatotypes in order to get a significant nationwide demographic cross section.

"Uh . . . okay."

"I personally like to put information into the ends of the bell curve, not the middle. I try to recruit real mutants."

If I had thought he was deliberately trying to fuddle me, I might have got mad, but it was obvious he honestly thought I understood him.

"Great!" I said. "Well, guess that let's me out, huh?"

"What makes you say that? A fella as large as you, you'd be perfect. Are you interested?"

"Huh. I guess—what's a mutant?"

Right then, Star came back through the swinging doors at the end of the room and Stevie and me both sat up straighter. The nurse behind the desk called my name out. Stevie gawked at Star as she glided toward us. "She is also definitely on the far end of the bell curve," he said out of the side of his mouth. "Mind if I recruit her?" He absentmindedly reached up and started toying with his earring.

Well, she had made it clear she didn't need no protection from strange men, and Stevie was about as strange as they got.

*   *   *

The fella that gave me my physical had a thermometer in his coat pocket that looked larger than I liked. I made sure not to get in too helpless a position during the proceedings.

When I came out, Star and Stevie were sitting on the couch chattering away like old friends.

"Well, great," Star said as I drew near. "Looks like we got plenty of time before afternoon rehearsals to get you into this research program of Stevie's."

"Uh . . . y'all been discussing the details of this deal while I was in there?"

Star nodded. "Oh, yes. Sounds like a great idea. For you, that is. I have regretfully declined, myself. C'mon, let's head on over to the Vet Building."

When we got there, we went through the front entrance straight on through to Hillary and her crew swarming over Sprocket. He ignored everybody while he watched the tee-vee, of course. I waved at Hillary, then went over and scratched above one of Sprocket's eyeballs until I got a reluctant groan of pleasure from him. I visited with him for a few minutes, then headed upstairs with Stevie and Star.

When Stevie unlocked his lab door and let us in, we found Billy Bob kicked back with his feet on Stevie's desk. He stood up. "Well, howdy, Star. You're looking wonderful today." He ignored me and turned toward Stevie. "We need to have a little chat, Professor."

Stevie sighed. "Whatever. I'm not even going to ask how you got in here. Excuse us, folks. Grab a seat for a minute." Him and Billy Bob went into his inner office and closed the door for only about a minute, before Stevie slammed it open again.

He looked angry. "You tell Coach Hanson that I

don't operate that way, and to forget the idea right now."

Billy Bob's nodded politely. "Thanks for your time, Professor." He turned toward the door. "Pleasure seeing you again, Star." Stevie was trembling.

"You all right?" I asked, after Billy Bob had vanished into the hallway.

"I'm fine," he said. "I'm just getting a little tired of Billy Bob and his aunt, that's all."

"His aunt? Is this coach his aunt?" Star asked.

That broke the tension for him. He laughed. "No, my boss is his aunt. You don't know her, but Henry Lee does. Coach Hanson isn't anybody's aunt. He's in charge of the football program here. Billy Bob told me that the coach thought he would be much too busy this semester playing football, so it was a good idea for me to hand him an A in the course he'll be taking from me. Without him ever really attending it."

"Maybe Billy Bob was trying to put one over on you without the coach knowing about it."

"That might be, but the coach is quite capable of coming up with that sort of suggestion himself."

"That don't sound right," I said.

"It isn't. But the jocks here are treated like they were the second coming. Football is big business at P&A. The professors get a lot of pressure from the athletic department and from administration to go easy on them academically. But this is the most outrageous demand I've heard yet." He snorted. "Didn't want to attend at all. What with having the coach and his aunt to cover for him, Billy Bob seems to have decided that he can get away with anything he wants to." He shook his head. "Well, never mind. Billy Bob and the coach probably can't do anything to me that the Magnolia isn't already contemplating. Let's get these samples taken care of."

He sent me to the bathroom down the hallway to make him some urine and stool samples into separate plastic cups. When I got back he had spread all his equipment on a marble countertop to take the rest of the samples with.

Star watched while he cut off a couple of pieces of my hair and carefully sealed them in a small plastic bag. Then he had me spit a half-a-dozen times into a plastic cup and sealed that one, too. He clipped my fingernails. He drew out a couple of tubes of blood from my left arm and put them in the refrigerator next to his desk.

"Oooh! Needles give me the crotchety willies!" Star said. But she didn't avert her eyes. Looked pretty interested in the whole process, matter of fact.

"Okay, skin off your shirt," he said. I tried to figure out what he needed next and couldn't think of nothing.

He had me raise my arm and used some teensy scissors, different from the ones he used on my hair and fingernails, to clip about half the hair in my left armpit.

He used a couple of Q-tips to rub out of my ears anything that might be in them. Then he stuck a couple more up my nose, which was kinda embarrassing. Didn't look like he got anything, but he sealed those in plastic bags, too.

Star asked him where she could find a drink of water and he referred her to the fountain out in the hall and down the left tee. Then he began to carefully scrape my forehead with a razorblade.

"Probably just as well she left for a second," he said. "You might consider the next bit to be private."

"Me and Star don't have too many secrets from each other," I said.

She came around the corner as I was trying to make it to the bathroom.

"Hey, Henry Lee, I thought he already had you do your business."

"Um, well, he needs some more samples," I said.

"What is it this time? He need some hairs from your—"

Then she spotted the teensy scissors and the two cups that I held in my hand.

She put her hand on my chest and urged me through the door behind me. It was a small, empty office with one wall covered by a huge picture of a waterfall dropping through the clouds into a pool, surrounded by heavy jungle.

Her hands had me unbuttoned before I knew what was what. She squatted in front of me. "Hand me that cup and them scissors. You shouldn't be using something sharp around such delicate machinery without help, anyways. Haven't you ever heard of the buddy system?"

She snipped away, cutting out a heart-shaped patch in the center. I didn't know that at the time, didn't discover it until the next day. All I knew is that she seemed to be taking her time and enjoying herself hugely in the process. I wasn't about to try and stop her. Them scissors *were* dangerous, after all.

That waterfall sure was grand.

"Am I supposed to fill up the second cup with hair, too?" she asked.

"No, ma'am. That's it for the hair."

She looked up at me and scratched her long fingernails along the area just above my bellybutton.

"Well, what's the other cup for?" Her voice had gotten sly.

"It's, uh . . . well, it's for . . ."

"Yes . . . ?" She reached around with her hands and started to scratch my cheeks.

"Dammit, you know what it's for!"

"Not me. Why won't you tell?" She looked about as innocent as a fox who owned her own chicken ranch.

"Well you just be that way!" I said. "What it is, I need to give a sample of my seed!"

"Oh, now I understand," she purred. She bent closer. "Well, I suppose I should help with that, too."

That was one hell of a waterfall in that picture on the wall.

When we brought the samples back, Stevie kept a straight face as he broke out another cup. "Well, looks like you've worked up a wonderful sweat. Good. I'd like a sample of that, too."

As he was handing me a questionnaire that he wanted me to fill out and get back to him in the next couple of days, the phone rang. It was the Stone Magnolia and she wanted him to meet her at her office ASAP to discuss her reaction to his proposed budget for the semester. We scooted while he pulled out some papers and started checking over which expenditures he could cut. He said she hadn't sounded like she planned to tell him that he hadn't asked for enough.

We went back to the camp and spent most of the

afternoon napping. The evening was devoted to rehearsing and getting to know some of the other folks in the camp. They weren't such a bad bunch. Everybody complimented us on how we handled the dirty dishes problem, even though they regretted the passing of what they considered a fun way to initiate newcomers to the camp.

About a dozen other bunches of gypsies had also entered the Grand Prix competition, and we listened to them practicing. Nobody didn't figure their rehearsals should be secret affairs. More like another excuse for partying. Star and me spent the evening and the night together, and things were like they had been before she started getting all moody and unpredictable.

The next morning, after breakfast, we piddled around for a while, cleaned out our rooms and cooperatively washed down the interiors and exteriors of Sprocket and Lady Jane and Big Red and Munchkin and her babies. One of the babies, named Thumper, took a half-hour to track down. We was getting worried before we finally found her in a field out behind the camp, playing a game with a bunch of other young'uns—human and otherwise—that looked like a cross between kick-the-can and aggravated assault.

It was another coolish, overcast day, so we set up around ten A.M. to rehearse some more. Doc wasn't entirely pleased with the sound he was getting out of us. Said we played the notes right, but not with enough feeling.

Stevie showed up around eleven-thirty. He wandered over during a break. We chatted for a while in the shade, and me and Star reintroduced him to Doc and Razer. Doc got us back in our chairs for more rehearsal on the second movement, which he said was supposed to sound a hell of a lot more melancholy than we could seem to manage.

Fifteen minutes into the session, Maureen and Sonny glided down from the low-hanging clouds and lit in front of Stevie, who was leaning on Sprocket as he watched us rehearse.

We'd spotted them flying southward high above the camp about an hour before sunset yesterday. I'd pointed them out and told the crew about them, but none of them had ever seen the dactyls up close before. Practice lurched to a halt while Stevie cussed them out for landing on flat ground.

He grabbed each one by the beak and pulled them close to make sure they were paying attention while he talked at them.

"You stupid chickens! I'm getting really tired of escorting you idiots around town! Now we gotta walk all the way back to the vet building and take the elevator to the roof. When are you going to learn? If there were still any saber-tooth tigers around you both would have been dactyl-burgers a long time ago."

"You think they understand you?" I asked.

"Of course not!" he said. "They're just a couple of stupid birds." He gave their beaks one final shake apiece before letting go of them. "But it makes me feel better for all the trouble they put me through."

They sidled up on each side of him and started rubbing against him, making pitiful clucking sounds. Their beaks dragged in the dirt all miserable-like.

Finally he sighed and put an arm around each one. "Why me? Why couldn't I have dogs? A pair of collies would be nice. I like collies."

He let everybody come up and stroke and scratch them, which seemed to improve their spirits considerably. The kids in the camp especially crowded around. After half-an-hour, Doc managed to get us back to practicing. Sprocket had slept through the whole foofaraw. I watched out of the corner of my eye while they climbed side-by-side up to Sprocket's top. One of his eyes twitched open for a second when they dug their claws into him and started scaling his body.

They perched like vultures on his head, rocking back and forth in tandem while we took it from the top on Doc's hour-long piece. Somehow we managed to get through it.

Doc tapped his baton against his kneecap and nodded. "It ain't the New York Philharmonic, but we're getting there. Ten-minute break. Then let's do it again."

I wandered off to the communal rest-room in the center of the camp.

When I got back I was treated to the sight of Sonny racing along Sprocket's length toward his nose. Maureen had hopped to the ground and stood there watching expectantly. Sonny came to the end of the runway and leaped into the air, flapping his wings frantically. For a second he actually went upward. Then he dropped like a rock. Right at our jungle of instruments and chairs and music stands. More than a dozen people stood in the crash zone, helplessly watching as he cannonballed toward them.

Sprocket's tongue shot out like an iron bar underneath him. Sonny fluttered wildly and managed to hook his claws around the tongue.

Sprocket yanked his tongue backward as hard as he could, simultaneously opening wide his drilling mouth. His tongue, with Sonny still attached, rocketed back inside him before it could hit ground. I was located at just the right angle to see Sprocket's tongue seat as far back as it could go. Sonny reflexively let go and bounced all the way down the hallway. Sprocket's mouth closed. So did his eyes. Far as he was concerned, the action was over and it was time to get back to his nap.

Maureen waddled agitatedly in front of him for a minute, then stuck her beak a few inches into where his nose would have been if he had one. He ignored her.

A few seconds later, his mouth opened again. His tongue was wrapped around Sonny's body. It deposited Sonny on the ground, dropping him fanny-first the last few inches. Then the tongue slid back inside and Sprocket's mouth closed again.

Sonny struggled to his feet and marched right into Sprocket's side. Me and Stevie held him for awhile until he got back to normal.

We practiced for the rest of the afternoon. Stevie stayed for dinner. The dactyls climbed back on top of Sprocket, who still didn't object. Matter of fact, during dinner, he began to hum contentedly while they scratched around his top, every now and then picking at him with their beaks.

I nudged Steve. He looked at them, puzzled, then nodded. "They're grooming him. They do that with each other all the time. It's instinctive."

"To do it with Drillers?"

"His hide is like theirs in some ways, leathery and tough. Maybe they figure he's a big, ugly dactyl."

"Ugly?" I said. "He's an extremely handsome critter! Now, on the other hand, they are the ugliest—"

"Now, Henry Lee," Star said. "Stevie is our guest."

"Um. Yeah. Sorry. I guess it's all in the eye of the beholder."

"I guess so," Stevie agreed. "I personally feel Sonny and Maureen are gorgeous birds."

"Takes all kinds," I muttered into my mashed potatoes.

The rest of the week was pleasant every which way. The weather stayed cool, with a short afternoon shower every day. Razer and Doc contributed to Stevie's research. They took Sabrina, and Razer's current honey with them, to help them with the donation requirements, which Stevie had told them more about than he had me.

"Forewarned is foreskinned," as Razer said. Doc and Sabrina and Razer's honey thought it was humorous.

The Grand Prix competition started on Wednesday night, and we all tried to attend most of the performances. They were held in the Rebecca Matthews Memorial Amphitheater on the east side of the campus. During the day we mostly hung around camp and rehearsed, since we were scheduled to perform Doc's composition for the judges on Saturday night. Doc said we was getting closer to what he heard in his head when he wrote the music.

Star was a bunch of fun to be around, happy and bouncy, and well—romantic as all get-out—to be entirely truthful about the matter.

Friday afternoon, she vanished from the camp for a couple of hours. Doc had given us the afternoon off so we could be rested up for the competition. We'd do a final run-through Saturday afternoon. I laid a towel up top on Sprocket and worked on my tan for awhile.

I was woken by a horde of kids playing Red Rover over by the tables that held the dinner dishes. Sometime while I slept I had got up the nerve to do what I had been avoiding all week.

I padded up Sprocket's length and climbed down into Razer's old room. He had been staying mostly aboard Munchkin, since him and Spivey had gotten together and I had been promoted to acting *segundo*. He'd moved some of his stuff aboard her, but had left most behind for the time being.

I looked around the mess that was his room and spotted his bookcase half-buried under a stack of dirty jumpsuits. Razer had not been famous for his housekeeping.

I thumbed through the books for almost an hour, getting more depressed and feeling stupider every minute. Symbolic logic. Differential calculus. Organic chemistry. Organizational structure theory. Transcendentals. Statistical Analysis. I couldn't understand a hundredth of the contents of the books. Hell, I couldn't pronounce the titles of most of them. No way I was going be able to learn this stuff.

Papa had been right. Tenth grade was about my speed. I'd always wondered a little if I was stupid, but on a farm it didn't matter much, long as you were smarter than the pigs. And it hadn't mattered on the crew while I was merely one of the hands. But I wasn't going to to make it as a *segundo*. I didn't have the brains. I'd reached too high, and now I was going to have to humiliate myself by asking Doc to let me go back to my old job.

Hey, that ain't too bad, I told myself. Being a hand on Sprocket's crew is a hell of a lot better than most other things. No, it wouldn't be too bad. I could handle it. I could handle being stupider than Doc and Razer and Sabrina. And Star.

As I was climbing back out of Razer's room to get

my towel, I looked up and made out Star's figure against the setting sun coming towards us. I slid down Sprocket's side and headed to her.

"Hi, babe," I said. "I missed you. Where you been?" I tried to hug her, but she wasn't cooperating.

"Can't I go anywhere by myself without getting the third degree?" she snapped.

"Well, sure, I just meant—"

But she had already stalked off. I stood there with my mouth open while she disappeared into Lady Jane.

Doc and Sabrina had set up a card table and a couple of folding chairs under a nearby tree, and were hunched over doing the bookkeeping for Sprocket and Lady Jane together.

Doc looked at me sympathetically.

"What'd I do?" I asked him. "All I said was I was happy to see her."

Doc's mouth twisted. "Yeah, that's what it sounded like to me."

"She's got a lot on her mind right now, Henry Lee," Sabrina said.

"Like what? If she's got a problem I'd do anything I could to help."

Sabrina didn't reply.

"Cute buncha kids, ain't they?" Doc said, nodding toward the mob playing Red Rover.

"Don't change the subject," I said. "If y'all know something—"

"All these kids around, you'd think you'd see more women that are with child. 'Course, with some women, it ain't all that visible. At least, not early on."

Sabrina punched him on the shoulder. "Goddammit, Doc, you promised."

I turned and headed toward Lady Jane's mouth. Behind me I heard them cranking up for a good one.

"Well, hell, the way she's been treatin' the boy, ain't hardly—"

"You just can't keep your big trap shut, can you?"

I scratched on her curtain and she came to it.

"I wish you'd have told me you was pregnant, Star," I said. So much for building up to things gradually.

She didn't even get mad, just leaned on her bedstead and pulled a cheroot out of the dresser drawer. "Sabrina told you. She didn't have any right to do that."

"Nope, she didn't do it. If her and you had your way, I'd still be stumblin' around in the dark, blaming myself, not knowin' how come half the time you act like I got hoof-and-mouth disease."

She looked at the cheroot and sucked on it for a minute, but didn't move to light it. "I only found out for sure today. Guess I oughta give these up for the time bein'," she said. "The doctor says—"

"Why didn't you tell me?"

"I ain't sure it's any of your business."

"Any of my business? It damn well is my business!"

Then I had a thought on how it might not be my business, after all.

"Is the baby maybe not mine? Is that what this whole deal is about? Well, I don't care whose it is; I'll still care about it like it was mine." Could be some other fella that got her in the family way, and she was gonna choose him? I didn't like that thought at all. "Whoever the other fella is, if there is one, he won't make a better papa than me," I said. "He won't care for y'all as good as me. I swear to God—"

"You're the daddy, Henry Lee," she said in a low voice. "That's one thing I know for sure."

To be honest, I was relieved to hear that. I wasn't lying when I said I would have loved it like my own, but this way would be easier and better. "Well, what is the problem, then? We get married and settle down."

"You never mentioned getting married before this, Henry Lee."

"Well—this changes things. It ain't just us we have to think about now. You're gonna need somebody to help take care of you and the baby."

She crumpled the cigar in her hand. "Don't you say that, don't you even think it! I ain't some empty-headed milk cow of a farm girl, lookin' to put a shotgun to some man's back. I wouldn't have a man that just wanted to marry me 'cause he thought he had to take care of me. I can take care of myself pretty damn well already!"

"Well, goddammit, that ain't why I said it! I personally would be extremely honored if you would marry me!" I shouted. I always was the romantic type.

She smiled and I smiled back, and it was okay for a half-a-second. Then she turned away. I sat on the bed and laid a hand on her leg. "Aw, come on, Star. We can work it out."

"That's the problem," she sobbed. "I don't know if I want to work it out."

"Huh?"

"I'm twenty-two years old, Henry Lee. I don't want to settle down and be somebody's wife. I don't want it a bit. We been seeing each other for almost two years, which is the longest in my life. I been getting with you like Sabrina is with Doc. That's fine for them—hell—they must be thirty-five or forty-years-old."

"But you're pregnant!"

"So? Maybe I won't stay that way." She popped the stump of the cheroot back in her mouth and sucked on it furiously.

It took me a few seconds to realize what she meant. "I can't believe you said that."

"It's my body, Henry Lee."

"This is our *baby* you're talking about!"

"No! It's a bunch of cells in my body that may become a baby in time."

"Do you really believe that?"

"Yes, I do." She looked at me levelly. "I had an abortion when I was seventeen, Henry Lee. It wasn't the best experience of my life, but it wasn't the worst, either. I survived it."

"But the baby didn't."

She turned white. "Oh damn, Henry Lee. That was a low one. I think you better leave now."

"No sir. If we're gonna stay together, you can't go killing our baby."

Then she was at me, crying and hitting me hard with balled fists. "Leave me alone, Henry Lee! Get out of here!" She shoved me into Lady Jane's corridor and against the far wall. "Get away from me!"

"Goddammit!" I roared. "I want to do the right thing for you and the baby! You can't do this!"

She backed away from me, every muscle in her body tense. "Fuck you! I never said you could run my life for me."

Then she disappeared into her room. Lady Jane wouldn't open the curtain again no matter how much I pounded on her.

* * *

The bleachers were empty, except for several couples smooching and hugging on the top row. A dozen people wandered around between the Driller and the mechanical rig, not doing much of anything. The mechanical rig was idle. I asked one of the guys over by the drilling floor, and he said they were having to replace a part before they could resume making hole. I sat on the bottom row of the bleachers and stared off at the horizon, listening to the Driller hum while he worked. I had brought my ax and the Pignose with me. I played quietly along with the Driller.

After a while, somebody sat down beside me and shoved a sack-covered bottle at me. I didn't even bother to see who it was, just tilted the bottle up and took a slug.

"Life sucks hard vacuum, sometime," Stevie said when I handed back the bottle.

"Yeah."

"You walk over here all the way from the camp?"

"Uh-huh."

"You in as rotten a mood as you look to be?"

"Yeah."

"Good. Me, too. How about we get so drunk we fall down and bark like dogs?"

"Sounds like a great idea to me."

We left Stevie's apartment, a block from campus, with a quart apiece. By the time we found ourselves on the roof of the Vet Building, each bottle was about half-empty. An optimist would have said they were half-full, but neither me nor Stevie were optimists at the time.

Stevie lurched over to the big chicken wire cage that the dactyls lived in. They rustled and ruffled their feathers and made clicking chuckles when they recognized him. Sonny hopped down from his perch and waddled over and stuck his beak through the mesh.

"These are my babies, Henry Lee," Stevie said mournfully. He reached in and scratched the back of Sonny's head. "I helped make 'em out of spare parts. Helped breathe life into 'em. They love me. Nobody else loves me, but they do."

"Aw, Stevie, they ain't the only ones love you." I was feeling pretty sorry for myself, because nobody loved me neither, so maybe I didn't sound real convincing.

"Yes, they are," Stevie said. "Only ones in the world."

"Aw, I bet . . . I bet your momma and poppa love you." I leaned against the wall and slowly slid down until I was sitting. I pulled the bottle up and took some more medicine.

"I'm a orphan," he said. "Left on a doorstep, like in a bad movie." He took some more medicine, too. "Even my momma and daddy didn't love me." He hiccupped sadly.

Maureen saw how upset he was, and came over and started licking his wrist with her purple tongue while he stroked Sonny.

"Nope, nobody but these stupid birds love me. An' I love 'em back. Done my best to take care of 'em." He put down his bottle and started stroking Maureen's ruff. Then he pulled back, picked up his bottle, and stumbled over to stand in front of me.

"You remember Billy Bob calling me the Herring?"

I nodded.

"That's me. The Red Herring of Romance. He noticed I never, ever had a girlfriend. No dates, no parties, no nothing. I'm so ugly and useless, no woman wants to come close to me."

"Awww . . ."

"I have been laid exactly twice in my life, and they were both pity-fucks. I used to take lessons all the time. Thought I could, you know, learn how to be attractive somehow. Dancing lessons, etiquette lessons. Bodybuilding lessons." He laughed. "Hell, I even took boxing lessons for a while. You know, the manly sport for manly men. Figured that might get me a girl or two. All I got was a broken nose. Still gives me trouble in bad weather."

He shook his head and staggered back to the cage. "To hell with it. I'm used to it all by now. I quit trying years ago."

"That why you're so depressed tonight?"

"Nope. Not exactly. I'm getting terminally drunk tonight because this afternoon the Magnolia figured out how to cut her losses with the dactyls." He opened the cage door and clucked at Maureen and Sonny until they waddled out to him.

He hooked an arm around Maureen's neck and hugged her. "See, they're a lot like me in one important way. They're failures, too. They're grown-up birds, look healthy, everything. Just like me. But they don't reproduce. Don't even try, as far as we can tell. They're a genetic dead end. Just like me. Ain't worth a fuck." He started to laugh again.

"Aw, Stevie," I said.

He got himself under control. "The Stone Magnolia's got me by the *huevos*, Henry Lee. We spent all sorts of money producing these dead-ends. Gene-grafting and cloning and all the stuff that goes with it is so horribly expensive you wouldn't believe it. She wants to see some results. Heck, I can understand that. I want to see some results, too."

He took another slug from the bottle. "She told me this afternoon, she wants to autopsy the birds to find out why they aren't reproducing. Then we can give the results to the rest of the other schools."

"Okay, so humor her," I said. I knew that an autopsy had been performed on Pegleg, but nobody had explained the exact procedure to me and I hadn't really thought about it that much. If anything, I thought it was merely a thorough examination, like the one I'd gotten at the clinic. And I sure didn't know it was only called an autopsy if the victim of it was already dead. I was being a dumb old country boy again. He looked shocked.

"What's the matter? This, uh, autopsy deal gonna hurt 'em?"

He started to laugh, collapsing against the cage. "Hurt them?" he choked out. "Hurt them?" Then he started to cry at the same time. Tears streaming into his scraggly beard, he turned and grabbed each bird by the neck. They could have torn him to bloody ribbons with their beaks and claws, but they only screeched and flapped uselessly while he dragged them to the edge of the roof.

I struggled to my feet, and lurched after him. Before I could get to him he'd pulled them to the very edge. He had to let go of Maureen while he shoved Sonny over the edge. She stood there and flapped in confusion until he grabbed her and sent her tumbling after Sonny. Stevie stood wavering and looking down over the edge. I was afraid he'd go over too, so I grabbed for him, but he slipped out of my hold and ran along the edge.

The dactyls both swooped in a sharp curve back to our level.

They looped and began to come in for a landing on the roof. Stevie picked up a double handful of gravel and threw it as hard as he could at them.

"Go away! Go away! Get out of here, dammit!" They banked away in alarm, then came back for another try.

I got a dozen yards from Stevie before he turned and threw a handful of gravel at me, too. A couple of fair-sized pieces hit me in the face. I flinched back and fell down in the process.

The dactyls had circled around and were trying to come in for a landing again. Stevie scooped up more gravel and flung it at them. "Get away!" he screamed. "Don't come back here! I don't want you any more!"

I got behind him while he was distracted and wrapped my arms around him. He struggled and twisted, knocking us both to the ground. He sobbed and hit at me while we rolled around on the roof.

"Goddammit, Stevie, just a minute, here!" I cocked a fist back. He was out of control. Didn't look like he was going to stop until I made him stop.

"Henry Lee, what they'll do in an autopsy—they'll kill the birds first. Then they'll cut them into little pieces and look at the pieces. Sonny and Maureen'll be dead and I'll be alone again."

We threw rocks for half-an-hour, until the birds banked into the darkness and disappeared, screeching mournfully. We waited another half-hour to make sure they didn't try to return.

By then, the bottles were both empty. Stevie said he had another one in the lab, so we fell down the stairs toward it. It was only one floor away, but it seemed like about ten. Neither one of us was navigating real well by that time.

After about five tries, he got his key into the door lock and we stumbled into the lab. He flicked on a light switch, and started rummaging through his desk drawers. I sat down in the doorway and leaned against the door frame to rest and get my strength back.

As he triumphantly pulled a fifth out of the lower left-hand drawer, I heard the elevator door opening at the end of the hall.

I leaned out of the doorway to check it out and slipped and hit my chin on the floor. Set the stars to whirling around.

A few seconds later, strong hands pulled me back up to a sitting position.

"Thank you very much," I said. "Very, very, very, very—"

"Poor fella. Looks likes he's really messed up."

"Yeah. Too drunk to even sit. Sad. Very sad."

I tried to focus on the speakers and finally succeeded.

It was Billy Bob and two other guys, each of them almost too big to fit through the doorway. All of them were in Kaydet uniforms, crew-cutted and ugly enough to make their mothers ashamed.

One of them marched over and picked up Stevie under one arm, neatly grabbing the bottle out of the air when Stevie lost his grip on it.

"Looks like the Herring is kinda out of control, too," Ugly Number One said.

Billy Bob bent over, put the heel of his hand on Stevie's forehead and pushed up until they were eyeball to eyeball.

"Hello. Anyone home?" Billy Bob asked pleasantly. He rapped on the side of Stevie's head.

"What you want?" Stevie returned.

"That C you gave me last semester looked bad. I want an A in your stupid course, little fart."

"Nope. Not 'less you earn it."

Billy Bob bounced Stevie's head up and down a couple of times. "I wasn't asking, little fart. I was telling. You give me an A or you'll wish you were never born."

Stevie chuckled weakly. "Too late. I *already* wish I was never born." He kept chuckling until Billy Bob started bouncing him some more.

I tried to stand up and Ugly Number Two absent-mindedly put a foot in my chest and shoved me onto my back. I grabbed the foot and tried to bite his ankle, but I didn't have the strength or coordination to pull it up to my mouth. He ignored me.

"I'm serious," Billy Bob was saying. "This is your extremely last chance to save your ass, Herring."

"Bite it, Billy Bob," Stevie said.

Billy Bob lifted Stevie's head once more and slapped his face, hard enough to send his glasses flying into the corner. Stevie yelped. His expression looked like he had been shocked sober instantly.

"I'm getting tired of asking you nice," Billy Bob said. He slapped Stevie on the other side of his face, snapping his head practically into his shoulder. I yelled and tried to sit up again, but Ugly Number Two shoved me back. "I can hit you all night," Billy Bob went on. "That what you want, Herring?"

Stevie's face crumpled and he wiggled frantically when Billy Bob raised his open hand again. Billy Bob watched while Stevie kept trying to squirm out of Ugly Number One's grip. Then he grabbed Stevie by the beard and brought his face close.

"You like this? You want me to keep it up? Or will you give me an A?"

Fresh tears dripped onto Billy Bob's hand. He raised his other hand.

"Don't," Stevie whispered. "Don't any more. I'll do it."

"You'll give me an A?"

"Yes."

"You know what happens if you change your mind or say anything about our fun tonight, don't you?" He slapped Stevie again, harder than the first two times. "That's what happens. Don't fuck me up, Herring."

Stevie upchucked on himself and Ugly Number One. Billy Bob backpedalled barely in time to keep from getting spewed on.

Cursing, Ugly Number One dropped Stevie on the floor.

Billy Bob's handsome face went ugly for the first time.

He kicked over the nearest table, sending glassware and other lab equipment crashing to the floor. Ugly Number One tossed Stevie on top of me, where he continued to heave spastically. The smell and the sounds of him made me feel awful nauseated, so I spent the next few minutes concentrating on not puking, myself. I hardly noticed the destruction that was going on around us.

Finally, Stevie and me both got ourselves back under control. We managed to stand up, supporting each other as we inched higher off the floor. God, he smelled awful.

Billy Bob had found a crowbar and was prying off the lock on the door of the refrigerator beside Stevie's desk.

"No! Don't do that!" Stevie shouted. Billy Bob

looked at him and grinned. The lock popped loose
and Billy Bob yanked the refrigerator open.

"Your big-time government research, Herring."

Stevie started to heave again and fell down.

"I got an idea, Herring," Billy Bob said. "You
aren't sure I really *deserve* an A, are you? Well, hell,
fella, I can mix up formulas with the best of 'em
when I set my mind to it. Watch!"

Billy Bob grabbed a half-gallon jug off the top of
the refrigerator, one of the few pieces of glass still
unbroken in the lab, and set it down on the desk. He
started grabbing test tubes out of the refrigerator and
emptying them into the bottle.

"Aha! Aha! Ze fiendish mad doctor in his lab,
going beyond ze boundaries of science!" he cackled.
"Ve vill create ze ultimate chemical and rule ze
vorld! Ha, ha, ha, ha!" His retardo buddies laughed
along with him.

He threw away about every fourth or fifth test
tube unopened, shattering it against the wall.

Stevie retched and moaned beside me.

When he had emptied the refrigerator of test tubes,
Billy Bob stoppered the jug and shook it vigorously.

He marched over and squatted beside Stevie. He
emptied the sludge in the bottle on top of him.
"Here you go, ol' buddy. Did I mix it up right?"

He straightened up. "I get an A in your course, or
we'll do this again, you understand?" He grabbed
Stevie by the hair and nodded his head up and down
for him. "Ah, you understand. Good. Sorry about
the mess. Shouldn't take you too long to clean up."

Ugly Number One kicked me in the belly before
he stepped over me on the way out.

Stevie didn't start to weep until we heard the
elevator doors close.

I didn't pay too much attention, because I'd finally lost my personal fight to keep my stomach full, when I got kicked.

We were still lying there all miserable when the campus cops arrived and arrested the hell out of us.

Doc bailed us out the next morning.

"Looks like you boys have about completely fucked up your lives," he told us on the front steps of the police station.

Bent over and feeble, we squinted up at him in the unbelievably bright morning light.

"Drunk and disorderly, disturbing the peace, creating a public nuisance, destruction of University property, assaulting a couple of police officers—"

"We didn't assault no police officers," I said softly, since I didn't yet seem able to speak louder than a whisper. "They assaulted us. 'Bout a half-a-dozen of 'em."

"Who's the judge gonna believe? The cops or a couple of drunk assholes? They threw the whole library at you two clowns."

"You mad at me or somethin', just say so, Doc."

He sighed. "Aw, crap. I was young and stupid once upon a time, too. C'mon, let's go have us a nice big breakfast. Some eggs and hash browns and pancakes, and maybe a juicy ol' steak."

He laughed when we both turned pale, stuck our hands over our mouths and started hiccupping.

"Well, maybe only some black coffee for you two big-time criminals." He took a couple of brand-new pairs of sunglasses out of a shirt pocket. "Here, I figured you'd need these. A good hangover'll make you blind as a hoot owl. Soon as you recuperate, we'll try to figure how we're gonna deal with this little setback."

It was after normal breakfast hours, so Doc volunteered to treat us our meals at the House of Pancakes near the campus.

What had happened, Doc said while we were walking, was that a couple of campus policemen had been making their rounds when they saw three Kaydets crossing the campus. One of them had vomit smeared all over his blouse, so they pulled over and asked a few questions. The Kaydets said that one of them had gone with his buddies to talk to his professor about a term paper he was thinking of getting an early start on, and they'd found the prof and a friend of his drunk and destroying the professor's laboratory. They tried to talk them into stopping, but the two drunks attacked them. The professor got sick on one of them, so they left.

"So, these Kaydets tried not to get you boys in trouble," Doc finished. "I talked to one of the cops and he says they practically had to drag the story out."

"Yeah," I said bitterly. "That was because they was making it up as they went along." Then me and Stevie took turns explaining what really happened the night before.

When we got to the House of Pancakes, the place was almost full, with students visiting each other freely between the booths. We were still waiting near the cash register before being shown to our booth, when the crowd shifted and gave me a clear sight of a face in the booth in the far corner.

It was Billy Bob. I nudged Stevie with my elbow.

"Look who we found," I said happily. "You want first crack at him?"

He glanced at Billy Bob, then looked at his feet. I nudged him again, but he wouldn't look up.

"No," he muttered. "I just want to forget about last night." It hadn't occurred to me that Stevie might actually be afraid of Billy Bob. I realized suddenly that life might be a lot harder in ways I'd never thought of, for a short, puny guy like him. After awhile somebody like him might just decide to quit fighting back, boxing lessons or no, because all it brought was more torment.

I had my problems, but that wasn't one of them. I knew just how to convince Billy Bob that the way him and his friends treated us last night was bad manners.

"Forget, hell!" I took a couple of steps toward Billy Bob's booth before Doc snagged my elbow.

"That's him, Doc! You remember. You saw him talking with Star at Jon-Tim's. He's one of the ones that done us dirty."

"Henry Lee, we're in the middle of the goddam House of Pancakes. You ain't been out of jail for a half-hour yet."

I reconsidered my plans for a second. "You're right. Okay, I won't bust up the place. How about if I merely set up an appointment with Mr. Dartmouth so we can talk later on? Someplace private. Like the parking lot out back of here, in two minutes." I took another step, and then the crowd opened up a bit more. Billy Bob wasn't alone in the booth. She was sitting with her back to the room and us, but I recognized her from seeing no more than her long dark hair.

Billy Bob looked up from saying something to her and winked at me.

I turned and ran out of the House of Pancakes. I jostled a couple of people who had been waiting in line behind us, but I hardly noticed. All I could think of was I had to get out of there before she turned around and saw me. If she saw me it would be more than I could handle.

Doc found me a minute or so later. I was sitting on the curb down the street, staring at the dust in the gutter. I felt like I had a golf ball stuck in my throat right beneath my Adam's apple. It wouldn't go down, no matter how hard I swallowed.

"I'm sorry as hell, Henry Lee," he said. "If I'd known they was in there—"

"Hey, it's all right. No problem. No problem." I swallowed again.

Stevie came up behind Doc. I couldn't stand the look of sympathy on his face, so I stared into the gutter some more. "We all went to Jon-Tim's for a while last night," Doc went on. "After the Grand Prix performances. Him and a friend of his come sniffing around. Must have been after their run-in with y'all. I guess he already knew you were in jail by then. Invited Star out dancin' to another club. I didn't know she spent the night."

"You saw them?" I said. "And you let him take her off like that? You didn't stop it?"

"Stop it? What was I supposed to do? Hog-tie her?"

I stood up. "You could have done something!"

"Dammit, she's a grown woman. I ain't her keeper."

"Fine. You're right." I started to cross the street, looking both ways for cars. "Thanks a bunch, buddy."

He called out behind me. "Hey, Henry Lee, where—"

"Just leave me alone for awhile, okay? I'll see y'all later on." I stumbled on the street divider, but recovered and kept walking.

I walked for hours. I kept wishing it would rain, but it didn't.

I fished a nickel out of my pocket and closed the door of the phone booth behind me. I'd written a letter home every couple of weeks and called every couple of months since Papa got the phone lines extended out to the farm.

I had to go through a lot of stuff with the operators, but he picked up at his end on the third ring.

"Papa?"

"Henry Lee? Damn, it's good to hear your voice. How you doing? When you coming to visit? You know we got a room set aside just for you in the new house."

"That's good. I was thinking of coming home for awhile, if I could."

"Are you all right, son? Is something the matter?"

"I'm not feelin' too well, Papa."

"Well, come on home. Your family'll take care of you. Let me send you some money. I can telegraph it this afternoon."

"No, I'm fine on the money part. I got some stuff to wrap up here, but I'll take a bus in a couple of days. Uh—you know Sprocket . . ."

"Sure as hell do. He's half of what you write home about."

"Well, he's—uh—he's hurt. It ain't for sure yet, but he might not be able to drill any more. Could we maybe pasture him if need be?"

"Hell, yes! Wasn't for him, we'd all prob'ly be livin' under a bridge someplace by now."

"I'm sorry, Papa."

"Hush. You just get here quick as you can. Bring that critter with you. Everything'll be fine."

I had a vague memory of having left my ax at Stevie's apartment the night before.

Stevie answered the door in his underwear after I banged on it for five minutes.

Neither one of us talked much. I found my ax and the Pignose behind his couch. He made me take a shower while he fixed coffee and a real late lunch for us both. Then he took a shower while I stared out the window, sipped coffee, and thought rotten thoughts.

When he got finished dressing and started on his third cup, he told me about his wonderful morning after we split up. He had been seriously eat on by the Stone Magnolia. She nearly exploded, he said, when he revealed that he had run off the dactyls. She let him know in her usual direct manner that as soon as she could put the paperwork through, he would no longer be employed at P&A, and after she made some phone calls, his prospects at any other school in the country would be as dim as she could possibly make them.

We cut past the football stadium on the way to the amphitheater. The parking lot was completely full of cars.

"I forgot," Stevie said. "The big exhibition game with the Longhorns is tonight. P&A's favored by ten points."

"What I needed to hear. We're screwed, but ol'

Billy Bob's gonna come out ahead all the way around, ain't he?"

"Yeah. I guess." Stevie stopped and pointed upward and over to the left.

"That's Rudder Tower over there, Henry Lee." About two hundred yards off I could see it outlined by the setting sun, a narrow stone spire with a bell enclosed in the top.

"Wow! Great!! C'mon, we're gonna be late."

Stevie just stood and stared at the tower.

"Sometimes I feel like that guy myself."

"What guy?"

"You haven't heard about Rudder Tower and Scott McCullar?"

I sighed. "Nope. I'm just a ignorant ol' country boy, remember?"

"Aw, heck, sometimes I forget. Anyway, a couple of years ago, a sophomore named Scott McCullar climbed up inside the tower one October morning. He was a Kaydet, as a matter of fact, just like our friend Billy Bob."

"Yeah?"

"Uh-huh. Well, Scott brought his Corps-issue M-16 carbine with him, as well as half-a-dozen boxes of ammo. He'd sighted in a sniperscope on the carbine."

I looked at the tower again. It offered a great view of practically the whole campus. I had a sick feeling I knew what was coming.

"He didn't—" I started.

"Uh-huh. He opened fire. Shot at everything that moved, for almost two hours, before the cops got to him."

"Oh, my God!" I breathed. "That's terrible, Stevie."

He nodded. "Yeah. Tragic. Could have been worse, though."

"Christ, how could it have been worse?"

"Well—he was an Aggie *and* a Kaydet. He missed everybody he shot at."

After a few seconds, I finally said, "How can you make jokes like that at a time like this? You're a very sick person, you know?"

I think he was still chuckling and wheezing too hard to hear me. Finally, he straightened up and looked at me soberly. "It's either laugh or cry, Henry Lee. Laugh or cry."

The Rebecca Matthews Memorial Amphitheater had been designed to look as natural as possible. From the low wooden stage, the grass covered ground sloped gently upward in an acoustically perfect curve for about a hundred yards. Dozens of oilfield critters circled the rim of the bowl. Most of them looked to be asleep. I spotted Sprocket and kept myself from going and stroking him for awhile.

The ground was covered with blankets and people and the crew was tuning up their instruments when we got there. Doc looked surprised when I marched up to the mixing board and plugged in. I got my sound levels checked out and my ax tuned and my fingers warmed up without having to look at Star more than a dozen times.

We began. Doc's was the last composition of the evening, and the last one of the whole competition. It was a compliment; the school knew Doc's work and figured we would turn in one of the better performances, so we got to provide the finale.

I guess I played okay in the first and second movements. I didn't blow any notes; mostly played rhythm anyways. But it wasn't your olympic-class guitar playing. Doc's composition was strong enough that it didn't matter, and the smooth work of the rest of the band covered my small part.

The last quarter of the second movement was a violin solo by Star. It was a slow, longing segment, but in the rehearsals it had never come across painful. She played it different this time; though she hit all the notes according to the score, they *hurt*. I never knew a violin could cry like that.

When she sat down, tears were on both our cheeks. She stared at her violin in her lap, wouldn't meet my eyes.

I almost missed the beat when the tempo speeded up. The final movement was a return to joy and good spirits. Out of the corner of my eye I saw shadowy motion on top of Sprocket. The white tube of his tongue slid out of his drilling mouth and strangely, snaked along the top toward his back. A minute later, it cracked forward like a whip. Sprocket hurled two dark balls high in the air. As they passed over the orchestra, leathery wings snapped open and they exploded upward into the night sky.

The balls were Sonny and Maureen! They had been hiding out with Sprocket. The audience gasped, and so did we, but we kept the music in time, although we were a little ragged for a measure. They looped high, then screamed over our heads again, side by side, both flapping in perfect unison with the tempo of the third movement.

I tried to figure where they could have been and immediately thought of Razer's empty room. They could have hid in there without anybody noticing. And Sprocket's trick with his tongue was ingenious, slingshotting them to airspeed velocity.

They swooped overhead again, still in tempo, and broke into song. I almost dropped out of my chair, and I wasn't the only one. The only sounds they'd uttered before were a series of unmusical, scratchy squawks. They must have listened carefully to our rehearsals earlier, not to mention being natural-born musical geniuses, because they accompanied and embellished on a thoroughly complicated classical score like it was a simple three-note repeat riff.

They owned voices like angels and they sang the ecstasy of heaven. Maureen was a high, clear operatic soprano with infinite breath. Sonny echoed her, occasionally running counterpoint in tenor saxophone, his voice never burred, but enriched by undertones one and two octaves lower than the melody line.

Together they made a music unheard on earth for millions of years. We all got caught up in it. Somehow our horns sounded brighter, our strings sweeter, the notes they produced crisper and more enmeshed; together creating a music Doc later said improved on the perfection that he heard inside his head when he wrote it.

Stevie slid down Sprocket's side a hundred yards away and made his way toward the stage. The dactyls stayed behind, preening and showing off their scraggly plumage to the admiring crowd that milled around Sprocket.

"It could go either way," Doc said beside me. "Either the jury disqualifies us entirely or they admit it was the damnedest performance they've ever seen and they hand us the Grand Prix." He took a gulp out of his champagne glass. "Either way, I'm glad it went down the way it did. I think us and the dactyls created a new kind of music tonight."

Star sat on the edge of the stage talking to some gypsies from one of the bands that played earlier and

I leaned against my amp and smiled emptily. I figured I'd probably best wait until tomorrow morning before I told Doc I was bailing out, and offering to pasture Sprocket in case he didn't get over his phobia.

Stevie's grin was wide and sincere enough to make him look halfway handsome. Him and a cute, bouncy-looking little blonde linked arms on the way to the stage and started chattering at each other.

Everybody in the place was feeling so great it was hard for me to hang onto being miserable. Somehow I managed to, though. I figured I'd seen about as much happy as I could stand for the time being, so I quietly unplugged and slipped away.

Jon-Tim's was almost empty, and the band was on break. I ordered me two beers at the same time and disposed of the first one in a gulp.

Jon-Tim jumped up on the stage and spoke into the microphone. "Thought I'd let y'all know. A friend in the press box just called me. Final score: Aggies 42, Tea-sippers 17. We kicked ass!" Everybody in the room started banging on their tables.

"Yayyy!"

"Gig 'em Aggies!"

"UT sucks!"

Billy Bob had it all now.

I was slumped back in my chair with my eyes closed when somebody tapped on my shoulder. It was Muddy, with Willie smiling beside him.

"Hey, Henry Lee. We're 'bout to go back on. How about sitting in?"

I took a sip of my beer. "Aw . . . thanks, but I ain't in the best mood of my life. I'd hate to bring you guys down."

"He say he got the blues," Willie whispered in

Muddy's ear, like I had spoke a foreign language and he was translating.

"Well, well, well," Muddy said. "You know the best thing to do when you got the blues?"

I thought about what the Chief said to me the first night he taught me about the blues. I smiled feebly. "Yeah, I guess."

"Come on. We'll play slow."

It hurt, but it was somehow sweet, too. For a half-a-dozen songs, I poured it out through the strings of Muddy's black Strat. Like Star had done through her violin, I guess. Toward the end of the set, we did a slow, grinding version of "You Can't Lose What You Never Had." That sure said it all for me. The band laid back and gave me plenty of time to stretch out on a solo. I got lost in it for awhile, maybe five or ten minutes, playing with my eyes closed, half-turned toward the back of the stage.

When I came back from wherever I had gone, I realized that Jon-Tim's had practically filled up, and everybody in the place was on their feet whistling and clapping.

Then I noticed that Star was half down the stairway at the far end of the room, and she was clapping, too. Stevie and the blonde I had seen him with at the amphitheater were a few steps down from her. Matter of fact, the entire crews of Sprocket, Big Red, and Lady Jane were scattered around the area. Doc and Sabrina stepped out of Sprocket's mouth at the head of the stairs. Doc was carrying the biggest gold trophy I ever saw. He looked at me and held it up, smiling.

Stevie was still grinning as hugely as he had been when last I saw him. He headed across the floor

toward me. Then his face went all grim and he
detached himself from the blonde. Billy Bob and
Ugly Number One, the one who had kicked me in the
stomach, had stepped in front of them.

I looked around the room some more. Half of the
new people in Jon-Tim's, maybe forty or fifty husky
boys, had the skinhead haircuts of Kaydets. About a
dozen of the others still had their helmets on. The
Aggie football team had come to celebrate their vic-
tory. You could tell they was in a serious partying
mood because they started breaking furniture and
throwing beer mugs as soon as the song finished.
Muddy and the band was in for a long night. I
decided I'd get the ball rolling myself.

I carefully unstrapped Muddy's ax and handed it
to him. "Thanks, Muddy. If the band knows any
fight songs, now would be a good time." I felt like I
was floating on the wind toward Billy Bob and Stevie,
my feet barely touching the floor. Both my hands
balled into fists. I realized I was about to do something I would muchly regret, and I didn't give a
damn. I might as well go out with a bang.

Billy Bob said something to the blonde, then raised
his hand, like he had the night before when he
slapped Stevie. Stevie flinched back. The blonde
grabbed Billy Bob's arm and said something to him.
She looked mad. Billy Bob patted Stevie softly on
the cheek, then turned away and said something to
Ugly Number One. They both laughed. Stevie
grabbed Billy Bob by the elbow and spun him around.

They stared at each other; then Billy Bob smiled
mockingly and grabbed Stevie's shirt front. The little
blonde said something again, looking even madder,
but Billy Bob ignored her. I was less than half-a-
dozen steps away by then, still gaining speed. None

of them had seen me. I was going to give ol' Billy
Bob a *big* surprise.

Stevie pulled free, tearing his shirt in the process,
drew a knobby fist back, and threw a punch that
knocked Billy Bob onto his back on the table behind
him.

For a second, the whole place went so quiet that
you could hear the tinkle as bouncing pieces of shattered beer mugs impacted on the floor. Billy Bob
shook his head, tried to sit up, and fell off the table.

Then all hell broke loose.

Athletic growls erupted from the throats of all the
Kaydets. They surged toward Stevie. I threw a body
block on about three of them at once. When I climbed
to my feet, Stevie had leaped at Billy Bob, who'd
managed to stand up. Stevie climbed Billy Bob like a
tree. I lurched over and cannonballed into Ugly Number One, going back to the floor with him. We rolled
over and over, pummelling each other wildly. I didn't
feel no pain at all. I barely noticed when I was torn
away from him by the crowd that swirled around us.

It quickly sorted out to being the gypsies, who
were pumped up from winning the Grand Prix, against
the football team, who were pumped up from winning the big game. Nobody was on the sidelines of
this game. Most of the football team had brought
dates, and them and the casing gypsies went at it, too.

The band struck up a tune with a heavy, jumpy
beat. I snorted when I recognized it. It was called
"I'm Ready." A couple of the lines go:

I'm drinkin' TNT, I'm smokin' dynamite,
I hope some schoolboy starts a fight.
Because I'm ready, ready as anybody can be.
I am ready for you, I hope you're ready for me.

The blues ain't nothing but the truth.

A few minutes into it, while I was putting the hurt to some football hero with more muscles than coordination, I glanced over to see Stevie shuffling around in a professional boxer's stance like you would see on the Gillette Saturday Night Boxing on tee-vee. Then he waded into Billy Bob again, hitting him fast enough to blur, fists alternating like pistons. Billy Bob tried to push him away and Stevie joyfully grabbed his wrist and invented some kind of judo throw that landed Billy Bob on his head. Stevie ducked as two full whiskey bottles flew through the air and crashed into the wall next to him.

About then, I realized he had pretty much gotten even with Billy Bob for both of us. The gypsy crews seemed to be holding their own against the football team. Everybody was generally having a great time blowing off steam.

The fun went out of it all of a sudden. I wasn't part of all this any more. I'd be just a fading memory to all these people by tomorrow night.

The hell with it.

I was near a stairway, so I slogged up to the top and circled the rim until I got to Sprocket. Sonny and Maureen was perched on his forehead, rocking back and forth and being entertained by the postgame, postconcert celebration. I patted him on the nose and turned for one last look below before going inside and starting to pack. Sprocket's tongue surprised me by snaking between my legs from behind, then humping up to lift me higher.

Before I could climb down, high-pressure water jetted from the ragged orifice at the end of Sprocket's tongue. It knocked down dozens of people in the pit. Sprocket chuckled and hummed to himself. The

birds cackled and ruffled their wings, enjoying themselves hugely.

I figured enough drenching might stop the fight,
which would be good for Star, so I didn't discourage
Sprocket having his fun. Stupidly, I had been worrying about her fighting in her delicate condition. But
that was none of my business either, anymore.

The jet trickled to a stop after only a few seconds.
"What's the matter, boy? Keep it up." I looked
back as Sprocket started to mutter unhappily. His
water bladder must have been almost empty when
he started, and he had run it dry.

I spotted Star and Sabrina on the far side of Jon-
Tim's, right past the bar. They had laid on their sides
four of the long tables that would normally seat a
group of eight or ten people and wedged them all
together to form a barricade in the corner. Behind it,
they sat on the floor, backs against the wall, and
chatted casually as if nothing was going on. They had
both apparently decided to sit out the festivities this
time around. Good for them. I felt relieved, not
having to worry about Star.

As I watched, a couple of Aggie girls tried to move
the tables to get to them, but the tables were heavy,
and Star and Sabrina had interlocked some chair legs
with the table legs to hold them all together. The
Aggie girls smashed half-a-dozen of their own chairs
to kindling before giving up and getting involved
otherwise in the whirling riot. All they had done was
make the barricade more bulky. Three or four bottles of liquor smashed against the barricade, but they
didn't get through, either.

I lost interest. Time to go start packing. In the
morning, I'd sell my shares in the Sprocket Limited

Partnership, find me a bus headed in the right direction, and get the hell out of Dodge.

I tried to climb down again, but Sprocket's tongue dipped and carried me to the small brick building a few yards away. The door in front of me said GENTLEMEN. None of those here right now. Sprocket's tongue-tip nudged a six-inch stainless steel elbow coming out of the ground and going through the wall into the bathroom.

He nudged it again and I got the idea.

"Yeah, there's water in there, but we can't get to it."

He hummed uncertainly. The elbow ended in big flanges mated to the rest of the pipe by one-inch hexhead nuts and bolts. They looked new enough to not be rusted together, so I probably could find me a crescent wrench or a socket and open them if I really wanted to.

"Nope, buddy. Forget it. I'm retirin'. Besides, way my luck is running, I'd likely get busted for vandalism or something. You and the birds just take it easy and watch the rest of the fight. Meantime, how about opening up and letting me in?"

I petted him sadly for a few seconds, while the birds loomed over me. If Sprocket got well, I'd probably never see him again after tomorrow. If he didn't, it would be good to have him pastured with us, but it couldn't ever be the way it was. Both of us would be broken.

I was inside his mouth and it was closing, when the screaming started. Mind, there had been a fair amount of noise, including high-pitched shrieks, all along. But this was different. A lot of people were panicking. I stepped back outside and looked in the pit.

The far third of the room was a wall of fire.

God knows how it started. A lot of flammable spirits had been liberated from their bottles and splashed all over the place, on the wooden furniture and the wooden panelling, not to mention soaking into the sawdust that was inches thick on the floor in places. Before the fight started, every table had on it a candle in a red glass vase. All it would take is one of those to shatter in a pool of whiskey.

But it had gotten out of control with unbelievable quickness.

People fought to get to the foot of the stairs leading to the surface. So many shoved, or slipped and fell, that they were completely jammed up. The college boys struggled to get to their dates. Half-a-dozen gypsies, among them Doc and Razer, had taken off their jackets and were futilely trying to slap out the flames with them.

My heart lurched when I realized why. Most of the people on the floor of Jon-Tim's place had stairways that they could get up. The fire was scaring them, but it was obvious they were going to escape.

But Star and Sabrina were trapped with no stairway, and the flames feeding on their barricade leaped higher than any others.

I could barely make out their shapes as the smoke grew thicker. They had moved back against the wall.

Stevie dragged a table forward. Him and Razer and Doc ran through fire and tried to use the table as a battering ram, but the other tables were wedged together too solidly. After a few seconds they were driven back by the heat. Stevie dropped to the floor and rolled until he killed the fire in his clothes.

I stood there like a fool. But Sprocket knew what

to do. We held fire control drills at least once a month on location.

His tongue slapped around the six-inch elbow. He grunted and the pipe snapped with a sound like an arm bone fracturing. The elbow came loose, with almost a dozen feet of pipe pulling free of the ground. He had broken it off down at the buried main. Water sluggishly welled up from the ground.

"All right! Get that water, Sprocket!" He stuck his tongue-tip a few inches into the hole and started to suck.

In a few seconds I knew that he wasn't getting a tenth of the water he needed. There wasn't enough pressure to feed it to him at a high rate, and most of it was migrating into the surrounding earth even before it got to the surface.

Jon-Tim's place would burn down before he was refilled.

There was only one thing to do, and I was afraid it wouldn't work. But I had to try, anyway. I gripped his tongue and pulled it out of the hole. Sprocket blurted in surprise, but I just stood there for a few seconds holding it loosely in my hands. I stroked it as soothingly as I could, then I carried it back to the hole and started feeding it in.

"You've got to go down to the main, buddy. That's the only way to fill up quick enough."

When he realized what I was doing, he jerked his tongue out of my hands and vanished it inside. He shuffled back a couple of yards, his eyeballs vibrating in panic.

I lost control. I banged on him, but he wouldn't open up, so I clawed my way to his top. All the sphincters up there were shut tight, too. From his back I could see the continuing madness in the pit.

The stairs were still jammed. Doc and Razer and Stevie were standing on one side of a wall of flames, trying to edge closer, with no luck. Star and Sabrina were trying to climb the walls, but there was nothing for them to hold onto. The walls had caught fire, and the flames were coming at them in a pincer movement.

I slid back down, halfway insane with fear for Star.

I pounded on him some more. "You asshole, don't do this! You can't give up! You can't be afraid! You gotta keep trying, no matter what! You can't—"

Then the last few days flashed through my head and I slid to my knees against him. "You can't give up," I whispered. "Like I did."

Star and Sabrina screamed. We'd run out of time.

I got up off my knees. I was crazy by then. I figured it was too late to save them, so I was going to go around the rim to where they were and I was going to jump in with them. I couldn't bear for Star and my baby to burn without me there.

Sprocket's eyes popped wide open as we watched the fire close around them.

He moaned. His mouth opened and his tongue whipped into the bubbling hole. He ran it in for dozens of feet, until it was easily into the buried main. Then it began to pulse at a high rate as he sucked the water up.

In only seconds, the ragged tip whipped back out again and he stepped to the edge of the rim. I grabbed his tongue and aimed it like a hose. He opened up on the fire and we deluged the barricade, knocking it apart, saturating the flaming walls until they didn't even steam anymore. Behind us, the dactyls sang their approval in thirds harmony.

Finally, he sprayed empty. I patted his tongue-tip

and turned to him. "Thanks, buddy. You got more guts than me. You're gonna be all right."

Star looked up at me from her corner. She was dripping wet, her long black hair tangled and plastered to her body. She walked across the floor to the stairway. She climbed it and was in my arms a minute later.

Sprocket dimmed his warts as soon as we were in my room.

"Star, we need to talk about—"

She put a finger to my lips. "Sssshhh. Not now. We already talked too much for our own good."

The lights went out.

She was still wet, but warm to the touch.

I woke up with sunlight streaming through the hole in the ceiling. Star was nibbling at my eyebrows. My whole body was one mild but bone-deep ache. I felt more relaxed and at peace than since I was a small child.

"I been thinking things over," I said. "On this deal with the baby . . ."

"Uh-huh," she murmured while she licked my nose.

"Well, I figured. Comes right down to it, I can't stop you doing whatever you want, anyway. And it *is* your own personal body, even though you've been generous enough to share the use of it on occasion. So . . . I wish you'd keep the baby and let's us get married, but—"

She bit my left earlobe. "I decided last night to go ahead and keep the baby, Henry Lee. Might as well keep you, too."

"Really?"

"Uh-huh."

"Well. That's . . . that's real nice."

"I was hoping you was still in favor of it. I been somewhat of a bitch lately."

"I wouldn't say that."

"I know. You're too sweet to. One of the reasons I love you so much."

"You never said you loved me."

"You, neither."

"Well, I do," I said. "Now about school, we got a problem here—"

"Later," she said. "Do that some more. It feels good."

About an hour further on, we managed to struggle out of bed. While we were dressing, I brought up the problem of school again.

When I admitted about failing eleventh grade, Star started laughing. "Is that what was worrying you? You just didn't have the right motivation. Believe me, if I can handle college, you can handle college."

I nodded, but she must have saw that I didn't believe her.

"Listen to me. I know lots of people dumber than both of us together that do fine in college."

"I took a peek at Razer's books," I said. I recounted the titles and subjects as much as I could remember. Before I finished, she was laughing again. "Those were *senior* texts, Henry Lee. You'll have, and need, three solid years of preparation before they throw them at you. If ever. Razer's hobby is mathematics. He don't talk about it much because it might ruin his image. Half of those books are completely unnecessary for a degree."

I must have still looked doubtful. She put her hand on mine and got serious. "Look, you said you were gonna try."

"I am."

"Then trust me. I know for a fact, from the way you picked up on oilpatch stuff and musical knowledge, that you can handle college. Try a semester and you'll see. I'm not saying it'll be easy, but we'll get you through. You ain't alone here, you know. Lots of people will be glad to help you with it. Me included."

As we passed by Razer's old room, I thought to check if the dactyls were still hanging out with us. When I tried to pull the flesh curtain aside, Sprocket resisted. Then I heard voices inside and called out, "Hey, who all's in there? Razer?"

"Henry Lee! Come on in!" Sprocket opened up the curtain then. First thing I saw was what looked like a burst bale of hay in one corner, with Maureen and Sonny squatted on it.

Second thing I saw was Stevie and the bouncy blonde he'd been with last night, lying in the tangled sheets of Razer's bed. The lady was a tad slow pulling the sheet up to her chin. There wasn't any doubt left that she was a mammal.

Stevie looked as much at peace with himself and the world as I had felt on waking. Matter of fact, all four of us radiated good will and cheer and lots of energy. Normally, people that are all happy and alert in the morning give me an urge to mumble and snap, but this time it was okay.

"Hi, guys!" Stevie said enthusiastically. "How you feeling this morning?"

"Just fine, Stevie," Star said.

"Us, too," Stevie said. "Oh—I didn't mean to be so rude. Henry Lee, Star, this is Doctor René Dartmouth."

"But y'all can call me the Stone Magnolia," she said. She extended a hand, barely remembering in time to hold the sheet in place with the other hand. "It is shoahly a pleasuah to make yoah acquaintance."

My eyebrows must have shot up into my cowlick.

Stevie squirmed. "Billy Bob is such a snitch," he said.

"Thought you two was mortal enemies," Star said behind me.

"Foah a while we were unable to fully appreciate each other's bettah qualities," the Magnolia said. "I believe we'll be working togethah more closely from now on."

"Ain't you mad about Stevie punchin' Billy Bob's ticket last night?"

She beamed at Stevie. "Not a bit. Mah nephew has needed somebody to straighten out his britches foah several yeahs. Billy Bob was a well-mannered boy until he got heah and began to associate with all those fullbacks and tight ends and such. He was most apologetic late last night. Ah believe Stevie reminded him that humility is a virtue."

Star and I had missed that part, being otherwise engaged.

Maureen and Sonny nodded together where they perched on the hay, as if they had understood her words.

I pointed a thumb at them. "This mean the autopsies are cancelled? You get to keep your job?"

They both nodded. "Go take a closer look at Maureen," Stevie said.

I stepped closer to her. "Looks fine to me."

"Poke her with a finger."

"She won't bite?"

"Don't poke too hard."

I goosed her tentatively. She hissed and stood up, spreading her wings a few feet, then settled back down. Not before I had seen what her abdomen covered. Two mottled brown eggs the size of canta-loupes.

"Well, I'll be! Us humans ain't the only ones been fooling around!"

"First two eggs in what we hope is a series," Stevie said.

Sonny picked up and waddled toward the ladder bolted into Sprocket's flesh that led through the hole in the ceiling.

Stevie leaned back and clasped his hands behind his head. "This is a huge breakthrough. I suspect they simply won't breed in captivity. I set them loose, and in the wild they immediately began to reproduce."

I looked around Razer's room. "Yeah, considering who used to live here, this is definitely in the wild."

Sonny vanished out the hole onto Sprocket's back. We listened, and a few seconds later we heard the supersonic whip-crack of another launch.

We climbed out the hole ourselves a few minutes later, joined by Stevie and the Magnolia after they got dressed. Sometimes during the night or early morning, Sprocket had trundled us back to the camp. Half a dozen of the crew, looking remarkably chip-per, circled a fire and sipped coffee and compared bruises.

A line of kids had assembled on the edge of the clearing in front of Sprocket and Munchkin. The kid at the head of the line, a redheaded girl about nine years old, marched into the center of the clearing and stretched her arms out from her sides. She looked up into the sky and whistled.

A dark speck dropped out of the blue, magnifying rapidly until it became Sonny. He swooped on the girl, grabbing her upper arms in his claws. We heard one delighted shriek from her before they skimmed over the camp out of sight. Then they climbed upward, Sonny's leathery wings beating effortlessly. The line of kids giggled and pointed at them. The kid newly at the head of the line fidgeted and took a few steps forward. He could hardly wait for his turn.

"Stupid birds!" Stevie said affectionately beside me.

Afterwards

It was an outdoors wedding, of course, since gypsies lead outdoors kinds of lives. The bride did not wear white. That would have been pushing things too far.

The actual wedding was small, less than fifty people, held in the garden behind the chapel at the university, but the reception afterwards was an entirely different matter.

Me and Stevie stood on Sprocket's head, carefully nursing glasses of champagne, watching the crowd swirl around the center of the camp. Sprocket danced in place and hummed along with the band. His tongue twisted out of sight through the crowd. The tip was inserted through one of the dozens of valves leading from a full oil tanker parked near the entrance to the camp. It had been provided strictly for the Drillers at the party.

All the men, including me and Stevie, had got all duded up in tuxes. The women all had on their best cocktail dresses. Stevie wore a flashy new gold and

273

diamond earring. Seemed like about three thousand people were in attendance. The sun balanced on the treetops and the reception was in the process of degenerating into the kind of party that you tell your grandkids about.

"Well, congratulations," Stevie said.

"Thanks." I scanned the crowd, looking for Star. She had been so busy dancing with other fellas that I hadn't seen her for about an hour.

"What you going to call the baby?"

"We haven't really settled it. I like Lewis Daniel if it's a boy. Star favors Rachael Victoria for a girl."

About that time, Star broke through the wall of people and walked toward us. She stepped on Sprocket's tongue and maintained her balance by holding a hand against his side. He hunched the tongue upward until she could easily step onto his back. It was a new trick he had picked up from another Driller in the camp a couple of days before. She kissed Stevie on the cheek.

"You certainly look splendorous today," she said.

He blushed. "Aww, well . . ."

"How you and your sweetie doing lately?"

"Better and better." He nodded toward the Stone Magnolia, who was dancing with Wiley the Wildman Throckmorton over by the barbecue pits. He shook his head. "I still have trouble believing she likes me."

"Takes all kinds," I said.

"Eye of the beholder," Star said, patting my rump.

"I guess so." He sipped the last of the champagne in his glass. "Enough about me. What about you two? When are you going to get married?"

Star and me exchanged glances. "Don't get us started on that," I said.

"Just 'cause Doc and Sabrina tied the knot today don't mean everybody in town has to," Star said.

"The baby's going to need a daddy," Stevie said.

"The baby's got one," I said. "And a momma who thinks she's still sixteen years old." I wrapped an arm around her shoulders and she hugged me around the waist in return. "What the hell. Who knows, maybe by the time we're both forty or so, with about five kids, we'll decide to settle down and be a boring old married couple."

The song ended, and the Magnolia beckoned toward Stevie to join her for the next dance. We started in that direction with him.

"In the meantime," Star said, "let's party!"

An excerpt from MAN-KZIN WARS II, created by *Larry Niven:*

The Children's Hour

Chuut-Riit always enjoyed visiting the quarters of his male offspring.

"What will it be this time?" he wondered, as he passed the outer guards.

The household troopers drew claws before their eyes in salute, faceless in impact-armor and goggled helmets, the beam-rifles ready in their hands. He paced past the surveillance cameras, the detector pods, the death-casters and the mines; then past the inner guards at their consoles, humans raised in the household under the supervision of his personal retainers.

The retainers were males grown old in the Riit family's service. There had always been those willing to exchange the uncertain rewards of competition for a secure place, maintenance, and the odd female. Ordinary kzin were not to be trusted in so sensitive a position, of course, but these were families which had served the Riit clan for generation after generation. There was a natural culling effect; those too ambitious left for the Patriarchy's military and the slim chance of advancement, those too timid were not given opportunity to breed.

Perhaps a pity that such cannot be used outside the household, Chuut-Riit thought. Competition for rank was far too intense and personal for that, of course.

He walked past the modern sections, and into an area that was pure Old Kzin; maze-walls of reddish sandstone with twisted spines of wrought-iron on their tops, the tips glistening razor-edged. Fortress-architecture from a world older than this, more massive, colder and drier; from a planet harsh enough that a plains carnivore had changed its ways, put to different use an upright posture designed to place its head above savanna grass, grasping paws evolved to climb rock. Here the modern features were reclusive, hidden in wall and buttress. The door was a hammered slab graven with the faces of night-hunting beasts, between towers five times the height of a kzin. The air smelled of wet rock and the raked sand of the gardens.

Chuut-Riit put his hand on the black metal of the outer portal, stopped. His ears pivoted, and he blinked; out of the corner of his eye he saw a pair of tufted eyebrows glancing through the thick twisted metal on the rim of the ten-meter battlement. *Why, the little sthondats,* he thought affectionately. *They managed to put it together out of reach of the holo pickups.*

The adult put his hand to the door again, keying the locking sequence, then bounded backward four times his own length from a standing start. Even under the lighter gravity of Wunderland, it was a creditable feat. And necessary, for the massive panels rang and toppled as the rope-swung boulder slammed forward. The children had hung two cables from either tower, with the rock at the point of the V and a third rope to draw it back. As the doors bounced wide he saw the blade they had driven into the apex of the egg-shaped granite rock, long and barbed and polished to a wicked point.

Kittens, he thought. *Always going for the dramatic.* If that thing had struck him, or the doors under its impetus had, there would have been no need of a blade. *Watching too many historical adventure holos.* "Errorowwww!" he shrieked in mock-rage, bounding through the shattered portal and into the interior court, halting atop the kzin-high boulder. A round dozen of his older sons were grouped behind the rock, standing in a defensive clump and glaring at him; the crackly scent of their excitement and fear made the fur bristle along his spine. He glared until they dropped their eyes, continued it until they went down on their stomachs, rubbed their chins along the ground and then rolled over for a symbolic exposure of the stomach.

"Congratulations," he said. "That was the closest you've gotten. Who was in charge?"

More guilty sidelong glances among the adolescent males crouching among their discarded pull-rope, and then a lanky youngster with platter-sized feet and hands came squatting-erect. His fur was in the proper flat posture, but the naked pink of his tail still twitched stiffly.

"I was," he said, keeping his eyes formally down. "Honored Sire Chuut-Riit," he added, at the adult's warning rumble.

"Now, youngling, what did you learn from your first attempt?"

"That no one among us is your match, Honored Sire Chuut-Riit," the kitten said. Uneasy ripples went over the black-striped orange of his pelt.

"And what have you learned from this attempt?"

"That all of us together are no match for you, Honored Sire Chuut-Riit," the striped youth said.

"That we didn't locate all of the cameras," another muttered. "You idiot, Spotty." That to one of his siblings; they snarled at each other from their crouches, hissing past barred fangs and making striking motions with unsheathed claws.

"No, you did locate them all, cubs," Chuut-Riit said. "I presume you stole the ropes and tools from the workshop, prepared the boulder in the ravine in the next courtyard, then rushed to set it all up between the time I cleared the last gatehouse and my arrival?"

Uneasy nods. He held his ears and tail stiffly, letting his whiskers quiver slightly and holding in the rush of love and pride he felt, more delicious than milk heated with bourbon. *Look at them!* he thought. At the age when most young kzin were helpless prisoners of instinct and hormone, wasting their strength ripping each other up or making fruitless direct attacks on their sires, or demanding to be allowed to join the Patriarchy's service *at once* to win a Name and house hold of their own . . . *His* get had learned to *cooperate* and use their minds!

"Ah, Honored Sire Chuut-Riit, we set the ropes up beforehand, but made it look as if we were using them for tumbling practice," the one the others called Spotty said. Some of them glared at him, and the adult raised his hand again.

"No, no, I am *moderately* pleased." A pause. "You did not hope to take over my official position if you had disposed of me?"

"No, Honored Sire Chuut-Riit," the tall leader said. There had been a time when any kzin's holdings were the prize of the victor in a duel, and the dueling rules were interpreted more leniently for a young subadult. Everyone had a sentimental streak for a successful youngster; every male kzin remembered the intolerable stress of being physically mature but remaining under dominance as a child.

Still, these days affairs were handled in a more civilized manner. Only the Patriarchy could award military and political office. And this mass assassination attempt was ... unorthodox, to say the least. Outside the rules more because of its rarity than because of formal disapproval. . . .

A vigorous toss of the head. "Oh, no, Honored Sire Chuut-Riit. We had an agreement to divide the private possessions. The lands and the, ah, females." Passing their own mothers to half-siblings, of course. "Then we wouldn't each have so much we'd get too many challenges, and we'd agreed to help each other against outsiders," the leader of the plot finished virtuously.

"Fatuous young scoundrels," Chuut-Riit said. His eyes narrowed dangerously. "You haven't been communicating outside the household, have you?" he snarled.

"Oh, *no*, Honored Sire Chuut-Riit!"

"Word of honor! May we die nameless if we should do such a thing!"

The adult nodded, satisfied that good family feeling had prevailed. "Well, as I said, I am somewhat pleased. If you have been keeping up with your lessons. Is there anything you wish?"

"Fresh meat, Honored Sire Chuut-Riit," the spotted one said. The adult could have told him by the scent, of course, a kzin never forgot another's personal odor, that was one reason why names were less necessary among their species. "The reconstituted stuff from the dispensers is always ... so ... *quiet*."

Chuut-Riit hid his amusement. Young Heroes-to-be were always kept on an inadequate diet, to increase their aggressiveness. A matter for careful gauging, since too much hunger would drive them into mindless cannibalistic frenzy.

"And couldn't we have the human servants back? They were nice." Vigorous gestures of assent. Another added: "They told good stories. I miss my Clothilda-human."

"Silence!" Chuut-Riit roared. The youngsters flattened stomach and chin to the ground again. "Not until you can be trusted not to injure them; how many times do I have to tell you, it's dishonorable to attack household servants! Until you learn self-control, you will have to make do with machines."

This time all of them turned and glared at a mottled youngster in the rear of their group; there were half-healed scars over his head and shoulders. "It bared its *teeth* at me," he said sulkily. "All I did was swipe at it, how was I supposed to know it would die?" A chorus of rumbles, and this time several of the covert kicks and clawstrikes landed.

"Enough," Chuut-Riit said after a moment. *Good, they have even learned how to discipline each other as a unit.* "I will consider it, when all of you can pass a test on the interpretation of human expressions and body-language." He drew himself up. "In the meantime, within the next two eight-days, there will be a formal hunt and meeting in the Patriarch's Preserve; kzinti homeworld game, the best Earth animals, and even some feral-human outlaws, perhaps!"

He could smell their excitement increase, a mane-crinkling musky odor not unmixed with the sour whiff of fear. Such a hunt was not without danger for adolescents, being a good opportunity for hostile adults to cull a few of a hated rival's offspring with no possibility of blame. *They will be in less danger than most,* Chuut-Riit thought judiciously. *In fact, they may run across a few of my subordinates' get and mob them. Good.*

"And if we do well, afterwards a feast and a visit to the Sterile Ones." That had them all quiveringly alert, their tails held rigid and tongues lolling; nonbearing females were kept as a rare privilege for Heroes whose accomplishments were not *quite* deserving of a mate of their own. Very rare for kits still in the household to be granted such, but Chuut-Riit thought it past time to admit that modern society demanded a prolonged adolescence. The day when a male kit could be given a spear, a knife, a rope and a bag of salt and kicked out the front gate at puberty were long gone. Those were the wild, wandering years in the old days, when survival challenges used up the superabundant energies. Now they must be spent learning history, technology, xenology, none of which burned off the gland-juices saturating flesh and brain.

He jumped down amid his sons, and they pressed around him, purring throatily with adoration and fear and respect;

his presence and the failure of their plot had reestablished his personal dominance unambiguously, and there was no danger from them for now. Chuut-Riit basked in their worship, feeling the rough caress of their tongues on his fur and scratching behind his ears. *Together,* he thought. *Together we will do wonders.*

From "The Children's Hour" by Jerry Pournelle & S.M. Stirling